"I saw ... ... the bright water—
and then hi... ..., brighter than the water, began
to rise. It came out cleanly, intact in every limb."

No, not weird fantasy—but a sober, factual
account of physical death in the world of *The Ring
of Truth*! Another universe—where natural laws are
different. Where all water shines, sunlight is heavy,
gravity works by repulsion—and the shape of the
world is an unsolved problem. Unsolved, that is, until
Prince Kernin and his companions set out on the
great Quest to the Mountain at the end of the world.

Here are satyrs, centaurs, intelligent reptiles, far
kingdoms, flying rafts, deadly battles—and that
Problem—all detailed in the saga of that reluctant
hero Orselen, the Prince's bard, who would far rather
stay at home that go exploring. And yet he too is
dragged, protesting, to the point where he achieves
the Ring of Truth. . . .

THE RING
OF TRUTH

David J. Lake

DAW BOOKS, INC.
DONALD A. WOLLHEIM, PUBLISHER

1633 Broadway, New York, NY 10019

First DAW Printing, June 1984

1 2 3 4 5 6 7 8 9

DAW TRADEMARK REGISTERED
U.S. PAT. OFF. MARCA
REGISTRADA. HECHO EN U.S.A.

PRINTED IN U.S.A.

Contents

TO GOD
If you have form'd a Circle to go into,
Go into it yourself & see how you would do.
                                    —*William Blake*

PART ONE

The Seed of the Quest

1

What god shall I call upon to inspire this new-hatched writing? Custom it is to call upon Her, the Dark One, Nami the Mother—but I cannot cry 'Sing, Goddess', because these words will not sing. They must not. When Kernin asked me to tell the tale of our quest, I first thought to make it in the manner of my ancestors: but when I began to touch my lyre, my fingers faltered, and a string snapped, and I knew that for a sign.

This story is too strange, too bitter to be sung by the sweet Goddess; and besides, it touches her own shape and being. About their own natures the gods are always silent. Rather perhaps do I need the aid of Firafax Half-god, beguiler of the market-places, the teller of fantastic tales. Yet he will not do either, for he deals largely in lies.

Come then Sinis, Lady of Sober Truth, guide of wayfarers to the end and at the end, and help me to tell in plain prose this history of Kernin's quest: of how the Prince of Aelvia sought and achieved the Ring of Truth; and yet how that achievement proved at last to be a hollow thing.

Using no artful words, then, I will begin with the egg, as the minstrels' saying goes. And in this case, also quite literally.

King Prahelek of Palur, Lord of the Four Quarters, Sacker of Cities, King of Infinite Space (and so forth), that mighty warrior of the Shorelands—King Prahelek, I say, had long been wedded to Queen Kandiri of up-river Nakhtos, and still for many Sky-Rings those two had no child. The priestesses of dark Nakhtos prayed to the Great Mother, and the priests of bright Palur offered up many a winged-ox to the Sun, and the rain-dervishes of the dry lower nomes performed their usual obscene orgies; but for many Ring-cycles, all to no avail.

King Prahelek vented his wrath, to some extent, on the wretched island-pirates of the Great Ocean—which at least proved useful to commerce in later times. Prahelek returned with his bloody sword, and a dozen pirate wenches as concubines, sailing by day and rowing by night up the holy River Sinolis from Palur to Nakhtos. Rumour had it that he purposed to wed the prettiest of his piratical slave-girls, and so beget an heir on her; and that would have spelt disaster to the River Kingdom. But as our dragon-prowed galleys glided into the crater-lake of Nakhtos, in the cool of Sunkindle, we were met by gaily decorated barges and jubilant bard-heralds.

The union of the Two Lands was saved: while the King was away, the Queen had brought forth.

Luckily, the King had not been away *too* long. If his campaign had lasted one Sky-Ring longer, the Queen's blessing might well have hatched worse mischief.

And even so, our first few days in Nakhtos were tense ones. Omren Chief Bard-Herald, my father and master, was particularly nervous. He did not often beat me, for (though I say it myself) I was a gifted pupil; but that third morning after our return, in the Blue Tower of the Nakhtos Palace, if I merely showed my native genius and originality in the slightest grace-note, he rapped me over the knuckles with his time-wand.

'By the Goddess!' he roared, as I was giving a particularly virtuoso turn to a hackneyed old learner's piece, 'you'll play the Sunquenching Hymn properly if I have to quench *you* in the process!'

He was tearing his hair with his free hand, twisting it round his head-peaks. He was also sweating, though the Blue Tower was airy and cool.

Suddenly he quietened. 'Orselen, dear son: I—I may not be with you much longer. Please, *please* prove worthy of your ancestors, the Bards of Nakhtos, and of your high calling. Ours is a noble tradition, which must be maintained as it has been for ten thousand Rings, indeed ever since the Land-taking. If—if not in this reign, then in another, you may yet live to be Chief Bard of the Two Lands. You have, I think, the family talent . . .'

I knew that, of course; but this was not the moment to tell my father so. I merely looked modest, and rubbed my knuckles.

'Orselen, my boy!' He embraced me, and suddenly I realised that he was trembling. Why was he talking of his death? He was still hale, in fact a little younger than the King. 'Son, whatever people may say of me hereafter, please believe what I tell you: that I have always done my duty to our people and our old ways. As it is written in Sakanek: "No greater good there is, far above

venture and victory, Than to serve holy hearth, woman and sib
and hatchling.'' Well, I have served, in my fashion—the good
old fashion of Nakhtos, which once used to be also the fashion
of Palur and all the Shorelands. In those days, Kings did not
pretend to own their Queens; nor, before Sakanek, did they
spend their time in wars and wanderings. My son, promise me
that when I am dead, you will maintain the old ways; and—and
if ever you are a counsellor to a king or prince, that will give
such a one the good, old-fashioned counsels: to cherish his
people and honour his lady wife. . . .'

All this began to be beyond my comprehension, for I was still
young and had not seen 200 Rings, or, as we say in the River
Kingdom, ten 'years'. But I loved my father, and I knew that at
bottom he was right. The old ways, the old tunes. Was he
attacking my novelties of playing? Grace-notes are all very well,
but the old tunes must be maintained under them. 'I promise—' I
began; but at that instant, in rushed Fiupen, the Second Bard.

Fiupen was a conceited ass (and a very indifferent musician). But
he was a Palurian, and at that time he prided himself on being
close to the King. Now his pomposity was struggling with his
desire to impart inside information. He made my father a stumbling (and insufficient) bow, and blurted out:

'Have you heard, Omren? His Majesty—to whom be life and
strength and victory—His Majesty, in his graciousness, has. . . .'

He paused for breath, for he had been running, and up the
outside stairs in all the heat and gravity of noon.

'His Majesty has what?' snapped my father, gripping his wand
so hard that his knuckles went white. 'Spit it out, man!'

'His—His Majesty has visited the incubator,' said Fiupen,
'and he has—acknowledged the Egg. The official ceremony will
be held tomorrow at Sunkindle.'

My father Omren dropped his wand. He swayed limply, and if
we had not been in the half-floating lightness of indoors, I think
he might have fallen. But instantly he recovered, picked up his
wand, and turned to me with a broad smile.

'Come now, boy—the Thanksgiving Hymn! And none of your
dragon-blasted *grace-notes*!'

Twenty Rings later—that is, after one whole 'year' of 402
days—another ceremony was held on the roof of the great Central Tower of Nakhtos Palace.

Everyone who was anyone in the Twin Kingdom was there.
The Black Priestesses were there, and the white-robed Sun Priests,
and the Chief Horner of the Rain Dervishes, and all the nome-

lords from famous Suoran on the Great Sea to little Kherilos
under the Aelvian Wall; and the King's courtiers, and the Queen's
courtiers, and the Menkinvian Girls' Choir, and the pipers, and
the harpers, and the Chief Bard, and the Second Bard, and the
ambassadors of Agnai and Rindos, and goddess knows who else.

Even I was there, though I had no right to be. I had smuggled
myself into the throng, peeping inconspicuously (I hoped) through
the gap between the last of the Black Priestesses and the first of
the Menkinvian Girls. I was coming to the age when I thought
the blonde Menkinvian Girls very pretty. But after a while, as the
public excitement mounted, even I took my eyes off the girls,
and looked at the great glass-plant dome in the centre of the roof.

It was astonishingly early in the day for a Hatching. In fact, it
was not yet really day at all: it was Last Toe hour, Sunkindle
was barely beginning, and the air was cold. I shivered, clasping
my hands over the gaps between my kilt and my shoulder-vest,
and looked up into the zenith, at the Sun.

Yes, the Sun was still a dull, copper-coloured ghost, with just
a faint red star-point, only visible if you knew where to look, near
the edge opposite the Ring. As for the Sky-Ring, she was also a
mere wraith—a wraith of a wreath, a faint orange-red oval line
like an empty gold diadem tossed against the sky; for this was
the night after Ring-ripe, the last of Olari's visibility. I heard the
girls whispering that this was a bad omen: a lusty young Prince
should be hatched in full daylight, and best of all in the middle
of the Ring-month, or at least with the Ring waxing. The whole
world seemed supernaturally quiet. Overhead the stars burned
bright, not yet paled by the Sun: 'the unchanging stars that stand
still, fix'd all the night time', those white lakes and rivers and
seas of the sky, whose shapes and names I already knew by
heart: Pelas Velnul so high up, the 'Sea of Angels'; Pelas Ranel,
'Sea of the End', the wide low white patch which sat over
World's End beyond the land of the Wise Centaurs. . . . There
were stars above, and stars indeed also below, for the assembly
on the roof were equipped with candelabras of light-plants. Just
occasionally a light-berry broke off from its stalk, and sailed
slowly up into the sky, a little star to the great stars; like a ghost
leaving its body. . . .

Hastily I suppressed that thought. It was no time to harbour
Death, even in similes: Ganthis-Ran comes, they say, when she
is called; and the little one was incurring ill-luck enough as it
was, by his bad timing. To distract my mind, and hopefully to

throw Ganthis off the scent, I looked backward over the Palace roofs toward the lower town and the country. Nearly everything there was pitch black: all but the soft silver radiance of the River, which wound like a snake of light-berries on the Ringright side of the city, dwindling at last upstream to a glowing thread snapped off by the Aelvian Wall.

As I first looked, the holy River was the only bright thing in the landscape; but then, in one eye-blink, there was another.

That other was over Khar Durnaran, the Farthest Mountain, which was so far inland and therefore so high that it seemed almost to touch the lower edge of the sky. Usually from Nakhtos the Farthest Mountain shows like a grey arrowhead floating above the highest blue hills, and at night like a black dragonfish fin swimming in the brighter haze of World's End; but just as I gazed at it in that predawn, I saw a bright spark rise from its top, a spark brighter than the world's-end haze. Another rising light-berry? Not at *that* distance! That bright point expanded as it rose, and grew fainter like a dissipating ghost, and blended into the haze. And then I knew that Khar Durnaran must have erupted.

I had never heard of the Farthest Mountain erupting before. There is nothing of that in the Myth-writings, or the Lays. For that matter, craters do not often burst out of the tops of mountains. This surely was an omen!

I was right: it was. But what sort of omen I did not learn till much later.

I looked round apprehensively. But nobody else had seen the fire of Durnaran. And now, just as Last Toe Hour gave way to First Finger Hour, and the Sun began to glow gold and the stars to fade, the fosterers flung wide the portal of the Royal Incubator.

In that sad-rich light of earliest Sunkindle, we saw the Egg.

It nestled in its down-straw nest in the middle of the dome, pale green and nearly spherical and taller than a man's forearm. For a Ring of Rings, four hundred days, it had grown in warmth and sunlight and fresh air, grown like a plant, and at first therefore it had been as green as a plant, but now it was faded nearly to white, since its growing days were over; and its shell had hardened to a ripe brittleness. As we watched, the whole big Egg trembled; and a great Oh! rose from the assembly.

King Prahelek took one step forward; Queen Kandiri took two. The King twitched as though he would advance further, but the Chief Black Priestess said something in a low voice. The

King scowled and fretted, but the customs of Nakhtos and the older customs of Palur were both against him. In all the upper River lands, it is the mother who must receive her child, and speak its name. Black-haired, beautiful, gracious, Kandiri was queen of this situation.

Then it happened so quickly that everyone was taken by surprise; even my father forgot to strike his harpstrings for the Prelude to the Hatching Hymn. The Egg simply tore apart right down its front, it burst as quickly as the earth bursts when sun-stuff erupts, or as a shield shatters in battle when it is smitten in the midst by a bronze-pointed spear.

And then the little one came out, *running*; and we saw at once that he was a boy.

Hatchlings, of course, are equipped with good strong nails for their necessary first effort in life. My father told me that in my time I was quite well endowed. But this little prince had a claw on his right thumb as long and strong as a phoenix-eagle's talon, and as he ran forward out of the dome onto the main roof, he held this thumb-claw extended as though he meant to do some of us a mischief with it.

He was heading nearly in the direction of the Queen.

Queen Kandiri beamed. Unthinking, she exclaimed 'Kernin!'— which means something like 'sharp one', or 'little Swordy', or 'Edger'—it is a word of the modern Nakhtian dialect, with no exact parallel in our Classical Shorelandish. The Queen uttered her cry spontaneously, in sheer enthusiasm at the endowment of her new-hatched darling.

My father Omren looked appalled at the Chief Priestess. The Chief Priestess nodded.

'Begin the Hymn for Prince Kernin, Heir of the Two Lands,' she said.

Unthinking, the Queen had named her son. King Prahelek began to mutter in wrath: the Royal couple had previously agreed to name their child, if it proved a boy, Pelenek. The kings of Palur had been either Praheleks or Peleneks for many centuries of years; yet now the Heir of the Twin Kingdom was landed with an unroyal un-Classical name, a dialect name such as one might give to any common soldier's brat; and a name, also, unfit for poetry—it would neither alliterate with those of his paternal ancestors, nor fit into the cadence of a heroic verse, being one syllable too short.

Meanwhile the Queen, ignoring her crime, was reaching out loving arms for her son.

The baby stood swaying there before her for one eyeblink; and then he side-stepped. He was remarkably nimble for a hatchling

not a hundred eyeblinks old. The time of day may have helped:
most hatchings take place when the Sun is white-bright and his
rays heavy. Now Kernin stood swaying on his little feet in the
gentle gravity of dawn, and he looked about at the people.

I think he now began to be dismayed. There was a whole ring
of the Establishment surrounding him; and the bards were playing
at full twang and the Menkinvian girls were singing their loud
paean of joy.

It was too much; much too much. He wanted out. He slipped
past his mother, and made for the only hole he could see in the
ring.

That hole was the gap between me and the last of the Black
Priestesses. He ran very straight, and in spite of the now growing
heavy light, quite nimble and fast; and he might have broken
through. The Priestesses were aghast, and dithering; the choir
girls drew away with squeaks of terror. But I—

On some obscure impulse, I stepped into the gap, and caught
that little naked child in my arms.

He looked up into my face, and I down into his. He was
beautifully formed, without the slightest buds yet of head-peaks;
and in the growing yellow sunlight I could see that his eyes were
not dark blue, as is most common, but a sparkling green. My
own eyes are a sort of greyish green; Prince Kernin's were a
little like that, but of a purer colour, like the sky in the first
minutes of Sunquenching or the last of Kindling; in fact like the
sky at that moment over Khar Durnaran.

And then he began to cry. Not loudly or violently; but he was
tugging at my arms as though he wanted to get past. He still
wanted out, and through his tears he looked up at me as though
in reproach for stopping him.

I will never forget that look; for I saw it again, in the greatest
moment of his life, and the bitterest. Kernin, one might say,
always wanted out; right from the start.

And then the Queen came flouncing up, all skirts and fluttering
stoles and outstretched arms, and the Prince's first adventure
was over.

2

For five years after that I saw little of Kernin, for I followed my
father, and *he* had to follow King Prahelek wherever he went,
which was mostly on campaign; for a war had broken out with
our chief rival, Rindos.

During those years I learnt to handle a sword as well as a lyre, and I became a man. I was grateful to the rough old sergeant-at-arms who taught me swordsmanship, for I soon found in that war that the Rindians did not regard bard-heralds as sacrosanct. Rocky Rindos borders on the coast of the wild Luzelish, and from those savages they had picked up bad manners; also, they were fond of high-leaping night attacks, in which with the best will in the world it was difficult to tell heralds from soldiers. But at last King Prahelek held the field after a notable night-slaughter, and the Rindians sued for a truce of 4000 days—that is, nearly ten years. Prahelek was minded to reject this, and press the war home to the gates of Rindos itself; but then we heard that Agnai was stirring behind our backs, and even Aelvia was raising that old question of their disputed border, so Prahelek saw wisdom and confirmed the peace.

I for one was not at all sorry. In that last battle I had had to blood my sword and kill my man: it was either him or me. But unlike some people, I have no love of carnage for its own sake. I saw enough in those five years to sicken me of that business; especially of the business between battles, when your glorious army is not fighting armed foemen, but making sport with poor peasants—looting, raping, murdering, and butchering eggs or stealing eggs to hatch out little slaves. Since that war I have come to wonder at the heroic lays it is my business to sing. I have never felt the old way about the epic Sacking of Suoran by Sakanek the Mighty. I can guess what *that* must have been like in reality, before it was put into metre.

And then King Prahelek returned in triumph to Nakhtos; and from there he carried off young Prince Kernin, now old enough to leave his mother, and dwelt with him mostly in bright Palur by the River's mouth.

Prahelek wished his son to be trained up as befitted a prince of warlike Palur. Some parts of this education Kernin took to very eagerly: for instance, even at six years he loved riding, preferably at full gallop till the groom stopped him. But in other things. . . .

'Splendour of the Sun!' roared the King once in my hearing. 'Why does this boy always ask "why"?'

It was true: Kernin asked 'why' about a lot of things. Why did living creatures die? Why were the common people poor? Why was King Prahelek's hair turning grey? (That was a bad one!) Why couldn't horses talk like people—since some of them were just as sensible as people?

Sometimes he got answers which half satisfied him; like when

he asked Fiupen why there was always an afternoon storm at
Nakhtos, but not at Palur. Fiupen said pompously: 'Because,
Highness, the Goddess Suori blows away the clouds from Palur.'
I added hastily: 'The Goddess is the afternoon sea-wind, actually.
Her breath doesn't reach as far inland as Nakhtos. That's why the
upper nomes are wet, but the lower ones dry.'

And sometimes Kernin asked questions to which there simply
couldn't be an answer, unless you told him a story out of the
Myth-writings. Once he stood by me on Palur citadel, at Last
Finger Hour, and looked up at the Sun as it faded.

'Why does the Sun quench?' This, with unshed tears in his
eyes.

I told him, so that the pretty stars could come out. He brightened at that, because already he loved the stars, and had got me
to teach him the names of the star-seas.

And then there was the time when I was playing to him on the
lyre Sulani's Lament, which I knew he loved. When I had
finished, he said: 'Why is music?'

It was in his ninth year that Prince Kernin received his tutor from
across the Great Sea.

The boy stood on the rocky cliff of Palur, where the citadel
juts like an out-thrust jaw between the river-mouth and the
ocean. It was half way through First Finger Hour, and the Sun in
the zenith had just turned fully yellow-white. Kernin wore only a
plain linen kilt—he hated stiff royal robes, avoided them whenever possible, and now he planted his bare feet firmly on the
rock against the thrust of the morning land-wind. I had been
playing for him a call on the horse-horn trumpet, Hinelen's
Challenge, a great ringing melody in which he now delighted.
Hinelen's herald had played that on this very spot centuries ago,
at the Land-Taking, when our ancestors sailed to the Holy River
from Menkinvia. When I finished, and the wind blew my last
note out to sea, Kernin gazed out over the ocean and laughed.

'When I am big, Orselen, I will sail over that sea, like the
Land-Takers. I will sail to Menkinvia and Old Menkinvia, to
Kherindorna and Kintobara. I will sail to the Land of the Centaurs!'
he boasted.

I was sitting nearly at his feet, ready to grab him if he
stumbled. But really there was no fear of that. Eight years after
his hatching, Kernin was not tall for his age, but very sturdy,
sure-footed and nimble. He was also brown as a peasant lad from
going so often half naked. He was a handsome boy, green-eyed
still, with reddish-brown hair nearly the same colour as mine,

and very small head-peaks quite covered by his fiery locks: he did not resemble his royal father at all. All the Court, except possibly King Prahelek himself, loved the young Prince. I was deeply happy that the boy liked me, and had chosen me to be his personal Bard-Herald. That charlatan Fiupen was extremely annoyed—but enough of that now. Among his many fine qualities, Kernin had excellent taste in music, and knew a true virtuoso when he heard one. Just occasionally, though, there appeared a tendency in Kernin which caused me some inward anxiety. He was showing it again now.

'Sail to the Centaurs?' I queried. 'Little Highness, you know, that goes well beyond the Land-Takers. No Prince of Palur has ever done that; almost no *man* has done it—'

'I would like to do what no man has done,' said Kernin, his green eyes flashing like sun-gleams on water-pools, looking at the sea. Little pools contemplating the great pool. Pelas Magha was dotted with white sails that morning. Now that King Prahelek had cleared the sea of pirates, there were merchant galleys coasting between Palur and the other Shore cities, and an occasional double-huller slanting in from Menkinvia. And beyond all, the great green Sea spread and rose until it faded into the haze of World's End; and above that soared the perfect blue dome of the morning sky.

Kernin's mood seemed to veer, abrupt as the little winds that herald the afternoon storm in the uplands. Our young Prince was like that: one moment a boyish boaster, the next—something else. Now he was gazing past all the ships, into World-End itself. I remembered the time he asked me, 'What holds up the Sky?', and I answered pat, 'The Hundred Pillars of Prah', and hoped that he would believe what I hardly believed myself.

Almost sadly now, his eyes sought infinity. 'Why does the far ocean seem to climb *up*?'

' "As far as a star, as high as the sky" ,' I quoted. 'That's from the Rhyming Proverbs of Rakpen. And the sage Rakpen has another proverb: "Where man stands is always low: The gods have wrought to keep him so".'

'But *why*?' The boy sprang about, lightfooted in spite of the full day gravity, and pointed inland. Over the River he pointed, toward dark Nakhtos of his birth, and the Horse Plains, and all of the Two Lands up to the Aelvian Wall. It was not the clearest of days, so we could see hardly anything of cool Aelvia, nor any hint of Khar Durnaran; indeed, the limit of visibility was no more than 200 miles; but even so, the rise of the far ground was obvious to me. Kernin pointed at the mist-blue notched ridge of the Aelvian Wall. 'Look, Orselen, I understand that the far *land* can be high, because it *is* high; but surely not *water*! If the far Sea was higher than Palur, it would all come flooding down on us in a fall, as the River floods over the Aelvian Wall there.' He made another quick turn, half left. Now he was looking along the curving line of the shore, where it leads toward Agnai and Menkinvia. 'No, that's not right, either!'

'You are quick, my Prince,' I smiled. Indeed, the flat lands of the Shore also seemed to rise slightly upward; and sea-girt Agnai, 160 miles away, stood nearly as 'high', to the untutored sight, as the foothills of the Aelvian Wall. At the line where the shore faded into the haze, the 'rise' was about one finger's breadth held at arm's length. There are some people who never notice this, just as there are some people who never bother to learn the names and shapes of the stars. But Kernin was a noticer.

'No,' I said, 'it is not *real* height we see on all sides of us, it is *distance*. That is one of the basic facts of life. I know, it is hard to understand, and I puzzled about it too when I was your age. But there are so many strange things in life, why bother with just one? Why does the Sun kindle every morning, and quench every evening? Why does the Ring shine for ten-and-a-bit nights, and then not shine for another ten-and-a-bit nights? For that matter, why does Time itself always go on evenly, like a river rolling ever onward, but apparently from no spring to no sea? . . . There is only one good answer for all such mysteries.' I paused impressively. 'It is the will of the gods.'

'Now you sound like Fiupen. What, are the gods envious of men, that they play such tricks?' His cheeks flushed with sudden anger. 'If I were a god, I would not treat men so. . . .'

Hastily I pressed all my ten fingers on the stony ground, to avert divine vengeance. I think the Goddess accepted my silent prayer. 'You must never speak like that, even though you are a Prince,' I scolded. 'I do not know if the gods are envious, but they punish insolent speeches; as in the case of . . .' and I rattled off three stock examples from the Myth-Writings. 'Besides, it is obvious that the laws of life are arranged for our benefit. If the Sun did not quench at night, we would all be roasted; if we had no Ring, every direction would be the same, there would be no Four Quarters; and every day would be the same too—no calendars, no festivals! And that's how things once were, according to the Menkinvians: that was the Slumber Time, the Egg Time, when there were no astronomers, no calendar-priests, no counting, no real culture at all. All these good things we owe to the birth of

Olari, the Ring-goddess; and that is why we have a Ring as well as a Sun.'

'There are two sorts of *why*,' said Kernin, 'and still, none of that explains why far places look high.' He was gazing out over the great Sea again, into the far, high distances. His eyes were clouded now, his mood dark; and then suddenly he brightened. 'What's *that*?' He pointed. 'Is it a ship—or a Moving Island?'

The thing was a hazy bluish shape, and indeed very big to be a ship at that great distance. But Moving Islands occur only in the Myth-Writings and the Elder Proverbs, and in the end as the thing approached it proved to be a ship indeed. Such a ship! At least four times the size of any ship of men, with deck above deck, and three great masts, and a forest-foliage of sails. But the ships of Kintobara have become more frequent in the Shorelands since that time, so I will spare a full description.

That galleon came in to the port of Palur late that same afternoon—and it seemed the whole kingdom was down at the quay to meet it. Queen Kandiri was not, for she was then dwelling in Nakhtos; but King Prahelek came down to the river-side with all his court; for this was a thing out of living memory, that the Shorelands should be visited by a ship of the Centaurs.

Oh, what a crowd that was! For it was not just the court, there were all sorts of hangers-on—city folk in smart wigs and shoulder-vests, and half-naked dock labourers and peasants come into town for the day, and a sprinkling even of foreigners—spies, no doubt, from Agnai and Rindos, and strolling minstrels from goddess-knows where—some of whom were probably spies too. There was one motley-clad Aelvian zitharist and his girl-piper. . . . My father Omren glared at this couple, but they had too much sense to try playing or anticking themselves, even on the out-skirts of the crowd, since all eyes were directed at the huge ship: so our official choirs were able to get through their hymns of welcome without competition.

The High Priest of the Sun sacrificed a fine winged-ox in honour of the visitors. The beast died quietly with hardly a wing-flutter, and as the body dropped on the altar the soul came out cleanly and preserved its shape for several eyeblinks. Then the blue-white phantom of the ox, clearly visible in spite of the full sunshine, rose smoothly almost to the height of a ship's mast before it began to dissipate. An excellent omen! The High Priest prophesied that the newcomers' visit would prove most fortunate for the Twin Kingdom.

Then the centaurs began disembarking.

We had seen centaurs before only in old faded paintings: the reality was something of a surprise. They were not really very horse-like: for one thing, unlike horses they had no horn in the middle of the forehead. Indeed, they had no horns or head-peaks at all, so that their heads and faces were rather like those of women—but very thick-necked, burly women. Their prevailing colour was brown: dark brown head-hair and short fur over most of their bodies except their hoofs, hands and faces. Exposed flesh was a rich ruddy brown, like a very tanned but healthy and prosperous human peasant. But what struck me most about them was this: though they were nearly naked, they did not seem like *animals*. They carried themselves with great dignity, and they wore things: little half-garments like pouched aprons and short horse-blankets, and gold-wire diadems in their hair, and heavy silver chains about their necks. These gold and silver ornaments were the insignia of the ship's officers. And there was one centaur who wore no gold or silver, but a very strange thing upon his nose: a pair of transparent discs which flashed in the sun, and through which he peered. The discs seemed to be made of glass-plant, but much clearer than the stuff which is used for incubators.

There were half a dozen centaurs altogether, all the ship's officers and their one passenger. The common sailors remained chattering on the great ship, some of them perched in the rigging, some of them swinging from the yards by their tails. No, they were not centaurs, of course! As all the world should know, the ships of Kintobara are managed mostly by trained flymonkeys.

I could see Prince Kernin beside his father in the front row of the welcoming party. He was formally dressed now in the style of Palur: a thick yellow royal wig, a stiff heavy shoulder-vest, a long crisp-pleated kilt, and high boot-sandals. He was obviously very uncomfortable, chafing, but sweating at least half through rapturous excitement. He could not take his eyes off those centaurs, and he was twitching as though at any moment he would break ranks and rush forward. King Prahelek gave him one thunderous scowl, and placed a heavy hand firmly upon his shoulder. Kernin looked up at the King then, with a spark of green fire in his eyes—a fire which he quickly controlled. Then he gave a small nod, and quietened, and looked back apparently more calmly at the strange visitors.

The great meeting got off to a rather bad start when we discovered that centaurs don't eat meat, and so the sacrifice of the winged-ox was rather wasted on them. King Prahelek immediately gave orders for more suitable refreshments—wheatcakes, wine, and so forth. The centaur captain explained their business,

which was mostly commercial: now that this reach of the great
Ocean was clear of pirates, thanks to the valour of mighty
Prahelek, Lord of the Four Quarters, King of Infinite Space
(etcetera), there was a good chance for the centaurs to trade not
only with Menkinvia, but also with these our Shorelands.

The centaurs spoke with great thick voices, and also with
broad Menkinvian accents. Naturally, since the Menkinvians
were the humans they had had most contact with in the past. As
my mother was Menkinvian, I knew the dialect well, and was
rather amused to hear this version of it.

And then the one with those glass eye-disc things stepped
forward. He attempted a bow—and a centaur's bow is a strange
sight. 'Faire syr kinge,' he boomed, in a very grammatical but
strangely accented Old Shorelandish, 'I hight Barundran—
Barundran of Kintobara, at your most gracious Maiestie's service.
Or rather, to phrase it more fitly, I would be at your Maiestie's
service if your Maiestie would deign to employ me in any office
that suiteth with your Maiestie's grace and mine own humble
qualities. . . .'

'What have you to sell?' said Prahalek.

The centaur seemed disconcerted by the abrupt question. He
took his eye-discs off his nose, and, holding them delicately by
their silvery metal rims, used them to emphasise his gestures.
With the discs removed, one saw that his eyes were grey, and
there were little wrinkles about them. It came to me then that this
centaur was not young.

'Nay, fair syr Kinge,' said Barundran, 'I have naught to
sell—if you will except knowledge, and mine own humble self. I
am a scholar—Maister of Physique Science of the Academe of
Kherindorna. Methought ye might have need, in these excellent
but newly settled Shorelands, of some scole-maister—put case,
to lesson some young nobleman—or to tutor a tender-aged Prince
or so—hnnnm?'

That last enquiring sound was suddenly, obviously inhuman.
The centaurs from across Pelas Magha are rightly called Learned,
and they had studied the language of men dilegently enough, but
still, their throats, their tongues, their nasal passages were not
quite of human shape. That last sound was more like a horse's
whinny. Prahelek took a sudden step backward, and looked put
out, if not a little angry. 'Newly settled . . . Passion of Prah!' he
muttered.

Indeed, for all his courtly flourishes, the old centaur had been
tactless. Or did he not know that by now there were more than
six hundred bronze Year-nails hammered into the door of the

temple of Olari, the Ring-goddess, on Palur hill? And each nail meant twenty Rings, and the first nail was hammered by Pelenek the son of Hinelen Land-Taker. Of course, the centaurs are an exceedingly ancient people, but still, 'newly settled'! Our King was not pleased, and Barundran's chances of employment were not looking good, when suddenly young Kernin darted forward.

'Master Centaur,' he said, looking up at the great man-beast, 'do you teach knowledge of the world? Of Nature?'

Barundran bowed again slowly, and held his bow so that his big red-brown face came close to the boy's. Those two looked each other in the eyes, bright green to faded grey; and now the grey eyes also seemed to sparkle a little.

'Indeed I do, fair young syr. The nature of substances dark or light, the kinds of beasts and fishes and both sorts of birds, the theorique of Astronomy, the mathematiques, the uses of the Cross-sighter and the Angulabe—which may be pratiques of no small use to an enterprising Prince, surveyor, or maister-builder; the making of maps—'

Kernin looked as though he were about to burst. Of a sudden, he gripped the centaur's big right hand in his own small one (thus nearly making Barundran drop his eye-glasses); and then he swung about and faced the King.

'Oh Father,' he cried, intense and desperate, 'I want him! I must have him! Take him on, please!'

And then as Prahelek was beginning 'Newfangled—', Kernin interrupted. Yes, he interrupted the King!

'The making of maps may be very useful to you, Father. We could maybe draw a clear picture of Rindos—and of the Aelvian Wall—you know, the disputed nomes.'

Prahelek looked thunderstruck. In an instant I saw his anger turn into something else. Our great Sacker of Cities was, after all, no fool. On the contrary, he was a politician.

'Son,' he said, softly sibilant, 'we will speak no more of this at this time.' Then he turned to the centaur. 'You, Master Barundran—we will speak with you this night, at our Palace, to which we most cordially invite you. . . .'

Well, the rest of the proceedings at the port did not last long. King Prahelek gave the centaur traders ample licence to bring in their goods, duty free—details to be settled later. He seemed in a great hurry to get away. He also beckoned to the Captain of the Royal Guard, and I saw from his gestures what was up. A squad of guards pushed their way through the dispersing throng, heading in the direction where that Aelvian minstrel and his moll had been perched on the steps of the River Temple.

But they were too late. By the time they reached the temple steps, the zitharist and the girl-piper were no longer there. The guards made no arrest, then or later. Aelvian minstrels are notoriously fly-by-night; they are as elusive as satyrs.

Next morning Barundran was appointed tutor to Prince Kernin, and technical adviser to King Prahelek.

3

Alas for the hopes of warriors—sometimes—when they turn to philosophers for new weapons! Barundran soon proved a sore disappointment to the King.

This was not apparent for the first few Rings. During this time, the learned centaur dazzled the whole court of Palur with his ingenious little gadgets. He had several large sea-chests full of these things, which were nearly all mathematical instruments.

Mathematics! He seemed to have a mania for measuring: and not only space, but also *time*. Well, of course we could measure time tolerably well before he came—we of the River are not Luzelish barbarians; but not even the smallest sand-clock would measure times shorter than half an hour—as if they mattered! Barundran changed all that. He produced a little ticking machine with a face as round as a crater-lake, and little metal bodkins on it which turned slowly, slowly. . . . There were hieroglyphs spaced evenly round this circle, and Barundran explained that they stood for the numbers 1 to 10, and these, for the shorter bodkin, signified the hours from Sunkindle to Sunquenching—or again, from Quenching to Kindle, which was a little confusing, but anyway, twice round the circle meant a day and a night. One very neat thing: this same metal clock worked at the same pace, both by day and by night, indoors and outdoors, for changing gravity didn't affect it at all. One had merely to twist a little lever at the back, and a spring would work the machine for a whole twenty hours—and save the labour of the serving-man whose duty it was to turn the sandclock twenty times a day! More than that: the longer bodkin went round faster, once round in an hour, and each tiny line round the circle was a *minute*. 100 minutes made an hour. And even—would you believe it—100 *seconds* made a minute! A second was about an eyeblink.

I think it was when Barundran lectured us about minutes and

seconds that King Prahelek began to suspect the centaur must be a little crazy.

However, his angle-measurers were a little more practical. The Cross-sighter gave you verticals and levels very neatly, out of doors, and also right angles on the level, all with one instrument of hinged and fixed metal rods: an obvious convenience for builders. And the Angulabe measured angles. Once more Barundran seemed to be splitting hairs: his Angulabe divided the right angle into 100 *degrees*. The point of that was not so obvious.

Barundran explained that by measuring angles precisely you could map a territory without actually walking over it. Even territory in enemy hands, for instance.

'Ah!' grunted Prahalek. 'Now you're talking some sense—I hope. But you must prove this. . . .'

So we made an expedition up the holy River, past Nakhtos to Kherilos and the Aelvian border. The Aelvian Wall is really two lines of hills, and the first is much lower; the land between the First and Second Cataracts had long been disputed between Aelvia and Nakhtos, and when Prahelek married Queen Kandiri he inherited that quarrel. The Interland is two nomes, Upper Kherilos and Under Aelvia, wildish places with few settlements away from the River, but rich in grass-plants and gas-plants and fine timber in the forests. The people are not really Nakhtian or Aelvian: they wear tunics like the Aelvians, but woven from Nakhtian riverflax, not Aelvian wool. Originally both nomes had adhered to Aelvia, but a hundred years back Upper Kherilos was betrayed by its lord to Nakhtos; since when Aelvia had a grievance. The Kings of Nakhtos replied by claiming Under Aelvia too. . . . I won't go into all the details, which are somewhat musty, and have to do with the positions of a minor watershed, and the wording of an ancient saga of the Land-Taking.

Well, now Barundran set up his instruments at various points on the First Wall, and squinted through the Angulabe . . . and four Rings later he produced a magnificent map, all painted in red and blue on the finest riverstraw paper, and covering both the disputed nomes. Those local officials who knew our side of the border well acknowledged that this bit of the map was very accurate. As for the enemy side. . . .

. . . Well, unfortunately Barundran's map-contours tended to support the claims of Aelvia. That is, if you could believe in the accuracy of the Angulabe.

'Well, I give you one more chance only, hornless horse,' snarled King Prahelek in our camp at Kherilos. 'If the ground slopes the way you say it does, our troops will have it a little downhill when they attack. . . .'

And we did attack. The First Aelvian War was a sudden, brutal aggression from our side. The Aelvians were quite unprepared, and our troops captured the land all the way to the Great Cataract. And then Barundran's map was vindicated: by the route the army marched, the slope *was* downhill at the vital points. By the saga we were clearly in the wrong; but Barundran's mapping had helped us find the weakest point for the attack.

After that, King Prahelek was quite pleased with the old centaur, and confirmed him as Permanent Tutor to his son. He also began to ask his advice about military technology. Surely the Wise Centaurs would have ingenious designs for siege engines, scaling ladders, battering rams . . . ?

'Alas, your Majesty,' said Barundran (who was speaking our language a little less rustily now), 'we people of the Middle Plain, we have no such skills, since we love peace, and our only enemies are the hordes of Thulor, who build no walls. Among ourselves, we have known no war for two thousand years . . .'

Then Prahelek saw that the case was a hopeless one. He ground his teeth, and gave up nearly all hope of useful help from Barundran. If it wasn't that accurate maps just *might* come in useful one day . . .

So Barundran was relegated to his other job, that of Tutor to the Royal Prince. Much to Barundran's relief and Kernin's enormous joy.

These were happy years that followed the Aelvian War, partly because the Court was mostly at pleasant Nakhtos, that being the most strategic centre from which to watch both Aelvia and Rindos. For five years our enemies, and those we had made our enemies, offered no hostile move, and the Twin Kingdom flourished. Queen Kandiri was no longer young, but was still a very gracious lady who permitted my father Omren to call her 'beautiful' in each New Year lay. She was very pleased to have her Chief Bard and her husband at home for so long; and rejoiced also to have the company of her dear little son . . .

. . . Who was now not so little; neither was he very often in the company of his parents.

He and Barundran now had a schoolroom and laboratory in the Yellow Tower, which has a doorway onto the great flat central roof, that place where Kernin had once begun his adventurous career. They used to conduct experiments and discussions both indoors and out on the roof, and I, as the Prince's herald and friend, was sometimes allowed to join in these activities. And even at other times, when Court functions dragged Kernin away, he would often whisper to me the exciting lore he was picking up from the centaur.

Once in the middle of a Royal hunt, on the Horse Plains near Nakhtos, he started chattering to me about zoology. We had killed among the thickets, first a Lesser Dragon and then a wild boar. The Prince loved the wild riding over the yellow-green savannah and among the sword-bushes, but rather disliked the moments of the kills; yet he was fascinated at the carving of the carcases.

'A Sixer and a Fourer,' Kernin nodded, looking at the dissected dragon and boar. 'Do you know, Orselen, Barundran thinks the two classes must have quite separate origins? Maybe from different seas.'

I gaped; and then he explained. Well, yes, it was obvious when you thought about it: nearly all animals had either four or six limbs. Men had four, centaurs had six. There were reptiles and mammals and birds of each sort. Only, there were no six-legged frogs, and no fish in our rivers or Ocean with three pairs of fins.

'The Centaurs say that all life arises out of water,' said Kernin. 'Because water shines at night, and the soul shines when it leaves the body; and our bodies are mostly liquid, anyway. Water is akin to soul-stuff, to life, to light . . .'

I laughed. 'That's not quite a new opinion, my Prince. In the Myth-Poems—'

'Barundran knows more than the Myth-Poems,' he said coldly. 'The Myth-Poems don't prove that all Fourers have the same basic anatomy, they don't notice that all Fourers lay green and growing eggs; whereas Sixers either lay small, non-green eggs, or no eggs at all. It's pretty obvious that all Fourers originated from fish in the Great Sea; but where the Sixers came from, nobody knows.'

'Not even the Centaurs—who are Sixers themselves? I thought Barundran knew everything.' (I am afraid I put in a touch of sarcasm there.)

'Not at all,' said Kernin, looking prim. 'Barundran says it is the mark of a truly wise person to know that he does not know.' He paused. 'The Centaurs have some myths, I believe, about their origins—but so far the Master will not tell me about those. He does not believe in encouraging superstition.'

I opened my mouth, and shut it again. The 'Master', I thought, needed a more liberal attitude to the more humane side of learning. I must get him, somehow, to tell me about Centaur poetry.

But for a couple of years at least, neither I nor Kernin had any such luck. 'Grammar must come before Rhetorique,' said Barundran magisterially.

In that room on the roof, he was teaching Kernin to read and write. And he a Prince! We had to keep this point a secret, lest King Prahelek should explode in wrath. By the time Kernin was twelve years old, he could scribe as well as any priest or bard, and he could read even Centaurish. Barundran lent him some of the precious scroll-books he had brought from over sea—beautiful things, all in that vertical graceful script which is like our own and yet not the same. Kernin would have devoured those books, but Barundran rationed his reading carefully.

'Observation!' he said. 'Direct Observation should come before Theorique. Now, let us proceed to Observe. . . .'

They rigged up the Cross-sighter and Angulabe on the broad parapet of the palace roof, and took the measure of True Rise and False Rise. I remember one very clear day, about Second Finger Hour, when the ground visibility was some three hundred and fifty miles—about the maximum ever possible. What a view that was! We seemed to see the whole world spread out and raised up around us. Ringright we could see past Agnai even to the Harpy Hills, beyond which lies Menkinvia; Ringleft past Rindos to the gloomy forests of Luzelana; Ringward we saw all the Shore, and then the Great Sea rising like a shimmering green bowl up, up into the World-End haze; and Ringback we could glimpse parts of Aelvia beyond the wall, and then the much more distant Wall of forbidden Rathvia, and then inland still beyond *that*, goddess-knew-what: dark bluish hills, perhaps the legendary land of Gagnar, named for Springer-dragons. And beyond again, like a ghost pausing on its way up the Sun, Khar Durnaran, the Last Mountain, floating grey against World's End.

Looking at it all, Kernin pressed my hand, almost speechless with joy. Especially he was looking toward Khar Durnaran. 'If there's any Pillar of Prah, that must be *it*,' he whispered.

'Moderate your transports,' said Barundran drily, 'and proceed to *measure*.'

He had already levelled the combined Cross-sighter and Angulabe, which is easily done: when the shadow of the upright rod disappears, the apparatus must be levelled, since the Sun is always vertical. Now he had Kernin squint through the sights, and take the apparent elevation of the last clear points along the coastline and the green rim of the Sea. Result: nearly three 'degrees', or as ordinary people would say, two finger-breadths held at arm's length.

The top of Khar Durnaran came out more than twice as much. 'But that, of course, is partly True Height,' said Barundran.

'What is the cause of False Height?' Kernin blurted out. 'Come now, Master, a bit of theory is in order *now*, I think!'

The centaur smiled, sighed, and removed the eye-glasses from his nose. 'Very well, young Sir. I must confess that Sky-science and Air-science are the least satisfactory branches of learning, but this hypothesis at least seems probable. . . . Have you noticed how an oar, inserted into water, appears broken at the point of entry? The sunken part appears more raised than it should.'

'Refraction,' said Kernin impatiently. 'We covered all that last Ring-month, you remember, and you said that's how your eye-glasses work.'

'Oh, did we? I must be getting absent-minded—old age impairs the memory.' Barundran gave a little laugh. 'But here's the point. Refraction works in air as well as water. The light-rays from the farthest points of land travel up a little into thinner air, and then into thicker air, since air thins with height, as hath often been verified by hardy mountaineers. So *all* far points are regularly raised up, and the farther the higher: a highly useful fact, since we can then directly calculate distance from elevation.'

Kernin looked half overjoyed and half dubious. 'But what about the rays that come to us level, directly through the lower air? They shouldn't be refracted.'

'Well objected, my pupil. I see that you will be a philosopher one day. But the fact is, the level rays do not reach us at all. They are stopped by the thickness of the lower air.' He pointed with his eye-glasses to the grey ghost of Khar Durnaran. 'Notice how we can see the top of that mountain, but not its base, nor the country round its base. Because the top must be in very thin, clear air. Even so . . . in the end distance overpowers all sight, along the flat land of Earth.' He sighed. 'If it were not so, we might see such things. . . .'

'Then the Earth really *is* flat,' said Kernin. He seemed almost relieved.

The centaur shot him a glance of astonishment. 'Why, of course. Apart from hills and mountains. Hnnnm! How could it be otherwise?'

'No, well, sometimes—I just wondered. Then—there's no reason why a man mightn't travel to the Edge itself, and look down into the Keelless Sea—if the World-End fires weren't too hot. . . .'

'Ah—hnnnm—well. . . .' Barundran looked uncomfortable. 'Suppose we take up a new study now, my Prince? There is this matter of Gravity. . . .'

Kernin seemed disappointed. He had a devouring curiosity about the far distances, the ends of things, World's Edge and all that. But I had noticed Barundran hedging about such matters before. I could guess his motives: by now he had learnt some diplomacy. He was hesitant to say anything which would directly contradict our Shoreland myths, the story of the hero-god Prah and his Pillars, the birth of the Earth-Disc out of the fiery Lower Sea . . . all of which are matters of religion. If word should reach Prahelek that he was teaching *atheism*. . . .

Barundran studied Gravity most ingeniously, with another little metal gadget. Sometimes indeed we used a simple shopman's balance, such as you find in any market-place, and by shading one arm and leaving the other in sunlight, he showed how much weight is due to the pressure of the sun's rays. The subject is not at all simple: it depends what shade you use. A single leaf from most trees will stop about one ninth, but a solid roof stops about a third, since a three-ounce weight in our laboratory doorway balanced a two-ounce weight in the sun. What a neat demonstration, and so obvious when you saw it, yet no one in the Shorelands had thought to be so precise about the matter before!

And then Barundran went still further—with this special gadget of his. It looked like one half of a balance, a single pan with a spiral of strong wire underneath, and a dial and pointer like the one on his famous clock. It was what he called a 'spring weighing machine'. You put a weight on the pan, and the metal spiral was depressed, and the pointer showed how much depression— that is, the *weight*. Barundran used this gadget indoors, on several different floors and at various hours of the day and night. The results were fascinating. Even indoors the Sun has influence: and indeed most weight is due not to visible light, but to some invisible and more penetrating rays. The dark rays which the Sun emits at night are the most penetrating of all, for we found very little difference at night indoors or outdoors, under one roof or all the floors of the Palace. Night weight outdoors was just half of full daylight weight; night weight in the Palace cellar was about four tenths. We proved these points again and again with Barundran's spring weighing machine.

When I saw these conclusions, I gained a new respect for the old man-beast. He might not be a poet, but there was a kind of poetry in what he had just done.

'The persistence of weight in the depths of the earth,' said

Barundran, 'hath perhaps some theorique consequences. Our miners have not yet found any depth where weight altogether disappears. It is possible that Earth hath some weight of *her own*, apart from the Sun, an attraction of dark substance to dark substance. Which casts doubt on the strange suppositions of the mystique Symmetrists. . . .'

'The Symmetrists?' Kernin snapped up the phrase as greedily as a harpy pouncing on a juicy wyvern's egg. 'Who are they?'

'I have o'ershot myself to tell you of them. Very well: they are a sect among us, very given to dark sayings, and indeed enamoured of darkness itself. Forsooth, they worship Night and the starry Sky, which they hold to be the true home of all living souls. And they allege correspondencies between the stars and Earthly cities: when a star twinkles, it would be sending us some Message. For them, the holy Sun is no friend, but the great Enemy, and withal a deceiver. Heaven would rush down to embrace Earth, and Earth would rush up to embrace Heaven, were it not that your villain Sun pushes them apart with his heavy rays. For Heaven is also an Earth, and Earth a Heaven, and both are intrinsically weightless. But these hypotheses do not seem to save the appearances; for every night, as the Sun's rays weaken, would not the stars seem to rush down toward Earth? Which no one hath observed.'

'Why do they say the Sun is a *deceiver*?'

Barundran looked uncomfortable. 'Well—because his rays do seem to behave in—hnnnm!—a peculiar fashion. Unless he is very distant indeed. And yet that cannot be so, he must be much closer than the night sky.'

'Yes,' said Kernin. We were speaking this time on the roof about Sunquenching; and now Kernin pointed up at the Sun, which was a lovely flame-gold colour, dim enough to be looked at directly. 'I have noticed. From here to Palur is about 120 miles, and as you sail along the River the Sun shifts a little against the stars. About twice his own breadth, I think. It's a bit more from Kherilos.'

'And much more from our own country, beyond the Sea,' said Barundran glumly. 'Yet the holy Sun is *always vertical*. The only hypothesis which can save the appearances is that the Sun's rays do *not* travel in straight lines. Or else when they reach our air they are refracted more than any other rays; and so are the rays from stars just behind the Sun. Thus, though the Sun cannot truly be vertical from all countries, nevertheless he *seems* vertical from all countries; and his weight is delivered vertically along with his rays.'

'Wow!' said Kernin, in most unprincely fashion.

'The wisdom of the Centaurs,' I said, 'indeed almost passes belief!'

Barundran cleared his throat—a strange sound, somewhat like a dragon coughing. 'Harrrumph. Well, there was one of our ancient philosophers, Gormarendran, who said: "Give me only Refraction, and I will construct the Universe".'

I think Kernin was about to say something else, but at that moment we were interrupted. A Menkinvian waiting-maid had appeared in the dusk around the curve of the old, empty Incubator.

'My lord Prince,' she said softly, 'your Highness is required in the Great Hall most urgently. It is the matter of the King of Agnai's daughter.'

Kernin said, even more softly, but loud enough for me to hear: 'Prah take the King of Agnai's daughter! What's a wench compared to sweet Science?' From which you might conclude that he was still young. True: but alas, even when he grew older Science was still for him an enemy of wenches, and much else beside. This will be the bitterest part of my story. Warm Suori and cold Sinis are rival goddesses even in our myths; they certainly contended for Kernin's spirit, and in the end nearly destroyed him. It is for this reason that I must soon speak much of Love.

'His Majesty is waiting,' said the maid, 'and Her Majesty, and all; the Court. I fear His Majesty is growing wroth. . . .'

'Oh, very well, very well, I'll come,' said Kernin.

4

The business of the King of Agnai's daughter was like this: Prahelek was looking for allies. The truce with Rindos would expire in another three years, and now Aelvia was decidedly hostile; if Agnai joined a coalition against us, the Twin Kingdom might be in dire peril. On their side, though, Agnai was afraid of *us*: King Prahelek's record of aggressions was a long one. So when the King of Agnai proposed a royal marriage—his daughter with Prahelek's son—Prahelek was very pleased indeed. The girl was not the heir to Agnai, but still, the marriage would mean a definite alliance. King Prahelek was all for saying Yes, at once.

I was in the Great Hall of Nakhtos when Prince Kernin tried to say No.

It was still early evening, and therefore rather warm, and the great round hall was ablaze with light-berries. The Ambassador of Agnai was there, a tall red-headed man with hardly perceptible head-peaks, for the Agnaians claim a large portion of original Menkinvian blood, and are proud of that. He was very splendidly dressed, as indeed we all were. Kernin was sweating under the whole Princely paraphernalia, including the new fashion (borrowed from the Centaurs) of a gold-wire diadem. But our carftsmen had made the circlet much heavier and thicker, like a full Sky-Ring.

'I am sure my son will be delighted. . . .' said Prahelek; and Queen Kandiri also beamed and nodded at the Ambassador.

'If you will excuse me, your Majesties,' said Kernin suddenly, 'I have never met this girl. I may not like her, or she me. Don't you think—at least we ought to meet first, and see . . . ?'

The Ambassador coughed. 'That will not be very convenient for a while, your Highness.'

'Why ever not?' said Kernin.

'Well, Highness, the Princess Mengiri is but one year hatched. . . .'

At this there was a slight but perceptible gasp around the hall, and one or two of the Menkinvian maids giggled. There was Kernin on his throne, a burly twelve-year-old, and his wide shoulder-vest made him look even burlier. He was strong, handsome, almost a man—and now he was being offered a hatchling as a bride!

'I—I would prefer to decline this marriage,' said Kernin. 'Ambassador, I have nothing against your Princess, she may grow to be a delightful lady, but—I might well meet someone else while she is growing up.'

'Passion of Prah!' King Prahelek exploded. 'What are you saying, boy? D'ye think royal wives are taken at whim, merely for leching with? You know nothing of this matter—be silent, I tell you! *I* will conclude this business, and to mine and your Mother's liking. . . .'

'Father, in any case I think I am too young to marry.' Kernin looked uncomfortable and mutinous. 'Why cannot this business wait ten years, till the lady in question may begin to be marriageable?'

Prahelek ground his teeth, and began talking quickly to the Ambassador. Unfortunately for him, though, a bridegroom's consent is required for a valid marriage according to the customs of Nakhtos, and Kernin had a very stubborn streak in him. The audience had to be adjourned while the King held a private talk with the Prince. When they returned to the Hall, a compromise had been reached: Kernin would not *marry* little Mengiri at this stage, but he would be officially betrothed to her . . . which, diplomatically, achieved nearly the same purpose.

At the banquet that followed, King Prahelek got rather drunk, and in his cups was heard to mutter: 'Passion of Prah! Too young to marry, is he? Too young? We'll see about that. . . .'

And again he muttered: 'Too much poring over sh-shtupid gadgets with that old hornless horse. Manly exercise, that's what he needs. Passion of Prah! Make a pricking warrior of him. . . .'

For the scene which now follows I have no detailed eye-witness account: I was not there. But I have pieced the evidence together, and I claim the privilege of the old saga writers, now and perhaps again in this history. It happened, then, thus:

Kernin's bedchamber that night was very dim, for he had put the thimbles over all the light-berries, and there was almost no Ring. He was restless; he always had trouble sleeping at the beginning of the No-Ring nights. This, the time of the month when he was hatched: it was possibly unlucky, but he did not feel unlucky, only over-excited. Maybe his rhythms were different from most people's—most people rejoiced at Full Ring, not now. And yet he loved the darker nights. Now you could really see the stars. . . .

He threw off the sheet and slipped naked from his bed to the open window. Leaning on the sill, he looked out and up. This window faced Ringback, inland, toward Aelvia and Khar Durnaran. Khar Durnaran . . . that he could hardly see now, unless it was that tiny black gap in the World's End haze-glow—but beyond Khar Durnaran, beyond the haze, ten degrees up began the Sky! Those bright lines like rivers in heaven, those single points, those broader patches of light like seas. If he looked high, about 70 degrees up, he could see Pelas Velnul, the Sea of Angels. Why not say 'Angelwards' instead of 'Ringback'? Angelwards would be directly inland, and you could use the Sea of Angels as your Quartermarker even when there was no Ring. Not precise, though. Pelas Velnul was the broadest patch in the high sky. But straight down from Pelas Velnul stood the Flickerfly star. A little one, a dim point, but very distinctive: the only *orange* star in the sky, unless you counted the Ring, and the only one that regularly twinkled. Or flickered—not quite the same thing. Definitely variable, too: one could never see it during No Ring. Tonight it was very dim. But yes, it was *exactly* opposite the Ring. 'Flickerflyward', then. . . .

He gazed up past Flickerfly at the unvarying, blue-white stars of Heaven. Unwinking blue-white hieroglyphs on black paper.

So the Symmetrists loved Black Heaven, it was a land like Earth, full of sweet dark-faced Angels? O to be winged like an Angel, or, if Angels didn't exist, at least like a phoenix-eagle, and fly right up into the black fields of the Sky.

He was disturbed in his musing by a sound behind him. Not loud—but there should have been *nothing*. He whirled, conscious of possible assassins, of his stark nakedness. . . .

In the dim downcast light of the thimbled berries, he saw a slim pale form in a flimsy linen kilt. 'Master,' said the girl softly, 'I—I am very sorry I startled you.'

She was clearly not armed, except with her own charms. Silver-braceleted, barefoot, bare—elsewhere; about his own age or possibly a year more; fair flame-gold hair. Menkinvian?

Then he noticed that she wore a little silver chain about her left ankle.

'Master, I was sent—by Their Majesties. Master, if I please you, let me stay awhile. . . .'

'What is your name?' Kernin's heart was thumping.

'Rini, master.'

'A pirate-wench?'

'Master, I was taken in the egg, when his Majesty made his glorious campaign upon the Great Sea. I have been raised in this Palace, but I am indeed of the blood of the accursed Goryai. But I do not remember any parents, only the slave-fosterers and trainers.' The girl approached half a step, and as if by accident her flimsy cloth began to slip off her hips. 'Master—I am well trained. . . .'

Well, she was, and Kernin found that night that he was not, in one sense, too young for marriage. But when they had made love the first time, he startled the girl by saying: 'Rini, I will have you freed at once!'

'Oh, master, *no*! Don't you like me?'

'Very much, my dear; and that's why. It's terrible—there are no slaves among the centaurs, so why among humans? Especially a sweet girl like you—*you* were never a pirate, after all! You *do* belong to me personally, don't you, like you said?'

'Your Highness' name is engraved on my chain,' said Rini, showing it.

Kernin felt the links of the chain, and shuddered. 'I hate all such things. Chains, crowns . . . I never even wear arm-rings. *That* must come off.'

'But oh my master, what will happen to me? Their Majesties will surely punish me, since you reject their gift.'

'I don't—well, I do in a way. People should not be "gifts".'

Kernin sat up, and looked at his bedmate, and thought. 'Are you really sure it would be dangerous to you?'

'Yes, master, I would be punished—and then another girl would be given to you. Their Majesties wish to keep you—satisfied—till the Princess Mengiri is old enough. . . .'

'I see,' said Kernin, and laughed shortly. 'Well then, I must keep you, Rini. For the time being, anyway. Later I'll see what I can do for you.'

'Then you won't change me for another girl? Master, I would rather not be changed. I like you. . . .'

'I like you too. No, I won't change you. Better the dragon you know than the dragon you don't.'

'I am not a dragon, I am a *girl*,' said Rini, who was somewhat literal-minded.

'Oh, well,' said Kernin.

After that Kernin began to be in better favour with his father the King. He was given much less time with Barundran, and was taken out of the Palace much more to the usual activities of Princes. He was exercised in weapon-play: I gave some help there, and he quickly became a fine swordsman. He also went out on Progresses up and down the River to the various nome-capitals. Kernin was surprisingly compliant; but I, being often at his side, saw that he was not turning into the usual wenching-drinking-hunting royal Prince at all. He went through the motions, for he was learning some cunning in handling his father; but his real interest was elsewhere. Whenever he could, he was inquiring into the condition of the people—especially slaves. There were not many slaves in the River Kingdom, and those only war captives or their children to one generation, but—

'*Any* slaves are too many,' said Kernin to me once, as our galley was rowing back toward Nakhtos.

'Well,' I said, 'that's a minor problem. You can solve it with one stroke of the pen, or the sceptre, when you are King.'

'Yes, but there's so much else. The peasants—their condition is abysmal. . . .'

This in fact was his social-conscience phase. It did not last long, I am happy to say; but while it did, I did not approve. The fact is that people are naturally *un*equal, and most peasants enjoy being peasants, and I told Kernin so. Once in a Palurian nome we were attending a festival of Gorlun the Storm-god, and the peasant farmers and the Rain-dervishes were all dancing in their rings, all reeling drunk, all pounding the wine-soaked earth with their bare feet in the gold light of Sunquenching, and the girl who represented Nami danced naked but for her copper-wire ornaments in the middle of each ring. Beautiful peasant-wenches they were too: the Rain-dervishes leered and pranced, the crops were going to be good. I said to Kernin: 'You want to take them out of *this*? They love it!'

'I asked one farmer how old he was,' said Kernin, 'and he didn't know. They haven't heard of Years, it seems, only days and Rings. They can't read or count above twenty, they know nothing beyond their crops and their nome and the next festival. . . .'

'Half the world is like that.' I laughed. 'The happier half. It's we who are the sad ones, my Prince. With learning, we have invented Time and far-off things. If we thought less of far-off things, and enjoyed the here-and-now more, I think we would be better men.'

'Animals, you mean,' muttered Kernin. 'When I am King, I shall improve education, and force the nome-lords to do more for the people. . . .'

That really made me smile. A descendant of Hinelen, talking like that! Later in that voyage, as our galley was passing a stretch of palm-woods, I said to him: 'If you're going to be *so* struck on equality and justice, why don't you hunt up the fellows who are doubtless lurking in there, and hand the land back to them?'

'What fellows?' He looked blankly at the dark forest.

'The satyrs,' I said, 'from whom we stole the Shorelands in the first place.'

Then he laughed. 'That's going a bit far. It's *our* land now. But is it true, what the Aelvian minstrels say, that there are still a lot of satyrs in Aelvia—and they're allowed to come into the towns?'

'Possibly. Aelvian minstrels tell a lot of lies.'

'It would be nice to see satyrs treated like *people*,' said Kernin. 'After all, they are not too unlike us.' And he gave a mischievous grin, and touched his head-peaks, which just emerged now from his hair.

I was scandalised. It was bad enough that some Menkinvians and Agnaians would say we of the River had satyr blood in us, that our head-peaks were nothing but *small horns*—but here now was Kernin almost *admitting* it!

His real cure was effected by Barundran, when we got back to Nakhtos. The King felt he could allow Kernin some more time with his tutor now—now that the Prince was a real manly man, a warrior, a user of his concubine. . . . I don't think Prahelek

knew the real state of things as regards Rini at all. Kernin had
had her chain taken off her ankle, and made into a nice necklace;
he also slept with her only when they both really wanted to—
which was rather less often, I'm afraid, than *she* wanted to. And
now he was returning to his real love—returning hungrily.

We found Barundran on the roof at Last Finger Hour, just
before Sunquenching. He was delighted to see us; but his welcome was a little hurried. For once, he was showing an almost
youthful excitement—rather more like Kernin's than his own
normal philosophic calm. He was fidgeting with—not a mathematical instrument, but a large pot-plant.

'Hnnnm! Fair sirs,' he whinnied, 'do you know this vegetable?'

I laughed. 'Of course. It's a gas-plant.'

The fat sausage-like fronds, about as long as a man's arm,
were bobbing up and down—bobbing up with the buoyancy of
the gas inside the pale green semi-translucent sausages, bobbing
down with the pressure of the sun's rays. The Common or Lesser
gas-plant is not rare in the country about Nakhtos: children chop
off the sausage-fronds and make toys of them.

'We have nothing like this in our country, in the Middle
Plain,' said Barundran. 'O, my voyaging hither was worthwhile,
after all! I shall indite a monograph and send it to Kerindorna.
But stay, let us see what happens when the Sun quenches.'

What happened, of course, over the next few minutes was
that, as the Sun's rays died, the fat fingers of the gas-plant grew
erect with their natural buoyancy. Kernin obligingly drew his
dagger and sliced off one, and it shot up into the air like an
arrow until its gas leaked out of the stem-wound and the deflated
skin flopped and feathered down to the courtyard below.

'It is assuredly a relative of the Light-berry,' said Barundran.
'And like the Light-berry, it seeks its kindly home in the noble
world of Light.'

'The noble world of light?' said Kernin. 'Barundran, Master, I
think it is time you told me all your philosophy. I am no longer a
child; nor will I, nor friend Orselen here, ever betray you to the
King or the priests. Come now, why is the world the way it is?
Are there truly gods? Why is there evil and suffering and cruelty
and slavery and death?'

Barundran sighed. 'Large questions. And you know, among
us there are many schools. And even the great Gormarendran
was forced to speak of these things, as it were, in myths. But
truly I believe thus: that God is Light, and his chief home and
symbol is the holy Sun, and his children are the stars of high
Heaven. Darkness—his Earth, and solid matter, which your

Black Priestesses miscall the Mother—all these low elements are mere emanations, fallings away from the High One. Do not exercise yourself overmuch, my Prince, over suffering and evil in this life: such things must be, while we inhabit this dark and muddy prison. But the purified spirit ascends at death to God—as even your White Sun-Priests confess. The Symmetrists blaspheme when they praise darkness rather than light. . . .'

Well, we argued for quite a while; but in the end, Barundran more or less convinced Kernin that evil was a necessity in this world. It could be lessened, but not banished altogether. And violent revolutions were not a good idea.

'No thinking being does evil except from ignorance,' said Barundran with a sad smile, 'but ignorance is stubborn. And therefore when you are King, my lord, it will be your task to enlighten your people—gradually.'

Kernin's natural impatience flared up at that. 'But I know so little myself! Barundran, I would like to visit your own noble land, where people are so much *more* enlightened! Why shouldn't my father let me make a short trip across the Sea—to Kherindorna, if not to Kintobara?'

I interposed. 'Because he wants you to fight in his next war. Because he wants you to marry the Princess of Agnai. Because he will not trust you to the huge and dangerous Sea. . . .'

'Because he will not trust me to myself,' said Kernin softly. 'Once in the Middle Plain, I might not want to come back—not soon, anyway. . . .'

'Quite so,' I said. 'It is what I myself would fear. Put such thoughts right out of your mind, my Prince. Your life is the keystone of the Kingdom. No, it's not just your father's aggressive ambitions: *you* are what holds the Twin Kingdoms together, or will do once your father is dead. You owe a duty to your country, not to desert it.'

'Orselen speaks truth,' said Barundran mildly. 'In this dark world, we are all God's soldiers. We must not desert our posts. It is not for us to seek the ends of the earth while our families perish.'

'No?' said Kernin, suddenly very sharp. 'Then why are *you* here, Barundran, so far from your home?'

The centaur laughed quietly. 'Well riposted, my Prince. I too have some itching curiosity. But I am a private person, no magistrate of any of our republics, and my dear wife is dead and my children all well grown and comfortable. It is a tradition among us, that old philosophers may wander . . . and so here I have wandered nearly to the end of the known Earth.'

'The End of the Earth!' Kernin had kindled now with the sparks of his old theme. 'By the Sword of Sinis, it is about time we talked of that. Where does the Earth end? Barundran, you must have some theories. . . .'

Barundran sighed. 'Theories aplenty. Well, I will fish out my scrolls, and we will draw diagrams; but tomorrow, good prince, tomorrow. Now, I think I see a fair maid come to fetch you to the Royal feast. . . .'

Next morning at Sunkindle I met Kernin in a corridor, dressed simply in a plain kilt and sandals, as coming directly from his bedchamber. He seemed excited—but that word is not adequate. His green eyes appeared slightly unfocussed, as if directed to an infinite distance. I thought of the title he would inherit one day—'King of Infinite Space'. No, he was not agitated. He radiated a calm joy.

'I have had a dream,' he said.

I smiled. 'Well, tell me.'

In his dream he had found himself flying. With outstretched arms for wings, but not flapping them, he had floated gently from a hillside. Below that hill there was a kind of sunken garden, full of the most beautiful flowers; and on the stems perched strange creatures—scaly things, something like grass-hoppers, something like springer-dragons. These creatures looked up at the flying Prince and envied him; yet he, looking down at them, rejoiced in their strange, unhuman beauty. Then in his flight he passed that garden—it might have been a small crater—and then, by the mere force of his will, he had flown higher, up another and higher hill.

'I did not flap my hands at all,' he said. 'I was flying with my *mind,* Orselen!'

'And then what happened—when you came to the second hill?'

He laughed, but ruefully. 'Then—I woke up. Oh, I know it sounds silly, but I can't express the sheer *joy* of that dream. The garden and its plants, the hills, the quality of the light—it was like a vision!'

'Had you slept with Rini beforehand?'

'Oh yes, we made love. Why do you ask?'

'There's a foolish theory among some physicians,' I said, 'that dreams of flying indicate a craving for sex. But I see this cannot be true. Much more likely it was touched off by the gas-plant you saw last evening, rising into the air.'

'Perhaps. . . .' he admitted. Then he shook his head as if to clear it, and laughed. 'Enough of such fancies! Now, ho for old Barundran, and the World's End!'

It was a clear bright morning when Barundran spread his charts on the table on the roof. Khar Durnaran stood like a mist-blue arrowhead in the white vagueness between dark Earth and bright blue Sky. Kernin made a small bow to the mountain, as if to an old friend, and then bent over the diagrams.

'There are two main theories,' Barundran lectured. 'Here you see the system of the Symmetrists. These two parallel lines are Earth and the Starry Heaven. That little disc in the midst between them is the Sun. Our country, the Middle Plain, lies directly under the Sun; left of it—that is, Ringward—are the hordes of Thulor, the wild centaurs; right of it lies the Great Sea, and then your Shorelands. You notice that the Known Earth occupies only a small portion of the lower line.'

'Where is the Edge?' said Kernin. 'Both lines run up to the end of the paper.'

'There is no Edge, either to Earth or Sky. Both are infinite, in all dimensions. The Sky is infinitely thick in the Up direction, the Earth is infinitely thick in the Down direction, and both are infinite toward all the Four Quarters.'

Kernin jumped as if he had been pricked with a dagger's point. 'Infinite!' he gasped. 'Infinite! You mean, you could go on wandering every way, and always finding new lands, new peoples . . . !'

'Precisely,' said Barundran. 'Unfortunately, the Symmetrists' scheme cannot be true: it does not save the appearances as regards Heaven. The stars which appear lowest in the Sky ought to be at enormous distances farther than the ones in the zenith, and this is clearly not so. Moreover, when one travels far—over the Great Sea, for instance—the stars *toward* which one travels ought to rise higher, whereas they do not. On the contrary, they *sink*. Conversely, by receding from one quarter of the sky, you can see *more* in that direction. For instance, the sky-sea which you call Pelas Ranol—that low, wide patch of light that stands in the sky in the direction of my country—we cannot see that *at all* from the Middle Plain. And on the other hand, we can see *another* wide Sky-sea lying in *this* direction, over *this* land roughly in the direction of Flickerfly star; and from here you cannot see that *at all*. For that matter, Flickerfly is much brighter from our country than here, yet you are *closer* to it. What does all that prove?'

'That the Sky is a dome, a bulbous dome, maybe three quarters of a hollow sphere.' Kernin looked depressed. 'The

open side of the dome hovers over the Earth-disc—and I suppose
it's held up by the Pillars of Prah, after all, on the Edge of the
Fiery Sea. This is merely what our priests have always told us.
Oh Barundran, you raised my hopes for a moment.'

'Hopes? What mean you, Prince?'

'I rather liked the idea of an infinite Earth,' said Kernin,
gazing inland past Khar Durnaran. 'Fancy how it would be, to
get on a good horse and ride, ride for ever, finding always new
things, new peoples, new life and beauty. . . .'

'And that may still be possible, in theory,' smiled Barundran.
'Now see this scroll, my Prince. This is the system of Gormarendran, which is the most accepted among us.'

The system of Gormarendran looked like this:

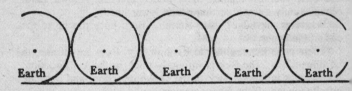

'Of course,' said Barundran, 'you must read this in two
dimensions, not just one. There are Skies beyond Skies in every
direction, like a layer of hollow eggs along the floor of an infinite
box. And in the middle of each Sky sits a Sun, and the flat space
beneath each Sun and each Sky is an Earth. There are Earths
beyond Earths for ever, just as there are Skies beyond Skies.
And, to say truth, there is some support for this theory from one
of our old legends, and from the biology which you know
already. We Centaurs perhaps originated on another Earth, beneath a different Sky, along with all the other six-limbed creatures;
for one of *our* Myth-writings tells, that before we were civilised
we lived on the shore of a far different Great Sea, with far
different stars—and by the by, very different animals, such as
huge flying men like the angels of your myths—before we
wandered from our old home to the Middle Plain.'

Kernin looked as if he could burst with joy. *'Can this be
true?'*

'It is only an hypothesis,' admitted Barundran. 'But it does
seem to save most of the appearances.'

Kernin was already tracing imaginary lines with his forefinger
over the diagram. 'Then there must be Inter-earths, places *between*
worlds, between Suns! What about these stretches between the

lower forks of the adjacent Skies? Are they lands of darkness? But I suppose some light would filter past the openings, under the edges of the skies. . . .'

'Our Myth has no tradition of a land of darkness,' said Barundran. 'But of course, the Skies could be partly translucent to the Suns, anyway. Or the gaps may be high enough to admit light all the way. Possibly at the mid-point between worlds one might look up and see *two* Suns. . . .'

'By all the gods,' said Kernin, 'I swear, I am going to find out!'

We others both looked at him aghast.

'It—it is surely not practical,' stammered Barundran. 'I will confess, Prince, that when I first came to this Shoreland, I too had some secret wild dreams. We of the Middle Plain are cut off, Ringward, by the very wild hordes of Thulor. This other way, I thought . . . but now here I find the way out of the Known World is blocked by great mountains and ghastly forests.' He gestured to the Aelvian Wall, the Rathvian Wall, Khar Durnaran, and so round to the Forest of Luzelana. 'Besides, we have little idea of *scale*. It may be thousands of miles.'

Kernin's jaw was firm, his eyes blazed green fire. 'There is only one way to find out how far: to *go*. And I am now deeply sworn.' He looked from one to other of us. 'This is the thing for which I was hatched: just this. What is a Prince or a King, a little lord of one warring city or another? Friends, we will all die one day and rot, and our kingdoms will rot with us. But to achieve the discovery of the *other Earths*—to find the peoples behind the Sky, the peoples under other Suns! That is a task worthy of a Man. . . .' He paused, and smiled at Barundran. 'And even, perhaps, of a Centaur.'

'Hnnnm!' Barundran made that queer noise; but this time there was also a tear in his old grey eye. Then he swallowed, and mastered his emotion. 'Well, my Prince, I see that we are two fools of the same sort. If ever—I do not think it can be done: there is your royal Father, and your princely duty to your country, and it will take years even to start—but if ever you do go, and I am still on these old feet—well, I will go with you, if you will have me.'

Kernin clasped his old teacher's hand. And then he was looking at me.

'I will not swear,' I said, 'for I fear all oaths, and all gods. Also, my Prince, I think this is a most disastrous fancy. What are the ends of the earth, or sunless lands, or even infinite worlds, to the one world we know?' I waved my hand over the roofs of Nakhtos, with their flower-gardens and incubators, to the holy River and the pleasant wheat-fields beyond, and the green-gold Horse Plains. 'Here is the plenty of the gods—wonder and beauty enough, and laughter and festivals and love.' I paused. 'But, my lord, I know your mind and your stubbornness. Well, I am your own Bard-Herald, and I claim my right of office, which is also my duty. Where you go, I must go too. If ever your challenge sounds in the worlds behind the Sun, it is I who must blow it.'

'Thank you, Orselen,' said Kernin, and took my hand also. 'My friend—I expected no less.'

Even the mightiest of trees, the angel-tree, queen of the forests, must grow from a tiny seed. And that blue-bright morning, on the palace roof of Nakhtos, there was planted the seed which grew at last into the great Quest.

PART TWO

The Prince of Aelvia

5

The Year 625 from the founding of Palur began with strange portents. A new crater erupted in the Kelan Nome, forty miles downriver from Nakhtos, precisely on Year-Nail Day at Sunkindle; and as we were all on the great palace roof for the New Year ceremonies, we saw the bolus of fire-stuff belched out of the bowels of Earth, and rising straight up to the brightening Sun. The Sun Priests held a hasty consultation, and decided the augury was a good one. But my father Omren told me heavily that he feared otherwise: a rising fireball is a natural symbol of a death. Well, certainly quite a few peasants died in the Kelan Nome, for the crater was two miles wide. If the Earth-mother had heaved out her fiery egg just a mile more to Ringleft, the crater would have touched the Holy River, with much worse consequences. Nami's 'poem', as the euphemism goes, might have proved a real tragedy.

Barundran told Kernin and myself, afterwards and in private, that this was no 'poem' of the goddess, nor any omen, but a purely natural and random occurrence. Sun-stuff streams down into Earth in the Sun's rays, and from time to time the fiery substance will accumulate underground, and then burst out almost anywhere, like a pimple on a man's skin. The eruptions of the fireballs are necessary, else at last the Sun would run out of light. The fireballs return to the Sun, and so feed it.

Barundran's explanation sounded reasonable; but I was not entirely reassured. Of course, as a poet I am naturally superstitious. But there were other portents, too. One strange piece of news from across the Great Sea: a horde from Thulor had made a sudden onslaught on the Middle Plain, causing some destruction before they were checked by the Wise Centaurs. The Unwise or savage Centaurs babbled to their conquerors that they had been terrorised out of their own territories by giant harpies, or flying chariots, or enormous gryphons—whether severally or acting

together the accounts were not clear enough to show. Barundran
muttered about 'poor savages—hallucinations. . . .'

'And yet those of Thulor are also centaurs,' I said.

'No race is privileged,' said Barundran. 'There are foolish and
wise among each. Doubtless there are even some wise satyrs, if
we could only track them to their forest lairs.'

Another portent: on Sinis-night of the Second Ring-month,
Barundran and Kernin were observing the stars from the palace
roof, when they suddenly noticed that two little yellow-white
stars were twinkling. Apart from the orange Flickerfly, it was
extremely rare for stars to twinkle: perhaps one would do so
every three or four years, always very small ones. Now on one
single night, two were twinkling at once. Or rather, not quite at
once: first the star-point above Pelas Ranol would twinkle and
stop, then the star-point under Pelas Velnul would twinkle and
stop; and then the first star again.

'It looks as though they are winking at each other,' said
Kernin. 'Passing messages, perhaps?'

'That is a possible hypothesis,' Barundran murmured reluctantly.
'But why should the blessed stars need such crude methods to
communicate? According to Gormarendran, they are the holy
souls of the dead, the purified children of the Sun. On the other
hand, I think it only fair to say that more twinklings have been
reported in the last twenty years than in all the previous century.
It will be interesting to watch, and see if the increase is
maintained.'

It certainly was. That same year, in the Fourth Ring, *three*
little yellow-white stars twinkled on Prah-night—and always, as
it were, taking it in turns.

The Black Priestesses declared that this portended a war, since
Prah is a war god: a war of three nations. But that was an easy
guess, for in the Sixth Ring the truce with Rindos would expire,
and there was that little grievance we had given Aelvia. . . .

King Prahelek's hair was now completely white, yet he began
the war with his usual energy: he crossed the Rindian frontier the
first day after the truce expired, and made long marches. He took
with him all his principal heralds, and also Prince Kernin.

Kernin was now fully fifteen years old, and fifteen years after
hatching a man is at his full strength. Kernin was quite as tall as
his royal father, but more slimly built, nimble, a fine swordsman
. . . and very handsome. All girls seemed to love him; and most
of our troops admired him. My father Omren was especially fond
of the Prince: on the night before our first battle, he embraced

him in my presence, and called him 'dear son'. Well, that was fitting: Kernin and I were on such terms now that in private we called each other 'brother'. We were hardly lord and servant any more: with Barundran, we were fellow conspirators. For a year now, we had been nursing our secret—Kernin's vowed Quest. We did not often speak of it, but I knew that Kernin had not forgotten.

He was a conspirator indeed. During the past twenty Rings, he had been at pains to gain his royal father's favour. He had hunted, he had trained hard. It seemed to me that he had hardened in more than one sense.

In that first battle, which flared up in daylight, Prahelek watched his Prince closely, hoping to exercise him in his first fight but not expose him to any great risk. Things did not work out that way. The enemy pressed hard right up to the Royal guards—and then, suddenly Kernin seemed to take fire. Eyes blazing, he leapt upon his great yellow stallion Goldhorn, and called to me to follow. He led a charge. . . . Truly the god Prah, Lord of Battles, had entered into him: I never saw anything so savage, nor yet so skilful. With his own sword and lance, Kernin slew and slew. . . .

And this was the boy who, a mere forty Rings earlier, had been squeamish about hunting a few wretched animals.

Well, after that wild charge through the full gravity of day, we held the place of slaughter, and the Rindian king fled for his life. Prahelek was overjoyed: his son was his son indeed! I had only one chagrin at the victory feast in our camp that night: that wretch Fiupen played the King's Praise-song. For my father Omren had been wounded in his right arm by an enemy arrow. It did not seem a dangerous wound, but he was now an old man, nearly as white-haired as the King, and he was shaken and unable to pluck harp-strings.

I played the Praise-song for my own Prince and friend; and by the way, my song was a masterpiece, far better than Fiupen's wretched effort, as all the unprejudiced listeners acknowledged. . . . But I digress.

The next day, Kernin demanded from his father that he be given an independent command. 'You have only indifferent generals watching Aelvia. Father, they will be attacking us there any day. Give *me* Aelvia.'

'What,' smiled Prahelek, 'will you scale the Aelvian Wall, up the Second Cataract?'

Kernin shrugged. 'I could try.'

*　　*　　*

We made swift marches back to Nakhtos, and then rowed up the Kherilos by night, when lower gravity makes the river's flow sluggish. And there we found that the Aelvians had already attacked. On Sinis-night, when there was almost no Ring, they had lowered themselves with rope-ladders down a sheer cliff-face of the main Aelvian Wall and had taken our guard-troops shamefully by surprise. Now they had captured a small foothold in the lower country, formerly their own territory, and they were tumbling reinforcements down the Wall as fast as they could. They were stocky black-haired warriors, rather rustically armed and weak in cavalry, but they made up for these defects in sheer fighting spirit. Instead of trumpeters, they were musicked into battle by girl-pipers—brave bare-legged wenches in short tunics of russet wool. The Aelvians allow great honour and freedom to their women, and at this time their war-leader was none other than their young Queen Niamwy.

When we arrived at the battle-front, Kernin curled his lips in a cryptic smile. 'Plucky folk: but we will take them.'

And we did. He rallied our disordered army and attacked at once, by night in the middle of No-Ring. That was an onslaught I shall never forget: it was like a dream. We charged with our right on the River, and the scene was lit only by the night-glow of water—the river itself to the side, and the very distant glow of Pelas Magha behind, and in our faces the tumbling sparks of the Great Cataract as it flung itself down from the notch in the Wall. But since it is the Sun's dark rays which provoke water to shine, and the cataract presents little surface to those rays, its light was not very bright; and Kernin had taken care that we had a dark wood in our rear, so the Aelvians did not see us till it was too late for them. Their troops below the Wall were still few and without horses, and we soon drove them up against the sheer cliff of Drycleve, away from the River, the place whence they had first descended, where there are no possible paths up, not even in night gravity. It looked like being a massacre.

But Kernin told me to blow the Retire. With me at his side, in the first light of Sunkindle he spurred toward the ruck of our defeated enemies.

'Yield,' he cried, 'yield! I give you life, and honour. Well have you fought. . . .'

It was a ticklish moment. The little dark men were milling about in front of their girl-pipers, and it looked to me that at any moment some of them might seize their chance and try and kill our Prince. I shouted: 'Your herald, ho! And I flourished my horse-horn trumpet to prove my own privilege.

Well, their herald emerged from the rout, and we negotiated.

'Nay, we will die under our Wall, look you,' said the stocky, black-browed harpist. 'And each of our pipers hath her dagger at her own throat, rather—'

'I swear by Sinis, trier of hearts,' said Kernin, 'none of you will be made slave, neither man nor woman, nor will I touch any lass's honour. You shall be our honourable prisoners for two Rings or three, and then—I wish for nothing but friendship with Aelvia. This war was none of my doing.'

Well, we swore great oaths on both sides, and then on those terms they yielded. Kernin kept every bit of his word, and we held a merry victory feast next night under the Wall, and in the Prince's great tent we were musicked by the three girl-pipers we had captured. Wild wailing stuff it was to my ears, but Kernin seemed to like it. Their Bard-herald sang a song of defiance: we had won a little battle, he chanted, but Queen Niamwy and her main army were still intact above the Wall, and would soon descend upon us and smite us like afternoon thunderbolts, or like Prah smiting the Elder Gods.

Kernin laughed. 'I like your spirit, my captives. But the gods, both Elder and Younger, may dispose otherwise.'

The war was now a stalemate. We sat under the Wall, and the Aelvians sat on top of the Wall, and neither side could get at the other, save for arrow shots. Kernin would spend his days riding along under the Wall, and his evenings alone or with only me beside him, brooding in his bed-tent over Barundran's fine map of the Disputed Nomes. He was looking for an easy way into Aelvia, but it seemed there was no such way: as the map made clear. Aelvia is probably the worn-down remains of a crater a hundred miles across, and its main Wall marches without a break right and left from the River till the Disputed Nomes end in two awful hilly tangles, the so-called Haunted Forests. There anything might lurk: sphinxes, harpies, springers—and of course, satyrs. No army could march through *those*.

At times Kernin would put away the map, and have the light-berries removed; and then he would gaze into a bowl of water. Under the thin roof of a tent, water at night will still glow very faintly: a fact which is sometimes used by wandering scriers. Kernin would gaze into the blue-white dimness of the water, seeking for inspiration.

I said to him once: 'Brother, why are you so set on attacking Aelvia? You know we wronged them, not they us. You might now arrange an honourable peace with their Queen, and rejoin your father for the main war.'

He said: 'Aelvia . . . I must have Aelvia.'

A disquieting suspicion began to trouble my mind. 'I did not think you were ambitious to be a conqueror. You always derided Sakanek.'

'I have not changed. But Aelvia—it is the last of the Shorelands. The way to World's End must begin there.' Suddenly he leapt to his feet. 'Brother, I have it! Gas-plants!'

The Aelvian or Greater Gas-plant is a giant of its kind, with sausage-fingers nearly as long and thick as the trunk of an angel-tree. The plants grow plentifully on the fringes of the Haunted Forests, and the children of the Disputed Nomes have games of riding on them, as one rides a horse. The game works best about Sunkindle or Quenching; by day one's weight pushes the plant down, by night the plant rises too much, and you slip off.

Kernin soon had great squads of his army, and of the local peasants, cutting off gas-plant stems. Once the stem was cut, you tied up the cut end with rope lashings. The main trouble was to ensure that the stem didn't get away and go sailing up into the air—especially at night. Once cut, roped and weighted, we stored the big stems in glades on the fringes of the forest, where they might not be seen by the watchers on the Wall.

But all this took time, and on occasions (especially toward No-Ring) Kernin grew restless. I saw in him a steely resolve struggling with his natural impulsiveness. He had got Barundran to join us now in the camp, and he vented some of his energy in philosophical discussions with the old centaur. He would also attend the festivals of his workers, New Ring and Mid-Ring and Ringripe, and applaud the pretty dancing girls. I suggested to him that he ought to send to Nakhtos for Rini. But he wouldn't have that. He had now given Rini her freedom officially, and was trying to marry her off to a suitable Nakhtian palace servant.

'I really haven't time for emotional wenches,' he told me. 'There are greater things.' And he gazed up over the Wall toward Khar Durnaran and World's End.

But young men are young men, no matter what their driving ambition may be. There came a time when one of the local dancers caught his eye, a girl named Velni, who was rather less Angelic than her name would imply. Black-haired, bright-cheeked, with a saucy look, she gyrated admirably at Suori's feast in her copper spangles and not much else. Next afternoon we found her acting as a water-carrier to the gas-plant workers—which did not prevent her from fluttering her eyelids at our Prince.

The inevitable happened. Kernin turned to me and said, in

some embarrassment: 'Brother, if you will not mind waiting
here, I wish to have some little time alone.'

'Here' was mixed woods and savannah, and the workers were
out of sight in the next glade whence we heard the thunk of their
axes; all but the girl, who was hovering near us with her water-
pitcher, on pretext of offering the Prince a drink. I said: 'Are you
sure it's safe? These are the Haunted Woods.'

'Of course. Our axe-men must have frightened all the monsters for miles around. We won't be going far, just to that glade
on the other side, with the bank of honey-berries. And Velni is
no spy or anything. . . .'

'I know that,' I said. 'Do you think I haven't checked? Well, I
will be within call, if you need me.'

'Not for *this*, I think.' He laughed; and then those two stole
out of the clearing.

Tarsh, formerly of the lair of Dharn, was angry. As he loped
through the forest he had played once a few notes on his reed-
pipe—and then flung the little instrument away into the heart of
a honey-bush. Time was—only two suns ago—he had played
that melody, the Come-come, outside the lair of Vhurn, and a
shani of Vhurn had come wandering out—young, snub-nosed,
with lovely furry legs and feminine, unclawed feet—and he had
enjoyed her again and again till the daystorm had surprised them,
and they had rolled laughing in the wet, rain dribbling between
her little conical breasts, or splashing off his horns—and then
she had taken fright, it was so late, she had to get back to her
Old One or face a beating. She probably got a beating anyway.
All the young shanis were always getting beatings from the old
males, their masters, just for doing what came naturally . . .
especially with young horners like Tarsh. Of course they would,
why not? The Old Ones kept all the girls, but they couldn't use
them right. They had only two horns that really worked—on
their heads. Lifehorn, lifehorn, thought Tarsh, looking at his
own lovely one, which lifted its head stiffly as he ran, what
trouble you've got me into. Thrown out of the tribe, just for
pleasuring too many shanis. Thrown *out*. And now, where shall I
go?

He might lurk in the forest, stealing harpies' eggs or pouncing
on little sphinxes, eating honey-berries . . . and hoping that an
occasional shani would come wandering into the deep forest
itself. Small hope, that. And anyway, that was no life for a
self-respecting *shath*, a nasty solitary life, and probably a short

one, for there were worse things than harpies in the forest. And no hope of making a name for himself in any Lair. . . .

Suddenly the forest was thinning. Here was an open glade with a lifehorn tree in the midst. He paused in the dark of the last thicket, listening to the lives of Earth. How safe was this place? His sensitive ears swivelled, picking up the great far rhythms. A long, long way off he could hear the low roar of the River of the Cloth-Wearers. Closer still, there was a faint tock-tocking like a woodpecker yet certainly not a woodpecker: surely some activity of the Cloth-Wearers themselves. But not very close to this glade. This glade itself was safe.

He loped out into the open, and leapt onto one of the stems of the lifehorn tree, straddling the great green bouncing thing as it swayed up and down in the bright air. He was facing out towards its end—and the huge green phallus put his own smaller one to shame. According to the Old Ones, there *were* no female lifehorn trees: hence the desperate erection and perpetual waving of these green-gold fellows. Big brother, said Tarsh inwardly, I am truly sorry for you, we are in like cases, you and I. . . .

And then he heard that tock-tock again, a little louder and nearer, and a thought struck him, and he leapt to the ground. The Cloth-Wearers! After all, they had shanis too . . . not very pretty ones, and they had this crazy habit of wrapping up most of their charms, but. . . . Yes, that had been known, there were tales told of it in the Lairs. He began creeping toward the tock-tock. He kept his every sense alert, as a good beast should, and at first his motive was simple desire and vague, half-conscious hope. But then as he approached the dangerous River edge of the forest, his mind shifted into clear calculation. That was a thing he was good at, too; and for that also the Old Ones had hated him.

The Cloth-Wearers . . . they too had Lairs, in their fashion, most elaborate ones, and they were such careless folk that they let their *shath*, their males, move *between* lairs, change their place and their tribe. From the forest edge he had watched them, sometimes. . . . Tarsh knew he had no future as a forest shath—once an outcast, always an outcast—but among the Cloth-Wearers it might be different. If he could somehow make friends with some Cloth-Wearer, do him a good turn, for instance—why, he might be allowed to become a Cloth-Wearer himself. For a time, at least. Tales told that that could happen, at least in the high country over the mountains. And afterwards—why, anything was possible. The Cloth-Wearers had such uncanny skills, if he could learn some of *those*. . . .

Hah, Tarsh, he said to himself, you may become the Old One of a Lair yet; or something even better!

He crept forward. And now, on the fringes of this next glade, he heard things which—well, some were exciting, but one was terrifying. That soft chatter—definitely the voices of two Cloth-Wearers, a male and a female. But that deeper sound which was not really a sound but a vibration through the earth! It was a Gagen moving about in its lair.

He peered out between the leaves. And then, to his amazement, he saw that the two Cloth-Wearers were now wearing no cloth at all.

They were lying in a loving embrace, right over the swelling of earth and honeyberries which walled and hid the Gagen's lair.

Satisfied and happy, Kernin had just given Velni an affectionate kiss, when the earth of the bank exploded under them. In the first second he thought it must be a crater explosion. In the next second he knew it was not. Out of the black hole beside the girl's head there protruded a monstrous ash-grey face: the face of a lizard, but a lizard bigger than a grown man. Its eyes were dull red, like a pair of quenched night-suns. They registered no emotion whatever, no more than the empty eye-sockets of a skull; they were merely deaths marking their prey for destruction. The grey jaws, the saw-like teeth—the Springer opened these vastly, horribly wide, and before Kernin could make the slightest move, clamped them shut over the head and throat of the girl.

She did not even manage to scream.

Kernin was naked, his clothes and sword at the edge of the clearing five yards away, and the girl was certainly dead or dying already. In unarmed combat against the Springer, he didn't stand the slightest chance. Logically he should have run for his sword and shouted for Orselen, but horror knows no logic. As the Springer started to back down its narrow tunnel, pulling the girl's body after it by the half-severed neck, Kernin began tearing at the earth with his bare hands, trying to widen the passage, to go somehow to the rescue.

The next moment a dark furry figure hurtled out of the forest, and began kicking at the earth of the bank on the other side. Kernin paused, stupefied. It was a satyr, and the satyr was using his powerful clawed toes to collapse the earth at high speed. Just once the satyr turned its face toward him, and grinned. Amazingly, it was an ally. And the next moment the creature had done its work, and it was diving down the widened tunnel into the Springer's burrow.

Now Kernin saw what he must do, and ran for his sword. And that was the point at which I, hearing strange and horrible sounds, came racing onto the scene.

'Come,' Kernin shouted; and against all my protests he led the way down into that blackness. Beyond the tunnel was a hollow big enough to stand upright in, but so dark that at first we could see nothing. We could hear, though, hisses, grunts, growls. I clamped my hand on Kernin's shoulder to restrain him, and then as our eyes adjusted to the dimness we saw that the satyr was locked in mortal combat with that monster. The Springer was trampling over Velni's dead body, and jumping backward and forward, its jaws clamped over one of the satyr's horns: apparently the satyr had tried to butt the reptile, and having failed at that he was striking furiously at the thing with fists and feet. But he was awkwardly stuck, and Springers have terrible clawed hands, and that ghastly boxing-match could surely end only one way. Then Kernin chose his point and moment and lunged with his sword; and I came in from the other side; and between us, horribly, messily, we won that battle.

The Springer fell over Velni's headless body, and its ghost followed hers up into the roof of the burrow. The girl's spirit I think rose intact through the earth, and I trust went up to the holy Sun; but the Springer's filthy ghost rapidly disintegrated, and wisps of it remained near the 'ceiling', allowing us the better to view the ghastly sights inside. The space was roughly spherical, like a hollow egg or a tomb. Kernin, naked with his bloody sword in his hand, was leaning against one curved wall, and beginning to shake. I have never known a braver man, but he always hated enclosed spaces. And no enclosed space was ever as hateful as this one.

There was another small creature in the burrow, hopping about in the background. Of course, a baby Springer: the big one had been a female. Indeed, male Springers are smaller, less dangerous, and don't build underground lairs.

'I think that Thing was trying to feed its child,' said Kernin.

Our strange satyr ally now made one bound, and pounced on the baby Springer. He swung it by the tail, but the walls of the burrow were too soft to brain it. 'No. . . .' said Kernin, stepping forward; but next moment the satyr had bitten out the little thing's throat.

'Why did you want to stop him?' I asked, as we all three retreated from that foul place into the open air.

Kernin shrugged. 'The little one had done no wrong All that was merely Nature. Kill and eat, or be killed and eaten. We do as much ourselves, to so many animals. I suppose Barundran would say all this is mere Necessity. But I cannot philosophise now. *I* was the one to blame; I alone.'

'No,' I said, 'I too. I failed in my duty, I should not have allowed—'

'We know so much less about Nature than the satyrs,' he said. 'As Barundran called them, the Wise Satyrs.'

The afternoon storm was just beginning, and Kernin still did not dress: he held himself naked and let the rain cleanse him and his sword. And then we had to take notice of our new friend. The satyr was a little frightened of the lightning, but once we had retreated to the cover of the trees, he calmed down and contemplated us, and we him. He was broad-nosed, almost black-skinned, and very furry. What made him look even uglier and stranger than most satyrs was this: he now had only one, or shall we say one and a half horns. The Springer had bitten off most of his right horn.

'I think I owe him my life,' said Kernin. 'We must reward him in any way that is possible. Few *men* would have done what he did.'

And then we realised that the grunts the satyr was making were really speech. He was slapping himself on his furry chest and croaking 'Tarsh'—which was his name.

He pointed back toward the Springer's burrow, and favoured us with a hideous grin. And spoke, at some length. I made out words which sounded like 'Tarsh—kill Gagen—revenge—you *shani*—no?' Then he pointed in the direction of our camp. 'Tarsh—go—wear cloth. . . .'

'Yes,' Kernin nodded. 'Certainly, Tarsh, if you wish.'

Tarsh grinned again, then touched his own chest and then Kernin's. The word he spoke this time sounded a little like 'Friend!'

I will say one thing about Tarsh—already at this stage in his career, he was no fool. As between us two, he sensed already which was the Prince and which merely the Herald.

When we returned to camp, all thoroughly wet, and we two humans rather shaken by our terrible adventure, we changed our clothes, and gave Tarsh some for the first time. He was delighted with a Nakhtian kilt, and wore it with some dignity, eyeing us all the time to see how he should behave. If he wasn't so black and hairy, or his toes so well clawed, one would have said he was very like a human peasant deciding to become a courtier.

After a day's study of his speech, Barundran was able to prove that the local satyrs' language was definitely related to Shore-

landish. 'There must have been much mingling,' said the old
centaur, 'between your two races—at the Land-taking, or later.'

Kernin had the Springer's burrow cleared of all filth and everything but poor Velni's body, and then lined the chamber with
clear white egg-stone, and walled the domed rise outside with
egg-stone also; and so made the peasant girl a regular tomb of
which a prince might have been proud.

And then we had another death to suffer.

Kernin left the war-front briefly to escort his Aelvian prisoners
to Nakhtos. He had good reason for not wanting them in his
camp now that the gas-plant operations were well advanced:
there was always the chance that one man might break his parole
and escape somehow up the Wall.

When we reached Nakhtos, we found there was now a lull on
the Rindos front too, and the King was there. And my father
Omren: his wound had poisoned, and he was dying.

His spirit went out of him at last in his old room in the Blue
Tower, in the presence of the Queen, Kernin, and myself.
Before that the Queen wept and caressed him and called him
'beloved servant—saviour of our Kingdom'. She also said certain other things, which I will not here relate. After that, Kernin
and I looked at each other in a way that was new and yet not
altogether so. We were, after all, already conspirators against
most of the world.

When the end came, Omren rose on his pillows, and embraced
first Kernin and then me.

'Elder son,' he said, 'see that you always do your duty
to—your Prince. Never leave him—he has need of your counsel,
for he is a wild one . . . wild. . . .'

And with that he smiled once upon Kernin, and died.

The whole Court came to the funeral outside the Ringleft
Gate, in the burying-place of the notables beside the Rindos
Road. When we had seen my dear father's body folded into the
spherical eggstone coffin, and that laid in its egg-shaped hole in
the earth, King Prahelek said to me gruffly: 'And now, Orselen,
I am minded to make you my Chief Bard-Herald.'

Fiupen, shifting uneasily from foot to foot in the background,
was looking green with envy and malice. This should have been
my moment of triumph.

I said: 'My lord King, I cannot leave my present lord the
Prince.' I swallowed. 'Second Bard Fiupen—he is in any case
the more competent musician.' (May Sinis and all the gods
forgive me for that lie!)

Prahelek grunted, suspicious. Then he shrugged. 'Well, no doubt you will not have long to wait your turn. I shall soon be following my old bard, your father.'

And then he turned to Fiupen, and appointed him Chief Bard-Herald of the Twin Kingdom—much to that wretch's astonishment.

As we rode back to the Aelvian Wall, Kernin said: 'Brother, I cannot thank you enough.'

I grinned. 'Let us hope you will thank me hereafter. I stayed with you because someone is needed to keep you in order.'

Kernin brightened. 'Now I hope all the evil omens are fulfilled. We have had enough of Death. Now, ho for Aelvia.'

He was looking up toward the far high places—not Aelvia, I think, but Khar Durnaran and World's End.

6

Drycleve is that place on the Aelvian Wall where ascent is most impossible. The cliff rises more than one hundred feet sheer, and even overhangs a little. It is probably a spot where the Holy River once had its fall, but a thousand years ago the river shifted, leaving this place bare. Half way up the cliff hangs a strange appearance, a figure thirty feet high, as of a winged woman. The rock of the cliff is mostly reddish, but the figure's body, limbs, and wings are pale, the face dark. The peasants of Under Aelvia say this carving was made by Prah when he conquered all the Shorelands from Luvilion to Agnai, and it represents one of the winged Elder Gods whom he overcame. We Nakhtians, however, call it The Angel. Barundran surmised that the carving was done by no man or god, but by the falling waters of the ancient departed River. Certainly the lines are rather vague, and it takes imagination to see them. All but the face: that is startlingly clear. It is a stern, dark face. The Aelvians reproduce it on their banners, and regard it as the guardian of their country.

Because Drycleve was so strong, it was patrolled by only a few Aelvian lookouts, and not much even by them, since the Wall rose higher on either side, affording better spy-places. No general in his senses would mount an attack on Drycleve.

Perhaps Kernin was not in his senses. I often suspected that, afterwards. But at least, there was always bitter method in his madness.

We chose a night of No Ring—Prah's Night, in fact, which may have brought us luck. Luck was with us even in the weather, which is sometimes unpredictable in and around Aelvia: a few clouds had survived from the afternoon storm, and these were wandering up and over the Wall on the last remnants of the sea-wind like monstrous straying sheep—a sight unusual enough to attract the eyes of the enemy lookouts.

Like an enormous black snake, our squads of soldiers and impressed peasants crept forward, sweating as they hauled on the ropes, but not daring so much as to grunt with the effort—for Kernin had threatened any offender with instant death, a quiet death, gagged and strangled, and had stationed Palurian executioners beside the column to show that this promise was not idle. Out from the nearest patch of forest crept the black-painted platforms, one behind the other, and assembled at last one behind the other, with the leading one a few feet from the foot of Drycleve. The black snake had become a straight black spear, pointed directly at the heart of Aelvia.

Then the signal was given from among the huddled black-coated forms upon the leading platform: the cry of a night-harpy which has just made a kill. The cry was so authentic that no watchman could have suspected it: it was uttered by Tarsh the satyr, who crouched on that platform beside me and Kernin. Tarsh wore no cloak, only a dark kilt: he did not like cloaks, and he was black enough in himself not to be easily seen.

Then the sweating peasants beneath us began to ease their ropes gently, gently . . . and our platform rose. There was no fear that it wouldn't rise, it was so rafted underneath with giant gas-plant stems. The real fear was that our rope-men might lose control and let go—in which case, we would go sailing up to the night-time Sun like ghosts long before our time. As that idea came to me, hurriedly I cancelled it, and thought instead of Prah rising gloriously in the body from the crater of Moma, victorious, a demigod becoming a god.

The platforms swayed sickeningly, and at times came near to fouling each other. The wind was pushing us in toward the undercut of the cliff, toward the overhanging form of that now invisible Angel. If we were caught with one edge under the rocks we would be in bad trouble. I was really afraid that Aelvia's guardian figure was about to deal us doom. But our rope-men had been well rehearsed in their forest-fringe training grounds, and at the last moment everything came out pat. We were level with the top, and down there, a hundred feet below, they were belaying for the moment of greatest strain.

Then I rose in my place and blew my triple trumpet-blast, the

Short Challenge; and Kernin drew his sword and leapt onto the soil of Aelvia.

By now every platform was made fast, each to each, and as every troop disembarked from the cliff-side platform, its place was taken by other troops leaping from the platform in rear. Within five minutes, Aelvia was invaded by an army one thousand strong.

When we encountered the enemy, I am afraid it was more like murder than war. We took most of their cliff-watchers from behind, and hurled them back over their own cliff. Kernin struck down just a few, and then would have given the rest quarter, but the Aelvians are proud and valiant. Most of them leapt to their death crying out in the Aelvian dialect 'Nyam nin!' (Our country) or 'Kenain Niamwy ki bhu!' (Long live Queen Niamwy). Meanwhile our rope-men had hauled down the empty platforms and sent them up again loaded with cavalry. We couldn't use these in the first assault, because horses will make noises. But now we had them, and Kernin mounted Goldhorn and led a charge against their main camp on the Holy River above the Cataract.

Well, we won, of course. We swept into that camp from behind in overwhelming force in the middle of the night. The Aelvians were crying out 'Treachery, treachery!' Naturally, they could not imagine how we came to be where we were. Yet still the gallant men were dying by their tents, sword in hand. The air was full of new-slain rising ghosts. With a sick stomach, I knew now what the legendary Storming of Suoran must have been like when Sakanek burst through the crater in the city wall. The only thing better here was that there were fewer women in the Aelvian camp, and no eggs or hatchlings. We could see well enough, it was nearly as bright as a burning city, for the cavalry had brought with them light-berries and flaming yellow torches of sunwood, and many of the Aelvian tents were also brightly lit or on fire. And the Holy River gleamed blue beyond, and from heaven the Sea of Angels looked down in calm ironic peace.

Tarsh loped along beside Kernin's stirrup. He had been humanising himself rapidly over the last few Rings, but he still was unhandy with a sword: for this night's murderous business he was relying on his bare claws, and one good bronze dagger. Who says that satyrs are always timid, peaceful folk? In his own forest, Tarsh had already killed males of another Lair; and in the wicked light of that stricken camp, his eyes gleamed red. With his grotesque uneven horns, his blackness, his ugliness, his bristling excitement, I thought he looked horrible—an emblem of lust and murder.

He grinned up at Kernin, and pointed with his knife at the Royal tent which now stood square in our path.

'There you take the great *shani* of the uplanders, yes?'

Kernin dismounted. 'Orselen: raise your lyre, and parley with them. I want to meet with their Queen.'

I faced a row of warriors in black leather, all with swords drawn; and there was a girl-piper behind them, stark naked and playing the Death-wail. I never saw men less inclined to parley. And then Queen Niamwy came out of the tent, and silenced the piper.

'You have killed my Bard already, look you, so I am my own herald. Nay, it was done before he could raise his lyre, so for that I do not blame you. And now, Prince of dark Nakhtos, what is your will with Deulyn's daughter?'

'Only to save unnecessary bloodshedding,' said Kernin. 'Lady, I mean no harm to you, nor to any man, woman, or child of sweet Aelvia. Let us call and cry a truce, for Suori's sake, the goddess of Peace!'

Niamwy was as black-haired as the great Goddess for whom she was named; about seventeen years old, blue-eyed, womanly. I have always thought her beautiful, in a quiet way; a little like Queen Kandiri of Nakhtos in her younger days, perhaps. That night under the stars, and in the flickering flames of her ruined camp, she wore black leathern armour and a bronze sword, and she looked superb. Now she said:

'Suori is also the goddess of Love; and I know what is customary on these occasions, and what was done at the goddess's own city of Suoran; and Sakanek was one of your own ancestors. Would you trick me now, Prince, so that I may not die first?'

'Lady, I swear by my heart, by Sinis, and the holy Sun. . . .' said Kernin.

'If you break that oath, you are a dastard for ever,' said Niamwy, 'and your Bard will not dare to set your name in his lay. Well, then, we shall call truce, and parley.'

Her own folk cried out in dismay, but she over-swayed them. There was to be a mixed guard of Aelvians and our troops outside the tent, and now, as soon as the fighting had been stopped through all the camp, Niamwy motioned to Kernin to enter.

'I have heard of your noble treatment before,' she said, 'as in the matter of those prisoners of ours you took four Rings back; and so, my lord, I shall trust you.'

They went into that tent alone, and held conference until Sunkindle. We, outside, several times nearly came to sword-play with the Aelvian guards, who muttered terrible things against us. They felt doubly betrayed.

As for Tarsh, he was restless and disconsolate. I thought at first that the sight of that naked girl piper had disturbed him. But I was wrong: human women did not attract him much. What really bothered him was the Aelvian soldiers: they regarded him not with surprise or fear, but with a sort of easy contempt. After a while he grew angry, and strode away between the tents, flourishing his dagger, which was red with the blood of one of the cliff-watchers. 'I kill,' he growled, 'yet I have not honour. I will have somet'ing honourable. . . .' I noted that in my mind: we would have to do something about Tarsh one day. An ambitious beast. . . .

And then, just as the Sun was turning from dull red to warm gold, out of the royal tent came Kernin and Niamwy, hand in hand. Both were dressed most splendidly, and curiously alike. Well, I had never seen an Aelvian noble in the garb of peace before. Kernin wore just such a purple tunic of dyed sheep's wool, and on his head a silver crown of most dainty wiry workmanship—exactly similar to the crown on Niamwy's dark locks.

'This,' said Niamwy to her astonished guards, 'is my betrothed husband, Kernin, whom I have created a Prince of Aelvia. Aelvia's Angel indeed brought him into this land, over Drycleve by mere miracle: our winged guardian welcomed him, so his coming is surely for our good; and so do I welcome him. There will be truce now with the Twin Kingdom, and a folk-moot must be held straightway at my high city of Eladon. If the people of Aelvia confirm my choice of man, well and good: there will be perpetual peace with the downriver Kingdoms, and when Kernin succeeds his parents, the Disputed Nomes will be returned to Aelvia. *Both* nomes, right down to the Lower Cataract, if the folk of Upper Kherilos agree, as I trust they will. But if my people like not my peacemaking, then I will go into exile in the lower country with my man; for I esteem him a right worthy hero, and dearer to me than any kingdom.'

The piper-girl had some clothes on now; this girl Hafren had been beguiling me all those cold dark hours as we sat outside the tent, telling me some Aelvian tales. She was a fine wench, nearly as black-haired as her mistress, but with some red lights in her locks. Now she stood up, and said:

'By the Sadness of Saeth, Lady, I think your choice a goodly one; and if I had had to suffer such persuasions as you have all this night-time, I am sure that I too would have been convinced to a peace.' And she picked up her ten-pipe and played a merry tune—which I later learnt to be a love-lilt. This seemed to us Nakhtians bold behaviour from a minstrel girl to her queen; but the Aelvians are like that, unceremonious to royalty; and Naimwy was making no jest about that folk-moot. Kings and Queens in Aelvia hold their crowns at the pleasure of the people; and now Niamwy ran some slight danger of being deposed.

'Nay,' said Queen Niamwy, as her black-coated guards muttered, 'I have been mindful all this time that I am King Deulyn's daughter, and my Prince and I have enjoyed no more than kisses; as I wlll offer to prove this day to any deputation of ladies who will wait upon me.' This she said with as simple a countenance as any milkmaid; and nobody laughed.

I found my voice. 'My Prince: I would like to congratulate you upon the choice of a very gracious lady to your royal bride; but have you forgotten the little matter of the Princess Mengiri of Agnai, and your father's possible objections?'

'No,' said Kernin, 'but I propose to ignore my father's objections. I was not *married* to Mengiri; and anyway, Aelvia is as good an ally as Agnai. Nay, much better.'

At that last remark, I felt a sudden chill, and looked searchingly at Kernin. He was smiling at his new lady, and pressing her hand. But—could he really have fallen so suddenly in love?

It was not like him to use women to further his ambitions. Not till now, at least. But by now he had certainly not scrupled to use men. Or to sacrifice their lives.

But later that day, I found that in my thoughts I had wronged him. Once the armistice had taken effect, and we began our ride along the green winding highway to Eladon, Kernin said to me: 'Orselen, things will be—different, for me, from now on. I have found a lady whom I do most dearly love; and I hope the gods will bless us with children, young princes.'

I was overjoyed, and held out my hand, and clasped his shoulder till the jogging of our mounts drew us apart. 'Why, this is joyful news, brother. I—as you know, I am not of the marrying classes; but I too could find it in my heart to love some Aelvian girl. This is a beautiful country, cool green Aelvia, and a fine place in which to enjoy peace and bring up hatchlings. As for old foolish vows, such as boys will make, the priests can doubtless dispense you from them, with a sacrifice or two.'

But then he looked sidelong at me, and I saw the old green, fire flare up in his eye. 'You mistake me,' he said, 'I need break no vow.' And he turned his head again, and looked along our road. He might have been looking toward Eladon, fifty miles away. Or again he might have been looking beyond, to the black Wall of Rathvia, the Forbidden Land, which is outside the Shorelands, and the beginning of the World's End.

The land of Aelvia is shaped like a pair of cupped hands, and the line where the hands join is the Holy River, which is here called Sinel. The Aelvians associate this, by a forced etymology, with Sinis, goddess of wayfarers through life and beyond life. There are also two big tributaries coming in from right and left, the Haf and the Aesk. The place where all three rivers meet, nearly in one point, is Eladon, the capital in the midst of the country.

We made our march to Eladon slowly, and Kernin brought with him, besides Tarsh and me, only a small guard, and they all Palurians. The land-quarrel had been between Aelvia and Nakhtos, who were neighbours and therefore (you might say) traditional enemies; but Palur had been allied to Aelvia only thirty years before in old King Pelenek's time, and the Palurian soldiers had almost no interest in the question of the Disputed Nomes, and they aroused very little ill-feeling now against us. We were clearly an embassy, not an invasion.

Kernin had already sent messengers speeding to Nakhtos, and a herald to King Prahelek on the Rindian front. He told the King he had won a decisive victory, and Aelvia would certainly not oppose the Twin Kingdom again for many years. He was also sending the King reinforcements, half his own army in fact, as fast as they could march.

He did not tell the King about his projected marriage.

One of the first messengers to Nakhtos had been Barundran, who was now returning from there with a small band of freed Aelvian prisoners: the Bard we took in the first battle, and all three girl pipers. The rest of the prisoners would follow as soon as peace was definitely made. . . . Kernin deliberately delayed our progress through Aelvia till Barundran and the four ex-prisoners could join us outside Eladon. The bard and the girls told everyone frankly how well they had been treated, and what an honourable gentleman was our Prince. Well, one girl did complain that during all the four Rings she had been prisoner in our camp and at Nakhtos, none of our officers or courtiers had made any attempt upon her honour; which she thought a little ungallant in the circumstances—'And I a well-favoured enough wench, look you, I suppose,' she said.

When this became known, Queen Niamwy eyed Kernin, riding at her side, with joy and love. 'I think there will be no objection now to our marriage, my dear. All my lords are saying it, that you are a hero of the greatest, greater and better hearted than famous Sakanek—great in the strange manner of your victory over us, and magnanimous in giving us peace when—'

'Nay,' laughed Kernin, 'in that, Lady, I serve my own interest.' And he reined in his stallion Goldhorn, and as the Queen also checked her mare, he kissed his lady as they sat in saddle, knee to knee. The Queen took that as a most gracious speech, and a loving jest. 'But truly,' she said, 'though our people be warlike at need, yet peace with honour and justice is better than war, and serves all our interests alike.'

And so we ambled along the green road beside the shining River. The road was green because the Aelvians do not pave their ways, but merely level them and then make grass grow short on them, so that we seemed to be riding upon a perpetual long lawn. But on both sides of the way, especially up the little rolling hills to our left, the grass was much longer. I enquired of Hafren, the Queen's piper-girl, how the roads were kept up, or rather *down*. Were the peasants not pressed hard to keep at this close mowing, or did gangs of slaves—?

Hafren tossed her dark hair with the red glints in it. 'No slaves. We keep no slaves in Aelvia. By the Fiddle of Firafax, we have no need of 'em!'

'Firafax is a liar, if I recall rightly,' I laughed. 'You do well to swear by such a one.'

'Nay, you shall see anon. Ah—there!'

We had rounded a bend in the road, and now we found our way blocked. There was a flock of goats grazing right across the highway, with a couple of dark goat-herds behind them. First I thought these were satyrs, but then Tarsh made a strange throaty sound—'Ahaargh!'—and I saw that these herders were not male satyrs but females, nymphs, *shanis*. Apart from being stark naked they differed from human women in only a few points: snub noses, somewhat more pointed ears, black-hairy legs, and strange long feet with very small side toes. Shanis do not have claws on their toes, in spite of what some downriver folk may think. These goat-herd nymphs were lighter of skin than Tarsh, and much less furry. I did not think them pretty, but neither did I find them repulsive.

Tarsh did not find them repulsive either. He was quivering all over with joy.

Alas, how ambition sometimes interferes with love! Tarsh now fully dressed in a Nakhtian kilt and shoulder-vest, with a fine sword girt at his side, and by his own request he was riding a horse—not well, but he was staying on. He was determined to pass as a man among men; and now he succeeded only too well. The goat-herd nymphs had got their animals off the highway, with many strange cries and tongue-clicks, and now as we rode past they showed no sign of recognising Tarsh as one of their own kind.

Hafren giggled. 'Mayhap he has *washed* too much.'

This, I later discovered, was a slander. The nymphs and satyrs of Aelvia are clean folk, and bathe often in the rivers and streams. There are many of them scattered about the countryside, for the Aelvians say that Prah never entered Aelvia, and therefore satyrs and Elder Gods still haunt their woods and fields. I do not know about the Elder Gods, for I never saw any winged spirits; but certainly satyrs aplenty. The Aelvians treat them almost like people, they grant them the freedom of the woods, and employ them (nymphs especially) as herders and even house-servants. But they do not ask their voices in the folk-moot: 'almost' can be an important word. The Land-taking in Aelvia was much less brutal than elsewhere, but it was still a Land-taking.

Tarsh jogged up and down now in his saddle. He looked as if he wanted to leap off his horse and accost the nymphs, but then he glanced at Prince Kernin and Queen Niamwy, and thought better of it. Humans did not behave so. Despairing, he turned sideways, and pointed up to his one remaining long head-horn. 'Ahaargh! Ahaargh, you shanis!'

The nymphs stared. Then one laughed. 'Why, it is half a man and half a shath! Fare thee well, One-horn!'

She spoke Shorelandish with a strong Aelvish accent, but as clearly as any Aelvian woman. Tarsh looked highly mortified.

'Shame!' said Kernin, wagging a finger at the nymphs. 'My faithful vassal lost his head-peak in my deadly quarrel—an honourable wound.' He turned to Tarsh. 'If you will, sir, we will get you a cover for that maim. A leather-worker could make a false horn—or perhaps like the Luzelish you could wear a two-horned helmet.'

'I take the helmet,' said Tarsh. 'A gilded one, yes?'

'Taras Goldhelm!' Kernin smiled. 'That will make a fine new style for you, my lord. . . .'

The days passed, and the nights. We never needed to pitch tents, for on this main road of the realm there were frequent villages. These were hedged about with plantations of sapphiras and sunwood, which are used in Aelvia not only for torches, but also for warming-fires at night. The Aelvian houses were strange to our eyes, having roofs that were not flat but steeply angled. This is so because of the weather in this wet, cool country, where the afternoon storm is gentle but long-lasting, often not clearing till just before Sunquenching; and even at night the air seems to hold some dampness, and the stars seem softer and less clear than on the lower plains. When Barundran joined us, he complained that the damp made his old bones ache a little; also, this country would not be so good for astronomy.

'Well,' said Kernin, 'the air may be clearer if we climb the high hills yonder.' And he pointed to the far dark Rathvian Wall.

'But that is not easy climbing,' said Queen Niamwy. 'It is much higher than the Aelvian Wall which you so magically surmounted, my lord, and there is no convenient cliff where you could repeat such a feat. And the Rathvians do not admit foreigners into their territory. They are a strange people, the last of human peoples, not Shorelandish even though they speak something like our tongue. But what of that? They are no danger to us, they have never once offered to attack us in all of four hundred years—no, not since the Land-taking.'

Kernin's face darkened at that. Then he smiled. 'Well, there will be time to make friends with them later. I certainly would not pick any quarrel with these neighbours of yours, if they are peaceable. But do they never allow even travellers to pass through their land?'

Hafren interposed. 'Saeth passed that way, according to our traditions, and returned also. But that was 350 years and more ago, when the hero Saeth was looking for Truth, and he found it, and was sad ever after, and made his Sons sad after him.'

I had heard a little of the Sons of Saeth already, and now I was interested to see the settlements of this sect of philosophers. When we came across the first one on the rounded top of a small green hill, I thought it was a clump of large tombs. But it was not: those rough-built beehives or eggs of grey stones were houses, each one a cell for one hermit. At Barundran's request a small party of us turned off the highway and climbed the down; and so we met the Sons of Saeth. They wore long grey wool gowns, grey as the stones of their huts, and as their hair, for they were mostly old men. They seemed morose enough for their reputation. I thought I saw a faint flicker of interest in the eyes of the youngest man when he saw Barundran—who was the first centaur, probably, ever to penetrate into Aelvia. But the forty-year-old philosopher quickly repressed even that spark of foolishness, and greeted the centaur with no more than ordinary politeness. I thought Barundran, for all his seventy years, seemed by far the younger of the two, at least in spirit. Indeed, he questioned the Sons of Saeth eagerly as to their doctrines.

'The truth is that all is vanity,' said the eldest of the hermits. 'Saeth saw the hollowness of this world. Life is a tale told by a lying minstrel, a brief light-berry which is soon burst. And philosophy is nothing but the practice of dying.'

'I have heard something like that opinion before,' said Barundran, 'in my own country.'

'If that's your philosophy,' said Kernin, 'why not kill yourselves at once, and have done with your misery?'

'That is no escape,' said the elder gloomily, 'else we should certainly do as you advise. At death the soul survives, as all men can see; and it may go up to the Sun, but surely it does not stay there, lost and merged. It streams back to Earth in sunlight, and then dives into the ovary of some woman, and then . . . the whole stupid process occurs again. The only chance is that by practising aversion from life, the soul may learn firmness enough to stay in the Sun; which is not even so an escape from the Egg of Existence, but at least an avoidance of its tedious circumference.'

'Do you never have any females in your order?' said Barundran.

'Certainly not. Women lack the needful dedication to Total Death. . . .'

As we came back down that hillside, Hafren burst out laughing. 'The Saethmen are welcome to their gloom. The tale tells that not only Saeth went on that journey, but also Firafax; and whatever it was made Saeth mourn, that only made Firafax the merrier. I am a Daughter of Firafax, myself.'

'Depressing Truth or merry Lies,' said Kernin, musing. 'But Sinis is goddess of Truth, and she is depicted as stern but beautiful. Do you not worship her?'

'We honour all gods as much as they deserve,' said Queen Niamwy, 'but we do not prostrate ourselves before any. We have no caste of priests or priestesses, we kill no sacrifices. I suppose of all gods we honour most the Four.'

We came across the Four at almost every crossroads: for these places were marked by a stone signpost ornamented with four carved and painted heads, each facing toward one of the four Quarters. Inland or Ringback stood the grey face of the Old One, the First One, the source of all being; Ringright the gold-yellow face of the Young Hero, champion of goodness, friend of the world, who reminded me most of Palurian statues of Hinos the Sun; Ringward smiled the Green Lady, who is Nature, the Earth, the Ring—indeed, all goddesses in one; and finally Ringleft leered the Dark One, the Enemy, who was carved much like a satyr, but uglier, with hollow eyes and a terrible smile.

'The Dark One is also a son of the Old Grey First God,' said

Niamwy. 'We do not like him, but we acknowledge his power, and his needfulness.'

'Necessity,' said Barundran. 'So, Lady, ye know him too? Truly, you are a wise people.'

And so at last we came to Eladon, which is a beautiful small city, approached by a medley of bridges. There are no city walls, except some tumbledown old ruins from the time of the Land-taking, now all overgrown with rubias canes and gold-flowered trumpet-weed; for the land of Aelvia was soon unified under one king. The houses of the city are not grand—even the Palace is only a slightly bigger red-brick hall with a dark tile roof, and the royal Incubator stands in a courtyard at ground level. Many of the streets of Eladon are as much 'grass-paved' as the country roads, and several times in our progress we were held up by cheerful satyresses with their mowing goats. These city satyresses wore little aprons which covered at least some of their charms, as the few city satyrs wore codpieces. There is truly no such capital anywhere else in the Shorelands: our nome-towns in the River Kingdoms are bigger; but they are not so beautiful as Eladon, their hall-doorways are not so quaintly carved, nor their arches so delicate. We passed by little market-placés, many cluttered up with zitharist story-tellers and their girl pipers. This now looked like a city fit for Bards! I fell in love with the place at first sight, and so I think did Kernin. It helped that we were both in love in the other way, too, and with girls of that place.

Well, I will cut a long story shorter. The folk-moot was held the day after we reached Eladon; and the six Earls and the six hundred knights and burgers confirmed the Queen's marriage, and perpetual alliance with Palur-Nakhtos. They acclaimed Kernin not as a conqueror but as a guest, since the Angel of Drycleve had helped him by miracle to fly into the country. But an old law of the land prevented Kernin from taking the title of King, since his own hand had shed the blood of some Aelvian freemen, albeit in honourable fight. He would be known as Prince of Aelvia, the Queen's Consort. And his children by Niamwy would one day inherit a Triple Kingdom—the whole length of the Holy River, since this rose from a spring in the Rathvian Wall.

And that night, which was auspiciously Suori's feast of New Ring—we went to bed with our women, my Prince and I. Bard-heralds of course are not allowed to marry—that custom is the same in Aelvia—but Hafren and I were very well agreed, and we had plighted private troth.

When she undressed in my new bedchamber, she laughed.

'It's not as if you haven't seen me naked *already*. You, and half your army!'

'I hope it isn't your custom always to go naked into battle,' I said.

'Only into this sort of battle,' she said, embracing me flesh to flesh. 'No, my dear; the fact is, your attack was so sudden that night I didn't have time to dress.'

7

When King Prahelek heard of his son's marriage, he was first furious, then exultant, and then furious again. But by that time there was nothing he could do to alter the situation.

He was exultant when he realised that he had now almost a Triple Kingdom; after all, Aelvia was as good an ally as Agnai, if not better. He became furious the second time when he learnt from his new reinforcements the full extent of Kernin's victory at the Aelvian Wall.

'Passion of Prah!' he exploded. 'The boy may be a tactical genius, but as a politician he's a fool. He could have *taken* that Queen and all her country with the strong hand—and when he had made slaves of them all, he could *then* have married into Agnai. But—as it is—'

Words failed the old king. As it was, Agnai had turned instantly hostile, so he could not now devote all his energies to finishing off Rindos, which he felt was almost in his grasp. Kernin sent him a message that he was marching with a mixed force of Palurians and Aelvians to cover Agnai—which might somewhat have mollified him; but when the herald read out the next clause of the Prince's letter, the King was enraged again. Kernin was advising him to make peace, a permanent peace, with the Rindians.

'If you make them desperate, you will only cause them to bring in the Luzelish barbarians as allies—and no one wants the Luzelish in the Shorelands,' wrote the Prince.

And it nearly came to that. Prahelek was on the point of besieging Rindos, when the old Rindian king made that final threat. A twenty-year truce—or a permanent peace—or he would marry his eldest son to the Luzelish High Chief's daughter, with all that *that* implied.

Prahelek settled for a twenty-year truce. There were those who said this showed he was really getting old: ten years, even five years before, he would certainly have tried to storm rocky Rindos before the barbarians could arrive.

Once the great Truce was proclaimed, the Agnaians slunk back to their city, and their king gave his infant daughter in marriage to a Menkinvian noble.

And then we had peace. Years of peace.

The longer I lived in Aelvia, the more I loved it. It is a neat, small country, but every mile of it is rich in legends, and its Bards—well, I have to admit that some of them are no mean lyrists, and I was able to learn something by studying their Myth-poems. Oddly, they have no tales about their main Four Gods, whom they call simply The Eternals; but they have other stories aplenty about the winged Elder Gods. Barundran said to me once, in his sage learned way, that legends of winged intelligent beings are very widespread in the Known World; and he speculated that these might be based on some truth. 'After all, on any theory the Earth or Earths must be infinitely wide; and there must be many species who have wandered across the lands from time to time. Hnnnm! And at least two sorts of dumb beasts have intelligent relatives, so why not three—or more?'

'Two sorts?'

'Hnnnm, yes. Did I never tell you about the handihorse, which is found in Thulor? It is shaped like a centaur, but cannot speak, and we use tame ones in the Middle Plains as draught animals. And there are also Dumb Satyrs, which resemble you men. Therefore, I see no reason why there should not be, somewhere in our Universe, intelligent handibirds, like great harpies. . . .'

'Or like Elder Gods,' I mused. 'A frightening thought.' For some of the tales of the Aelvian woods were dark ones, vague stories of Night Hags, snatchers of little boys. I wondered if Night Hags had wings. But the more I questioned our satyrs of Eladon, the less I believed such fables. The satyrs said our little woods were happy places. And looking out from my palace window, I thought so too.

From my bedchamber I could see Ringright over the roofs of the little capital, over the river Sinel, over suburbs and meadows, then up Hafdale with its rolling green downs and little blue Haf river, and finally to the Var Forest and the mist-blue mountains that ring the whole country only fifty miles away. That is an uneven line of mountain wall, the rim of the ancient crater, rising to several small bumps: Mount Whale and Bow Wave, Chalky Top and Long Table. I got to know that view better than

the view of the Horse Plains from Nakhtos of my birth; almost as
well as the strings of my lyre, or the contours of Hafren's sweet
body.

On the right of Long Table the mountain ring gradually rose,
and when you could see no more of it from my window it had
become Rathwall, the high border of the Dark Land. I could not
see Khar Durnaran from this window. And I was glad of that.

Better still, perhaps, the Royal Bedchamber of Queen Niamwy
faced Ringward, and its casements looked out over the Shorelands,
down to the great blue-green haze of the Sea, from whence the
trinkets of civilisation were now seeping into Aelvia: centaur
steel and goldwork, and clocks, and illuminated books . . . all
the things that might make glad the heart of Prince Kernin, apart
from his gladness in his beautiful and gracious wife. I rejoiced to
see with my own eyes (and Hafren, who was the Queen's
confidant, confirmed this) that Kernin was very much in love;
and the Royal couple used the Queen's bedchamber on most
nights.

A year and a few Rings after the marriage, their first child was
hatched, a little boy whom Niamwy greeted with the name
'Aelenek'—a diplomatic compromise, since the first part of the
name was Aelvian, but the rest Palurish—a right royal name for
a Prince who should be the first King of the Triple Kingdom.
There was no hitch at this hatching: little Aelenek came out in a
bright morning just after New Ring, beaming amiably, and
stumbled straight into his mother's arms to suckle immediately
from her shapely breasts. He was black-haired and blue-eyed, a
very normal little boy and not in the least troublesome. Old King
Prahelek was delighted with his grandson, for now the dynasty
seemed assured. Moreover, the Queen had already brought forth
again; and next year that child was hatched, a healthy girl who
was named Deuren.

These children charmed all our little Court, from their humble
nymph nursemaids to the proud visiting Earls of the six Shire-
Towns of Aelvia. Kernin also took huge delight in his children,
and often played with them. Once he said to me, amazed, as
though it had just occurred to him: 'You know, Orselen, every
new child is a sort of new world, nearly infinite in possibility—
wonderful.'

I rejoiced when I heard that. After all, Kernin was approaching his twentieth year, when a man loses the last traces of
boyishness, and usually forgets foolish, impossible dreams. And
I think that if only Kernin had been no Prince—if he had been a
mere nome-lord, or an Aelvian shire-lord, he might have been

gradually absorbed in the cares and joys of daily life, in local politics, in watching his crops and children grow. For mere Shire-lords in Aelvia boast only one bedchamber, which they share with their lady-wife.

But the King or Prince in Eladon by custom has his own private room, on the opposite side of the Palace's upper floor from that of his wife; and Kernin's window looked inland, toward Rathvia and World's End.

He was not often in that room for the first year or so, and almost never at night; but there were times. . . . Especially toward No-Ring, the palace servants told me he had trouble sleeping. Then he would get up, and steal from the Queen's side, and go to his private chamber and look out at black Rathwall and Khar Durnaran and the blue-white eternal stars.

In the second year, Kernin introduced a new sport into Aelvia: air-rafting. Most of the rafts with which we had conquered Drycleve had been dismantled or hidden in the woods of the Disputed Nomes. King Prahelek had belatedly realised that they would make excellent siege-engines for storming a city such as Rindos—or Nakhtos, or Palur. He almost wished now he had not sworn that truce; but in any case he did not want to give his enemies ideas. Kernin, on the other hand, took one of the rafts and greatly reduced its buoyancy, and brought it into Aelvia. It did not need any rope-men now to keep it from flying up to the Sun: it could be controlled, after a fashion, by the crew on board. It had bronze grapnels like a ship, and large and small gas-plants arranged *above* the raft, not underneath, nearly all around the square perimeter like bulwarks.

You boarded your raft just before Sunquenching, and then as the sun died and its rays stopped pushing you down, the raft rose, and you hauled up your grapnels and metal pegs, and then you were away, drifting, drifting up toward the bright blue stars, one thousand feet, two thousand feet, till the houses below looked like children's toys, and the Three Rivers of Aelvia appeared like thin blue shining snakes or the three longest fingers of a hand, and the city of Eladon, with all its berry and sunwood-lighted streets, dwindled to one bright-misty patch like a star of heaven. And then the whole dark-and-shining map would shift under you as the night wind took you, wafting you nearly always downriver toward the Aelvian Wall.

The first time we tried this—Kernin, Barundran, and I—Queen Niamwy cried a little, and besought her Prince not to risk his neck on so rash a venture. We were assembled on those subur-ban meadows between the Sinel and the Haf, hard by the main crossroads of the realm. The Sun was fading to dark gold, tingeing with warm splendour the grass, the line of noble angel-trees by the nearest road, and gilding almost pleasantly the grinning carved face of the Dark One on his post at the cross-road. There was a large crowd on the meadow, held back from the raft by a line of black-coated royal guards.

Kernin leaned over the gas-plant bulwark, and embraced his Queen. 'My love, there really is no danger. My wise Tutor has made every calculation and test.' Indeed, we had already sent up that raft with sandbags and lead bars equal to our weight, and we were quite confident. And the Queen was a brave wench. 'Go then, my hero,' she said; and then, to me: 'and you, Bard, make sure you set down in your lay that Kernin, Prince of Aelvia, was the first man to fly like a bird or an Elder God.'

'Fly like a bird!' said Kernin. 'I only wish we could. A bird can choose where he's going. Now if only we could tame a harpy or a gryphon to tow us. . . .'

Everyone laughed at that, for as we all knew, the great birds of the Known Earth were all incurably wild. 'Harness about a million falcons,' shouted one wit from the crowd.

Hafren, standing beside the Queen, tossed her dark locks, and the red glints in them glowed in the late sunshine. 'Up with you, Orsu,' she laughed. (This is the manner of Aelvia—they will shorten names most ridiculously.) 'Just make sure you don't overbalance, if your hornless-horse friend takes it into his head to try a gallop.'

'Hnnnm—' Barundran began to protest; but then Kernin and I tugged up the anchors, and between two eyeblinks, we were gliding *upwards*. It was not at all the same sensation as that time at Drycleve, that jerking up on the straining hawsers. We hardly felt we were moving at all. But there below us were our friends and lovers, their little upturned faces growing littler and dwindling in the dusk, and then the trees and the roads also dwindling, and Eladon and the Three Rivers turning rapidly into something very like their painted forms on a map.

'By the holy Sun,' breathed Barundran, 'I never thought to see this, I never thought to feel it. This is *flight* . . . !'

Kernin said nothing: he was too moved, too enraptured for speech. He lay with his arms spread crosswise along one bulwark, looking ahead and down. It was now rapidly growing dark, and the Ring and the stars were coming out in dark blue heaven, and the waters below were beginning to shine blue-white on the darkening Earth. At about five hundred feet I suddenly became alarmed: we were still rising, and much faster than we had expected. Were Barundran's calculations wrong? I slashed open one of the smaller gas-plants, and then indeed we stopped rising, but instead began to sideslip. It was worse than being on a ship in a storm on the Great Sea. Barundran made a startled movement to come to my aid, and then the shifting of his great weight nearly overturned us.

'Lie down, you old fool!' I shouted. Luckily he heard me, and came down heavily like a felled horse in the middle of the raft; and Kernin slashed another gas-plant, and—we righted. By this time we were drifting low toward the summit of a green down—a green down with greyish egg-shaped knobs on top.

We nearly hit the monastery of the Sons of Saeth. Some of the hermits came running out of their huts like angry bees disturbed from a hive, and then we had grazed past them and were floating higher over the next valley.

'I think we nearly helped some of those fellows to Total Death,' I said.

'Hush,' said Kernin. He was lying quiet along the leading bulwark again. And then I remembered.

'Why,' I whispered, 'brother, this is merely your dream—that dream of so long ago, when you were a boy in Nakhtos. You *are* flying by the power of your mind—for your mind devised this flying raft; and we have floated down a hillside, and will doubtless float up another. . . .'

'But I do not see the beautiful garden,' said Kernin quietly, 'nor the envious insect-things below, unless you count those hermits. Also, in my dream the second hill was *very high*.'

We certainly passed no very high hills that night. We drifted, with dim Flickerfly flickering orange over our stern, and the lovely Ring burning orange high over our bow; and finally we bumped to earth at Sunkindle, as the bright heavy rays pushed us down, just outside the Shire-town of Dythlorn in Lower Aelvia— much to the astonishment of the local Earl and his yeomen, who nevertheless gave us a tremendous welcome.

That did it! The Greater Gas-plant is not very common in Aelvia, but it *is* found in the Var and Ruren Forests. Soon all the Earls and their sons had built their own rafts. One of the greatest charms of the sport, for these lordings, was that you never knew exactly where you would land—and this air-wandering by night was like some adventure out of an old romance. Barundran was kept busy trotting from shire to shire, making sure that every lord used a safe design. But he did not try aeronauting himself again for quite a while: his great weight was clearly a hazard.

Kernin made many more ascents. I think he might have gone

up alone, but the Queen vetoed that, and so did I, so he had to take me. We quickly gained useful experience: for one thing, we soon found there was no real danger of soaring indefinitely up to the Sun and a fiery death: the air got thinner the higher you went, and at three or four thousand feet your smaller and weaker gas-plants began to explode under their own internal pressure, and down you came again. So we lashed on some little plants deliberately chosen for their weakness: these we called our 'safeties'. With these, we could glide at a comfortable three thousand feet, well clear of the rolling downs of Aelvia. At that height the air was less moist, and the stars as bright and hard-blue as we had seen them from Nakhtos.

Kernin preferred to go up during No-Ring. He would lie on his back, gazing up at the stars, or making measurements of their positions with the Angulabe. He made no new discoveries, but it amused him to confirm for the twentieth time what Barundran had long pointed out; for instance, that Flickerfly was never visible during No-Ring; and when it *was* visible it was *precisely* opposite the Ring, on a line passing through the dull red disc of the night Sun in the zenith. This, according to Barundran, was a fact which was true *everywhere* in the Known World; moreover, the angle between the centre of the Ring and Flickerfly was always and everywhere precisely *one right angle;* in lands where Flickerfly was higher the Ring was lower, and vice versa, but the distance between them did not change. Most curious.

Kernin also verified that the night Sun drifted across the background of the stars exactly in proportion to the length of our journey. One night we drifted clean out of Aelvia, over the Wall between Drycleve and the Cataract, and saw the Holy River dropping like a shower of blue sparks down the fall . . . and we came down at Kherilos after a journey of seventy miles; and before the Sun grew too bright we reckoned its centre had shifted one whole degree.

'Which is a *constant,*' said Kernin, almost angrily. 'Within the limits of experimental error. Barundran says it's exactly 63 of our miles to a degree, both in his country and ours and over the whole Known World. Amazing what Refraction will do.'

And then once he said: 'If only the winds would drift us *the other way*.' But they almost never did. Night winds are land-winds over all the Shorelands, and even through Aelvia, though here the winds are gentler. Barundran once explained this to me, something to do with air-pressure and the heat or cold of land and water; but I am content to leave all such mysteries to the gods, or as the Aelvians say, to the Old First One, who devised our world the way it is.

Barundran, by the way, was fairly happy in these years. He was excited as a child about air-rafting, and hoped one day to take it up again himself, when the techniques were better developed. He also travelled a great deal, studying Aelvia and the Aelvians, both humans and satyrs; or when the damp got too much into his bones, he would go downriver to Nakhtos and Palur, and meet his own countrymen, the centaur traders from Kintobara. In this way, he brought us a lot of news.

Item: the Wise Centaurs were in trouble again—they had had to fight off yet another horde from Thulor. Curiously similar rumours: this horde too had been affrighted by sword-waving Harpies, and air-borne chariots. 'Hnnnm! I wonder,' said Barundran. 'Mayhap some barbarian chief, in the lands beyond the Great Sea, hath also invented the air-raft. And yet the Gas-plant is not known in the Middle Plain. As for the Harpies: well, a harpy hath hands, but clawed ones, which are not good for wielding a sword. Could it be that those—hnnnm!—Elder Gods are returning to the Known World?'

Item: Winking Stars were becoming more frequent. We also had observed this, and our observations checked with those of the centaur astronomers beyond Pelas Magha. And it was always the *same* four or five yellow-white stars which were involved.

An item from nearer home: Barundran had made friends with a lot of Aelvian satyrs and satyresses, and they had humoured him in his curious investigations of their own persons. And so at last he reported to Kernin: 'Hnnnm! My Prince, I must confess that in the eyes of Science, well—Men and Satyrs are cousin-beasts.'

'That is a beastly thought,' laughed Kernin. 'And you had better not publish it in the Shorelands, my old teacher; for I know my peoples and their prejudices. Send your monograph to Kintobara, in the decent obscurity of your own majestic language. Up to now you are well loved in Aelvia, and I would hate that to change. But I might whisper your notion to Taras Goldhelm; it might cheer him up.'

Taras-Tarsh was now outwardly as civilised a gentleman as it was possible for a satyr to be. He spoke perfect Aelvian, with only a certain gruff quality to his voice which betrayed his race. He dressed usually in a fine wool tunic, and high boots which hid his long feet and toe-claws, and either a tall burger's hat or that shining gilt helmet. For all that, he was not happy in Aelvia. Everyone knew what he was; and the burghers of Eladon would comment loudly that he should be stripped down to a codpiece.

And then he would snarl, and rush out of town in a fury, and go to his 'own' people—and mostly they rejected him too. Even if he stripped naked, he was still merely Tarsh One-horn, an odd foreign satyr from the low-river country. He did manage to couple with various nymph-maids, such as those of our Palace, who rather liked him; but that was no great consolation to him now. Whether he called himself 'Taras' or 'Tarsh'—and he did both, as the mood took him—he was still an oddity without a place in society.

'One day I will *show* them,' he growled. 'Nay, I will show you all. . . .'

We four were strolling in the meadows beside the Haf: Barundran, myself, the Prince. It was a bright, clear morning. Kernin seemed to be only half listening to the rest of us: he was gazing inland toward the dark blue-green Rath forest forty miles away, and high Rathwall rising beyond, and beyond again the farthest uplands of Rathvia, and dreadful Gagnar named for Springer-dragons, and last of all the floating mark of Khar Durnaran. Suddenly Kernin roused himself. 'What would you truly like to do, friend Taras Goldhelm?'

'Call me Tarsh!' The satyr ground his teeth together, and his reddish eyes glared. 'If we were not truly friends, Kernin, and if my people in Aelvia were not such a bunch of hornless shanis, I would rouse 'em against you *humans* and take the land back for ourselves. But enough! I despise 'em now as much as you humans do. I must make my fortune elsewhere. Elsewhere, anywhere! Perhaps over yonder mountains.' And he nodded toward Rathwall.

Kernin started. 'It is high time we investigated Rathwall, I think.'

'Rath Forest is impassable,' Barundran protested. 'By the holy Sun, but I have tried. 'Tis all giant angel-trees and sword-bushes and spinners' webs. The source-spring of Sinel is the best way, but beyond the spring the forest closes in. 'Tis said there was a way up once, but since the Rathvians were so discouraging to travellers, the forest was allowed to grow over the path. . . .'

'Let it be cleared again!' Kernin's eyes were bright, with that green flash I had seen in them in his boyhood. Indeed, the tall handsome man seemed suddenly younger again. 'Barundran—Tarsh—will you two take my seal-ring, and be my envoys to the Earl of that Shire? Show him the Angel signet, and bid him have that path hewn open again. We have been tarrying too long! What of the Lands Beyond the Sun? You have not forgotten, have you, the oath we once swore?'

Tarsh pricked up his long ears—thereby nearly losing his tall hat. 'Call me Taras, like a gentleman, dragon-blast you! But what's all this about lands beyond the Sun? And what oath . . . ?'

'Hnnnm—child—my boy,' said Barundran sadly, 'I think none of us exactly swore an oath, except you, and foolish oaths, they say, the holy Sun always forgives. My boy, it is hopeless. I have been considering the evidence. The Known World from Thulor to Rathvia is 6000 miles across, and I reckon that Khar Durnaran is a mere 300 miles beyond the last point we can see at ground level; and in all this wide world there is no sign of any change in the great features of Nature. The Sun is always vertical, the Sky is always far, far away. We might have to travel another 6000 miles across desert plains or plains haunted by barbarians and dragons, and still come to no singularity. My boy, I am seventy-three years old: we centaurs are a long-lived race, and yet I am coming to the end of my days, and perhaps I am learning wisdom. Why seek infinity at the end of the world, when perhaps it is not there to find? Or perhaps, better still, if you are of a good spirit—"well-souled", as we say in Centaurish—you can find infinity anywhere: in your own Palace garden, in the eyes of a child—'

'Oh, hang your philosophy,' snapped Kernin. I was shocked: I had never heard him speak so rudely to his old tutor before. And immediately he relented. 'I'm sorry, old Master; but you began to remind me of the Saethmen. *I* am not ready to philosophise and die yet. We can but *try*, or begin to try. Suppose we could get through Rathvia, and march a thousand miles? A thousand miles might be only a couple of Rings' march. And if we *still* saw no change in the Sun, we might at least refute the system of Gormarendran . . . and a negative result in Science is still a valuable result—as you yourself have often told me, old Tutor, haven't you . . . ?'

Well, the upshot of this conversation was that Tarsh and Barundran went on that little mission up-country. As we saw them leave, Tarsh was talking animatedly to the centaur.

'I think we will have one more recruit for the Quest,' said Kernin, with a grim smile.

'Brother!' I said, 'I thought you had forgotten, I wished you had forgotten. And now that you have two little children, and a third in the egg. . . .'

'But that, Orselen, is exactly *why*.' His eyes were hard, the way I had seen him look in battle when ordering men to follow him to their deaths. 'Now I have done my duty. Now our Kingdoms have peace, and the succession is assured. If I should die on the Quest—oh, don't dig your fingers into the earth, the gods are not so jealous of words, and facts are facts, whether spoken or not—if I should die, I say, my life could well be spared now. I am nearly in old Barundran's case. By the Sword of Sinis, I was *twenty* last Ring—'

'And I nearly thirty-one. Brother, I am *middle-aged*,' I said, 'and beginning to feel it. And yet I would go with you to the ends of the Earth—if the Earth has any ends. That's the real point, Kernin. What's the good of marching forever? It's not as if there looks to be anything *interesting* beyond Rathvia, except that one enormous mountain—and as for that, I think mountains look prettiest from a distance and below. And above all, you are *not* yet in the situation of Barundran. He has no young family, no loving wife. If you are lost, I think your Queen would die of grief.'

Kernin's chin was disdainful and stubborn, his green eyes mocking. 'Don't exaggerate, brother. I love Niamwy, yes, and she loves me, but it is four years now, our first raptures are over; and no one dies of grief, let alone a strong-minded woman like my dear Niamwy. I think she would marry again, some very suitable Shire-lord, or one of my mother's cousins from Nakhtos, a faithful protector for our children till it be Aelenek's turn to reign—and till then both Niamwy and my father can still lead armies.'

My mouth went dry. Here he was, calmly discussing his own death, to be brought on by his own mad act! I went down on my knee to him—but he jerked me to my feet. 'Get up, get up—that's not fair, we are not on *those* terms, Orsu, and you know it!'

'Well then, as friend to friend,' I said. 'You are not seeing things straight, Kernin. Your children are *too young*, and your father—I mean Prahelek—he's too old. What if he should die before your return—*if* you return at all? "Woe to that hapless land Whose king's too young to stand"—you know the Rakpen proverb, and it's true!'

'Rakpen lived in a barbarous age, he fought with Sakanek at Suoran, and all that. Things are changed now. Who would attack us? The King of Rindos is as old as Prahelek, and he's sworn to a *twenty-year* truce. The Agnaians are all bluster and cowardice. And my mother and my wife have tolerably good generals.' Then his mood lightened, he laughed, and clapped me on the shoulder. 'Well, let's forget all that for now, anyway. I am not about to tear you from sweet Hafren's arms yet, Orsu. Let's go back to the city—it's Nami's mid-Ring feast this evening, remember? I hear there's a famous minstrel come back into town—don't snort, my dear distinguished Bard, I *like* "mere minstrels", and this Wilifern, they say, is a great story-teller, a liar of the best. And the young Earl of Rurenva is going to make a raft-flight from Aesk Ward market-place. We'll slip away, hm? Niamwy won't mind, there'll be time for dinner at the Palace after.'

8

'Hahai!' cried Wilifern the Minstrel, and struck his zithar a jangling crash; and he plunged his blazing sunwood torch under the sapphiras-coals of his brazier, and his girl-piper blew a piercing blast on her shrillest tube. Even so, it was many eyeblinks before those two could attract the eyes and ears of the crowd down to street level.

Apart from the now-kindling blue fire of the brazier, Aesk Ward Market Square was all a-twinkle and a-gleam with light-berries on the sides of shops and houses, some planted in pots on the plank counters of stalls, some held up on candelabra-poles for the benefit of their masters by cod-pieced satyr servants or aproned nymph-maids. And then there was also the dying light of the Sun, and the growing light of the Ring. In all these mingled lights, cold blue and warm orange, the silver-painted raft of the young Earl made a glorious show as it lifted from its scaffold in the centre of the square, and rose smoothly above the peaked roof-tops, the Earl and his herald leaning over the side and waving their hats in acknowledgment of the crowd's hurrahs.

In opposition to all the jollity, in a corner of the square stood a hooded and grey-robed Saethman, looking morose as Saethmen always do. He was exhibiting a cage with a treadmill, and on the treadmill a squirrel-mouse trying always to reach a morsel of sheep's cheese. As the mouse mounted, the treadmill turned, and the poor little beast never got anywhere nearer to the cheese. The Saethman was intoning a monotonous poem, alleging that his treadmill was an emblem of human life. But no one was listening to him. Apart from the air-raft, there was the attraction of Wilifern the Minstrel.

'Hahai!' cried Wilifern, striking an even louder-resounding discord. 'All right—ladies, gentlemen, and satyrs—gather round now, come all you merchants and prentices, and yeomen and yeowomen, nymph-girls and girl-girls—come to the second and better half of this eve's entertainment! I grant you that floating about in space is a glorious thing for a man, but, by Firafax, it is not new! Will you believe me when I tell you, that else-upon-a-place there are whole *worlds* that float—rocks and mountains, plains and seas, and all with their crews of peasants and kings upon 'em—going about their daily business quite calmly, eating and going to stool, raising crops and raising children, making war and making love—and all while their lands raft about in nothingness, just as you saw those two young gentlemen take to the air even now?'

'No, we will *not*,' chanted the crowd joyously. But this was the ritual response for the beginning of any Firafax tale. The crowd were now properly assembling into the usual ring—Kernin and I had made sure of getting into the front row—and there sat Wilifern on his tripod beside the blue-flamed brazier which is sacred to Firafax the Liar. Wilifern was said to be one of the best liars in the business; unfortunately he had been wandering abroad ever since the great Peace and Kernin's marriage, some said in Agnai, some said even in Menkinvia. Now I saw that, unlike most Aelvians, his hair was naturally red (doubtless he was of mixed blood, as Minstrels are most casual in their matings) and so his hair still showed at the roots, but above those the mass of it was dyed blue as is the custom of his calling. He was snub-nosed, dark-faced, with erratic eyebrows, and seemed neither old nor young. Slander said there was satyr blood in his ancestry—but that must be a jest; and anyway, his eyes were merry, human, and blue. The people loved him; and even I, though as a Bard I must despise Minstrels—even I had to admire his artistry.

'You will not believe? Well, may the Dark One damn you for philistines and fools,' Wilifern retorted equally ritually. 'Know, you idiots, that when Firafax jumped into the Keelless Sea of blue fire, for fifty years he was out of time-and-space as we know time-and-space. Gloomy Saeth had to return without him. In that time which was no time and all of time, the Dark One and the Old First One showed Firafax all the ten thousand things of this world, and also all the Million Things which are not of this world. And one of the Million Things was the Universe of Empty Space.'

'What is the Universe of Empty Space?' said the girl-piper from her place in the shadows beyond the brazier: obviously a rehearsed question.

'What is the Universe of Empty Space? Well, you know that our universe is about half-and-half heavy stuff—matter—and light stuff—sunrays and ghosts and air and sky. 'Tis said by the Sons of Saeth—may they gloom themselves to Total Death—

yes, you too, Brother Unvar, in your corner yonder, you with your squirrel-cage—'

The Saethman from his corner raised his voice louder. 'As above, so below: Seek no path, there is nowhere to go. . . .'

'Rot you, your poem's not worth a sheep's turd,' said Wilifern amiably. 'But now, all you freefolk and fornicators, listen! As I was saying when I was so rudely interrupted—even the Saethmen admit that the solid Earth goes down for ever beneath our feet; and what thing Heaven may be I will not say now—'

'As above, so below,' chanted Unvar.

'Die and dissipate,' said Wilifern. 'But Heaven is surely of an airish nature, since it floats above us even now in the night-time when the Sun is not keeping it up with his rays; so *our* universe is surely half Earth below, and half Air-Light-Space above—'

'That's obvious,' said the shopkeeper in the front rank of the crowd. 'Get on with it, Wili!'

'I *was* getting on with it, you savage,' said Wilifern, shooting a hideous grimace at the heckler. For a moment he looked a malicious image of the Dark One, just as he is carved on Aelvian signposts. 'And by the way, it is not *quite* obvious—but I will let that pass for now, true philosophy is no game of mine. Well, the seventy-third universe that the Dark God showed to Firafax was like this: it was nearly all *nothing;* with just a few bright specks floating about in that black nothing, and a few dark greyish specks buzzing around the light specks like flies round a corpse. And the Dark One said to Firafax: "How d'ye like this little world, my son? Isn't it the daintiest, wittiest thing?"

'Firafax said: "The beauty of this nearly-nothing is not quite overwhelming. What are those little light-berries, and those blow-flies near 'em?"

' "My son," said the Dark One, "the light-berries, as you call them, are each one a Sun, and the blow-flies are each one an Earth. Come closer to one of them, and you will see. . . ." And then he took Firafax right up to one of the darkish specks, and lo! it was round as an egg, and half its surface was lit up by the Sun which floated in the nothing not far away from it, and the other half of the egg-shaped world was in utter darkness. This egg-world was also spinning smoothly, smoothly, just as any one of you can make a hard-boiled handibird's egg spin with a twist of your fingers—but this egg-world was spinning *on nothing*, so it wasn't slowing down. And it was a whole world full of people, *very* much like our people. There were just a few trifling differences—their ghosts were quite transparent, so you couldn't see 'em easily or be sure when a man was dead—oh, and the men had no head-peaks, and the women brought forth their young alive like winged-cows do among us, and the sheep had horns but the horses had none—things like that. But on the whole they were just like us; and when they spun into their Sun's light, that was Day, and when they spun out of their Sun's light, that was Night—'

'Come on!' shouted the same front-row merchant. 'That won't do, Wili! The people and the animals would *fall off!*'

'No they wouldn't—they didn't,' the minstrel retorted, 'because in *that* Universe, there wasn't any *down*. Nor did the Suns' rays push people off the edges of the egg-worlds, because their rays *had no push*. The people and animals just naturally stuck on, just as you or I might stick on a spinner's web in Rath Forest, or as a fly's feet stick on a wall or a ceiling. "Down" for them was toward the centre of their little egg-world—which wasn't so little either, it was nearly twice as thick through the middle as from this Aelvia of ours to the land of the Centaurs—so big in fact that except on a very clear day those people couldn't notice that their world was round at all. But even so, since that Egg-world was spinning in the middle of *nothing for ever and ever,* and its Sun was shining in the midst of that same *nothing for ever and ever,* it wasn't all that impressive, and Firafax, even merry Firafax, shuddered a little.

' "Why, don't you like the Seventy-Third Universe, my son?" said the Dark One.

' "I have seen better," admitted Firafax.

' "I made this one *all by myself,"* said the Dark One sulkily; and with that he flung Firafax out of the Seventy-Third Universe, and out of the Keelless Sea, which is the Sea of Dreams at the World's End, altogether; and whereas Saeth had to make his way home from World's End by the hardest ways, Firafax now found himself home at once. He was standing on a pleasant lea in Aeskdale, between Rath Forest and the upper Aesk River, on a fine bright morning in New Ring, and near him were girl-maids keeping their sheep, and nymph-maids mowing a road with their goats; and Firafax saw that our own world and our own country were so beautiful that he began to laugh; and he has never stopped laughing since. And the girl-maids and the nymph-maids, when they heard him laughing, drew round him in a ring, and asked what he was laughing about; and since he was a liar, he told them he was laughing at the marvels of World's End, and then he began telling them tales of some of the Seventy-Three Universes and the other Million Things, until the girls also laughed till the tears came to their eyes, and they gave him in return all their wealth—as I trust my generous listeners will now also do for this humble son of Firafax. . . .'

The piper-girl began making her round with the base of a harpy-egg shell held out as a collecting box, and the people laughed, applauded, and threw in copper or silver plain-rings, which are the common coin of Aelvia. When the shell came to Kernin, he threw in a plain-ring of gold. He was dressed like any burgher in a sober russet tunic, but the bystanders knew him, of course. Everyone knows everyone in Eladon anyway. But the folk made no fuss around their Prince: this is the Aelvian way, and a good way too, I have come to think. The merchant who had been heckling scoffed when he saw Kernin throw in the gold ring.

'By'r Green Lady, you waste your money, sir Prince. Tales are tales, but this one of Wili's was such nonsense. Sun's rays with no push, indeed!'

'Oh, I don't know,' said Kernin. 'The fiction had a certain logic to it. If a story-teller can invent an entire universe, he can surely arrange for it to have whatever physical laws he likes. One can *imagine* weightless light—or, by the by, dark water that doesn't shine at all at night, and so forth. And if the Old First God made this universe, why not others? Why shouldn't there be seventy-three universes, or a million universes, all with different laws of matter and spirit?'

I laughed, and supported Kernin. 'The important thing is for the minstrel to be consistent. If he invents laws for his world, he must not break them after—not in the same story, that is. . . .'

As the merchant went off shrugging, Kernin turned to me. Suddenly, in the flickering shadows, he looked and sounded serious. 'Orselen, I would like to know this fellow Wilifern better. Come now quick, before he vanishes.'

We got there just as the minstrel was folding his tripod-seat and packing his zithar into its leather case.

'Minstrel,' said Kernin, 'I liked your tale very much—very much indeed! A world of infinite space. . . . Do you know, one of my father's titles is that boastful one, "King of Infinite Space"? It is an idea I like, not to be bounded. . . .'

Wilifern bowed, and then looked from Kernin to me and back again with a curious grin. 'I am honoured. Even that time I saw Your Highness in Palur—what, is it ten years, or twelve?—I said to myself then, "Wili, that young lad will go far—or burst in the attempt". And *I* am such another, too. As one wanderer to another—'

'What,' I cried, 'was it *you*, that day Barundran landed, and King Prahelek tried to arrest you as a spy?'

Wilifern chuckled. 'Ay . . . and if he had nabbed me, indeed he would've had the right of it. I skipped upriver that time, and warned old King Deulyn to beware the Prince of Palur and his man-horse tutor; but our old King would take no heed, and now from the Sun when he looks down he may be surprised to see himself become your Highness' father-in-law.'

'Is it the same girl too?' I asked. Then the piper-girl came out into the light of the brazier, and I saw that she was young.

'Nay, girls come and girls go,' said the minstrel carelessly. 'A yeoman will apprentice his needy daughter—but there are few girls who will pipe for long on the minstrels' road. This one's a good wench, but. . . . Women start yearning for husband and hatchlings, and then they leave me.' He shrugged. 'It's just as well. That way, my pipers are always young and sleek and pretty—and *that* helps draw a crowd like nothing else.'

'Do *you* never think of marrying any of them?' said Kernin. 'You are not a Bard, and therefore you may.'

'Wanderers should not marry.' His eyes in the brazier light were doubly blue—blue as precious sword-steel from beyond sea. Now they fixed keenly on Kernin. 'It is not my fate to die in a woman's arms, that I know without needing to look into any bowl of water. As for you, my lord—'

'You will not prophesy, I hope?' I broke in, horrified, perhaps just in time. Aelvian minstrels sometimes play also at fortune-telling; and from what I have heard in recent years, some have a true gift. The professional liars sometimes see bitter truth in visions. But it is the law of Aelvia that none shall foretell a Royal fate—unless the monarch or prince should himself demand it. Wilifern now simply raised his crooked eyebrows in mute inquiry.

'No,' said Kernin, 'I will hear no prognostic. I never wanted anything less than to know my future; for that would destroy my freedom, which I value more.'

'Well, I will speak only of present things,' said Wilifern. 'You, my lord, have also the wanderlust incurable; and yet you are married—much married. You will be torn—you are already torn. I am the wiser of us two.'

'That's enough, fellow—' I began angrily; but Kernin put me aside with the back of his hand against my shoulder. He seemed to be passing into a dream from which I was excluded. As for Wilifern, I wanted to kill him.

'Tell me now,' said Kernin, 'the *whole* of this legend of Saeth and Firafax. I have till now heard it only in part, and in contradictory fragments. Firafax is a god—or half a god, no? And yet the Saethmen place their founder's journey in a real year—the year 249 by Palurian reckoning, which is less than four hundred years ago, well after the Land-Taking, and not long before the Siege of Suoran. They went through Rathvia—by magic, or how? And where did they stand when Saeth lost all his mirth, and Firafax lost all his sadness?'

'I have answers to all those questions,' grinned Wilifern, 'but since I am a Liar, how will you believe me?'

'Speak, anyway,' said Kernin, tight-lipped. 'I have studied much since I met Barundran, and I have come to believe that most legends contain truth.'

At that moment Unvar the Saethman shuffled by us with downcast eyes, holding his squirrel cage. 'As below, so above,' he chanted hollowly, 'He who seeks truth will sadness prove.'

Wilifern made a face at the retreating hooded form. 'Would you believe me, Prince, if I tell you that that fellow is my actual blood-brother? But he is, we were both sons of one mother . . . so you see, I have at least a *brotherly* acquaintance with Truth.' He paused, and grinned strangely. 'You asked me for the story of Saeth and Firafax.'

I gripped the hilt of my sword in impotent anguish; for I had made more searching inquiries than Kernin, among the Aelvian Bards and elsewhere; and I knew what he might now hear, and what I had for many Rings been carefully concealing from him.

'Know,' said Wilifern, 'Firafax was not a god *before* he made that journey. He was a man of Aelvia, or a satyr, or something betwixt the two. Perhaps he was a minstrel like me. And Saeth was a princeling, heir to the Earl of Ranelon, a proper young man, but a man with this itch to *know*. And they two did make a journey through Rathvia—the Rathvians will sometimes admit very small parties through their land, I have heard—but only men, not women—men whom they find sufficiently amusing. Saeth and Firafax charmed the Rathvians, and won through right to the Edge of the World—'

'What!' cried Kernin.

'—or at least to the summit of Khar Durnaran, the highest mountain in the world; and there they found the magic Ring of Truth, which Saeth put upon his finger; but Firafax laughed, and threw it away to his friend, and jumped from Kahr Durnaran into the Keelless Blue Sea, the Fire of Dreams beyond World's Edge, which it seems is just beyond Khar Durnaran.'

And when I had heard that, I knew to what journey we were doomed.

There was a silence of many eyeblinks. Kernin had taken Wilifern by the shoulder, and was gripping him, looking through the night out of the square, between the pleasant homes of Eladon, to where a certain dark arrowhead floated against the World's End glow.

Then at last Kernin spoke. 'From so high a peak one might see many things clear. If I were to climb Khar Durnaran like Saeth, would you come with me like Firafax, my good Wilifern? We would have need, on such a high hard march, of merry tales such as yours.'

Wilifern laughed. 'As a son of Firafax, I should know this is folly. Lies and warm beds in Aelvia are better than Truth. And yet, I have long known that this would be my fate. Yes, my Prince, yes. . . .'

'And to think,' said Kernin, 'we did not know it, but there were already four companions of the Quest assembled together, that afternoon in Palur.'

PART THREE

The Way to World's End

9

At first Kernin did not tell his Queen what he had in mind to do, nor did I tell Hafren. That next Ring-month, till Tarsh and Barundran accomplished their mission, was a poignant time. The third Royal child was hatched, a boy who was named Kandelen, and much resembled his brother.

Wilifern was now invited often to the Queen's feasts, and he quickly became popular, making Queen Niamwy often smile, and three-year-old Prince Aelenek cause the rafters to ring with his merry, childish glee. Wilifern and his piper-girl became immediate favourites with the royal children; the piper, Inanwy, was especially good with hatchlings. 'Wench,' said the Queen once, 'if ever you need to leave your present master, know that there will be a place for you in my household.' At that Inanwy looked suddenly melancholy. 'Your Majesty, indeed I may have to accept your kind offer, and that soon. . . .' She looked at Wilifern as she said that; but he replied only with a mocking grin and a slight shake of his head.

It seemed to me that Eladon and our royal palace and my own bedchamber—and especially my dear Hafren—had never seemed so beautiful. Hafren had at last decided that her own years as a young piper were coming to an end, and she had ceased to eat the so-called Maiden's Weed which is so well known to Aelvian females; and consequently she was at last about to bring forth. 'King Aelenek will need a Chief Bard too, one day, Orsu,' she laughed.

I nearly told her then, that I would probably not be present at the hatching of our first child. She took my emotion for mere surprise and paternal pride; and we made love most passionately.

'Oh my dear, my dear,' I said, 'if I were not a Bard, and you the daughter of a Bard, we would be husband and wife; but still, if my Prince should go on an expedition, I would have to leave you, and follow him.'

She laughed. 'Nay, we are both bastards of many generations' standing . . . and it is just as well, my love. This marrying was not the oldest custom in the Shorelands, as you well know. And I am bound to my Queen, as you to your Prince. Indeed, I think you are bound to your Prince by a dearer tie, are you not? You two are so alike in feature . . . I take it your mother, that sweet Mankinvian singer, she caught old Prahelek's eye while worthy Omren looked the other way. . . .'

I was startled. 'No, no, that is impossible! I was hatched *before* the union of the Twin Kingdom, at Nakhtos before Prahelek's time.' I regarded her with a certain fear. 'What are you saying?'

'Nothing,' she smiled. 'Stop my mouth with kisses. . . .'

And so I did.

Then Tarsh came riding back into Eladon, with news. 'The forest path is clear,' he grunted, 'and Barundran and I have climbed that mountainside, right up to the Rathvian Gate.'

Kernin sprang to his feet in his Great Hall. 'Well: what then?'

The satyr grinned. 'Nay, you must come and see for yourself. The Rathvians—you will see them, and you will not see them. They—but I cannot describe them: they showed very little of themselves to us.'

'What is this, my lord?' said Queen Niamwy.

And then Kernin told her that he was thinking of making a friendly visit to Rathvia.

Niamwy laughed. 'If you can achieve *that*, you will be evidently the greatest hero of Aelvia since Saeth and Firafax. But I do not see the point of visiting that forbidden and forbidding land.'

'Women never see that sort of point,' said Wilifern. The Queen took that impudent speech in good part; but Inanwy looked sad. She had of course been Wilifern's bedfellow, whenever those two could boast of a bed in their wanderings. And now their ways were parting.

I told Hafren that night, 'We ride for Rathvia at tomorrow's Kindle, my dear. And I do not know when I shall be coming back. The Prince is talking of a journey of two or three Rings. But it is the gods who determine the time of a traveller's return.'

She laughed. 'I think you may be back much quicker than you think. The Rathvians have let in nobody that I know of in three hundred years. But if you succeed sufficiently in your mad venture, do not delay your return too long. I am not a spirit, to sleep alone for ever like the dead in the holy Sun. Nor, I think, are you. Doubtless you will bed with some Rathvian wench. As you know, the old stories say their ladies hold great power, so that may be but politic, and I will not blame you. Neither should you blame me if I should fancy some handsome young Earl's son if you stay away overlong. That lad of Rurenva, for instance, the gallant raft-man. My first hatchling will be of your getting, Orsu; but the Green Lady only knows who will get my second.'

I groaned. 'I will try to come back. . . .'

But as things turned out, our entry into Rathvia was considerably delayed. In any case, we were not really ready for the great march: our first journey was merely a reconnaissance.

Rath Forest is the greatest of the Three Forests of Aelvia, and its first copses begin only a little way beyond the Shire-town of Ranelon. We were met at the gate of Ranelon by the Earl, a sober man of my own age, and a leather-coated guard of honour—and Barundran.

'Nay, no ceremony, my lord,' said Kernin hastily. 'I thank you most kindly for your welcome—and even more for your path-cutting. Let us on, at once.' And as we trotted through the little town, he turned to Barundran. 'I cannot get much out of Tarsh. Old Master, what . . . ?''

"Hnnnm!' Barundran's old grey eyes were shining. He seemed suddenly youthful: I thought he might at any moment break into a canter, or a caper. 'Why, they are the strangest-mannered Two-Leggeds I have yet seen. They wear *masks*, and they have no hor—I beg your pardon, my Prince, I should say, they have no head-peaks.'

It was bright morning when we entered Rath Forest. At first we rode beside the narrow stream that danced and bubbled over its bed of mountain pebbles—the hatchling river that lower down became the mighty Sinolis. The path rose steeply, and the great angel-trees spread their wing-like green fans overhead, making a roof over the path and the stream so that we seemed to be riding up an endless green-lighted tunnel. Luckily the great leaves were so thick that they noticeably cut off some of the sun's gravity, so our ascent was that much easier. But at last the ground rose abruptly, and at the foot of that hill we saw the end of Sinolis—or its beginning. There was a mist-blue pool under the hill and shaded by the angel-trees, bubbling and in the dimness giving off bluish vapour: and that was the source-spring.

We dismounted, and Kernin led us in a prayer to Sinis. 'Lady of Truth, of wayfarers, guide to the end and at the end, protect us on this journey, whose end You alone know; and if our bodies should fall, receive our spirits and guide them also, to the holy courts of the Sun: those courts where there is no falsehood, where all is known, both the secrets of the heart, and the secrets of every world's shape and end. . . .'

Kernin had always a great devotion to Sinis: I think she was the one god he truly worshipped. During this prayer I tried not to remember that her dark sister is Ganthis, Death. Sinis receives the soul, but Ganthis-Ran devours the body in the egg-shaped tomb.

When we rose to our feet, Wilifern laughed. 'Methinks I should pray also to Firafax, to give us good sport on our way, and perhaps not too much Truth.'

Kernin looked angry at that, and the minstrel desisted. Then we began to climb on foot, leading our horses. Barundran, of course, was his own horse, as you might say; he puffed a bit, but was surprisingly agile and hale, and a good climber for all his years. He had a new pair of gold-rimmed eyeglasses on his nose, but otherwise he went nearly naked, stripped for action. 'Why,' he panted, 'this minds me of my young days, when I was in the militia of our republic of Kintobara, and we patrolled the hills toward Thulor. I could handle a bow then, my boy, let me tell you.'

'Well,' said Kernin, 'you may yet need to handle a bow again.'

The forest closed in on us now, and there was barely room for one person to go before another, single file up the steep. On either side, the spaces between the great trees were blocked by sword-bushes, and higher up by the cords of spinners' webs. I was glad we were not doing this at night, when one could easily stumble into the sticky rope-like webs—and when the black, many-legged spinners come out to seize their prey. They eat mainly birds and small flymonkeys, but still. . . . Tarsh, however, swivelled his ears—he was wearing his fine two-horned gold helmet, which left his ears uncovered—and now he told us that there was no deadly creature within half a mile of the path.

'Prowess of Prah!' said Kernin, smiling. 'I see you will be a useful companion upon our journey, Tarsh—or is it Taras, today? You with your ears, Wili with his second sight . . . why, we are surely better equipped than poor Saeth and Firafax.'

Three thousand feet, four thousand . . . the forest climbed up Rathwall higher than any air-raft had yet flown. And then in a minute the trees thinned and were gone, we were flooded with sunlight and weight—and there, not two hundred yards further, or a hundred feet higher, we saw the Rathvian Gate.

This was a narrow valley between higher hills; and the pass

was blocked by a rough castellated wall of large black stones. The wall was not much higher than a tall man, and in the middle there was a sort of stone stile leading up to it: so the whole thing was hardly a formidable defensive work.

In the gap between the middle castellations, we saw faces. No, we did not, not exactly. Barundran was right: every one of the Rathvian guards was *masked*. Black masks covered the whole face, with mere slits for eyes and mouth, and above that were either black leather helmets or, in one case, a helmet-like mass of night-sky-black hair. True, this warrior seemed to have no head-peaks; but he could have small ones under that black mass. As we came right up to the wall, we saw that the soldiers also wore black tunics, and carried black-painted spears. Yes, even their bronze points were blackened! This panoply was like Aelvian war-gear, only more ancient-looking and more deliberately sinister. Truly, Rathvia is well named the Dark Country. I have never seen warriors who looked stranger or more uncanny.

Kernin made his followers wait some way back, with Wilifern, Tarsh, and Barundran slightly in advance of the Earl's party. Then he boldly ascended the 'stile', and I clambered after him, most apprehensive, my hand upon my sword-hilt. We carried no shields; if one of those guards decided to cast a spear. . . . But no. All that happened was that the one without the helmet stood up in the midst, and spoke:

'Back, Lowlanders! The Dark Land beeth no countrie for such as ye.'

That voice! It was smooth, dark, warm: it made me think of the Black Priestesses of Nakhtos when they chant the hymn for Ganthis-night, the last of No-Ring, or at a prince's funeral. The language, too. . . . I barely understood it, and Kernin at first did not at all: it was the oldest kind of Shorelandish, High Pelenic, in fact, like the eldest of the Elder Proverbs, but with a strange thick accent, a difference.

I became Kernin's herald now indeed, and interpreted for him. 'We come as friends to Rathvia, not as warmakers. The high and mighty Prince Kernin, Consort of Aelvia, Heir to Prahelek of Palur and Kandiri of Nakhtos, requests friendship with whoever governs goodly Rathvia—and free passage through your country for a very small party. Only four men—nay, three *men*, and one satyr, and one centaur: who would follow in the footsteps of famous Saeth of old.'

When I had done my message, in my best High Pelenic, the helmless one regarded us all, as enigmatic behind that mask as Death herself.

'I be Lord of the Gate,' said that voice. 'We seek neither enmity nor friendship with the men of the Lower Countries. And in seven thousand and more Rings we have let none pass this Gate. Why should we now break our custom for *you*?'

It was now past noon, yet at five thousand feet on that pass the air was cold. I shivered, and thought of a proverb: 'Some halls have wide entrances, but narrow exits.' Suddenly I knew I did not want to get into Rathvia at all.

But Kernin felt otherwise. He was getting to follow that strange dialect, and now he spoke up for himself. 'For curiosity. If you are human, you must know that emotion. Have ye ever spoken with a centaur? Or a satyr who wears human clothes? Or for that matter, with any *man* of the countries by the Great Sea? I take it you, sir, are not seven thousand Rings old. If your ancestors let pass Saeth and Firafax—is that known in your traditions?—why should not you then let us. . . .'

It seemed to me that that dark voice changed a little. Could that mask be concealing a smile? 'It is told in Namurai and Luvanash that Firafax amused our ancestors sufficiently. 'A was a conjuror . . . and had other talents, too, as did noble Saeth. Well, this is our Gate-law, Prince: any whom we let pass must amuse us now yet more greatly than Saeth and Firafax.'

'My minstrel can juggle and tell lying tales; Tarsh the satyr can hear a dragon cough in its lair a mile away; Barundran the centaur hath the great lore of Oversea—' Kernin began.

'Na, na!' said the Black One. 'I am Gate-Lord of Namurai, and 'tis my privilege to impose the feat ye must accomplish to pass into Rathvia. Let us see. Be these the five of you?'

The other three had been edging forward; and now the dark Gate-Lord contemplated us in silence.

'Hear my sentence,' he said at last. 'We will not let you pass this Gate on foot or horse, and if you bring an army to force your way in, we will defeat you: we have a magic powerful enough for that. Let us see if ye have any magic too. Your pass-feat is this: ye must all five ride over Rathwall through the air, on mounts that fly. But as for your centaur friend, since he is half a horse already, we will enjoin him merely to fly himself.'

At that, I could not help being angry. I seized Kernin's arm, and whispered in the modern Nakhtian dialect: 'I don't believe in these people's so-called magic: for that matter, I've never seen any magic that ever worked. They're bluffing, brother. We could teach their insolence a lesson with a few troops of soldiers, and then maybe, if you must get into Rathvia, you could do it in safety, with force behind you.'

Kernin whispered back: 'There'll be no need for that. And I am heartily sick of killing. Conquering Aelvia was bad enough. No brother, I'm not going to offer violence here.' He turned to the Gate-Lord, and in a loud voice he cried:

'Sir, I accept your Pass-feat. Ye shall see all five of us flying over your mountain ere ten Rings are out.'

The Gate-lord took that boast calmly enough. 'Well, we shall watch for you when you take wing. And if you accomplish *that*, Prince of Aelvia, be sure our monarch will welcome you to Rathvia's high-city of Luvanash.'

As we rode back down the mountain and into the forest, I said: 'Kernin, if you're thinking of what I'm thinking, forget it. No raft has ever soared this high; and we are supposed to *ride*; and the winds at night are always contrary, always blowing seaward.'

The Earl of Ranelon was close behind us, and now suddenly he spoke up. 'Your pardon, Herald; but you are wrong about the winds. The other shires scoff at us for being backward in this new sport; but the fact is, the winds after Sunquenching are often treacherous in our country. The first raft that flew from Ranelon buried itself in the worst of Rath Forest.'

Barundran said excitedly: 'I have been studying the Airish Science in these parts, my boy. When the afternoon storm is unusually prolonged, the daywind also is prolonged into the first half of the night. If we could go high enough, I think we *could* drift into Rathvia. But how to climb higher than five thousand feet?'

'We haven't really wanted to,' said Kernin. 'Suppose we use the very strongest of gas-plants, and build a huge raft—*with no safeties.*'

Wilifern loped over to Kernin, and gripped his hand. 'By Firafax, but I like your spirit, Prince. I would follow no one else to my death.'

I groaned, and grabbed ten-fingered at the earth.

'Nay,' said Wilifern, his blue eyes a-gaze into the dark distance of the forest, which was now turning darker with the beginning of the storm. 'I did not say the *Prince's* death. I seem to see my lord Kernin standing upon a great height, and one other with him. If I were to prophesy—which by the laws of Aelvia I am forbidden to do—I would say, by Sinis! I think the Prince will achieve his Quest. But since I must not prophesy, I say no such thing.'

*   *   *

It did not take ten Rings to build the big raft, but only five. Long before that, of course, the true scope of our great Quest became public knowledge in Aelvia. Kernin broke it first of all to Niamwy, on our return from that reconnaissance.

She took it like a great Queen. At first she tried to reason with her husband: that the journey to Khar Durnaran and the climb up the mountain were probably impossible, and in any case useless for any practical purpose. But when he said, 'That is not the *point*,' she repressed her tears.

'I should have realised long ago, what it means to marry a Hero. Well, my love, I see it is your fate to go. And it is mine to stay, and keep Aelvia safe, and our children, and maybe your old parents too.'

It was only once that she burst out, when she was alone with Hafren: 'O, if only *men* would understand the meaning of Duty, and the true meaning of Honour!'

Hafren reported this speech to me. 'I know, I know,' I said. 'And I am of the Queen's mind in this. But I do not blame Kernin: I blame the gods, the Old First One especially and the Bright One, who fashioned men the way they are, and made some to be Heroes. Sakanek was a Hero of the first class, and he achieved his Honour by the sack of Suoran, the slaughter of all his cousins, the tears of ten thousand women and children dragged into slavery—and his own death. All very glorious, very Honourable. Kernin is not so bloody-minded, his ambition is nobler, but I fear it will prove deadly to some; I hope, only to some of us Questers.'

Hafren wept a little, and clung to me. 'Well, it is a Bard-Herald's honour to follow his Prince, even into the most doomed battle. Go, my love. At least, when you stand on Khar Durnaran, make sure the Prince *comes back* from there.'

'Why,' I said, 'how should he go further? It is said, that mountain overlooks the End of the World.'

'Then make sure he does not jump past the End of the World,' said Hafren.

10

The Quest started on a New-Ring night, the first of the Year 631 in the calendar of Palur. In Palur and Nakhtos they would be hammering the bronze nails into Olari's doors, and in Eladon folk would be rejoicing in Suori's feast of Love. But it had been a sad little celebration in the Shire-town of Ranelon; and in those fields at Sunquenching we left our women-folk, and all the royal court of Aelvia, and began to soar. It had been a long, rainy afternoon, and now as the Sun died the winds were exactly right. As we rose over Rath forest, we must have made a shining spectacle: for Kernin had had the raft painted silver, and stuck with light-berries at every peak and post.

'We will not do this thing in a corner,' he said, and laughed. He had even tucked light-berries into the harness all over his horse.

Yes, he was mounted—on his stallion Sunhorn, and foal of Goldhorn, who was now too old for this journey. Sunhorn was carefully tethered to the bulwarks of the raft, as were our other mounts; in fact with all those traces, we had as much rigging as a ship of the sea. Barundran stood firm beside Sunhorn, and spoke soothingly into the horse's ear: he had a good way with nervous animals.

The rest of us were mounted not on horses, but on sheep.

Nakhtians may despise sheep as travelling mounts, but the fact is that the Aelvian breed is as big as a pony, and much more placid. Sheep also will give milk and wool—and, when necessary, mutton. We had half a dozen aboard as mounts and pack animals and general reserves, in case we could not get supplies of food at some stage in our journey. But that was not likely: we were all skilled hunters except possibly old Barundran, and he assured us he could learn. We were well enough armed too, with Aelvian long-bows and Centaurish short-bows, and round target-shields and leathern armour—and precious steel swords of Kintobara. Kernin's sword was the longest, a beautiful weapon with a gilded basket-hilt: he had named it Trier, in allusion to the Sword of Sinis, with which she judges souls, and either pierces and scatters the guilty ghosts, or dubs the good her servants and protects them on their journey to the Sun.

We were well wrapped against the cold, Barundran in his blanket, the rest of us in thick wool cloaks—all save Taras-Tarsh, who was relying largely on his native fur and a tunic which left his legs and powerful clawed feet bare. Now that he was possibly going into violent action, he was reverting to his preferred weapons, his claws and his bronze dagger. And yet he looked swagger enough in the sword he wore for show, and his great gold two-horned helm.

All in all, we were carrying a lot of weight; but that raft was truly enormous. We had smuggled its basis out of the cache in the Disputed Nomes, and then added more buoyancy, the strongest-shelled giant gas-plants we could find in Var and Ruren Forests.

'If we were to fall overboard, we and our animals,' said Kernin, 'I think this Flier of ours would jump right up to the Sun.'

'By the Goddess, my Prince,' I said, 'if you are seeking a clear view of the world from a height, why didn't you merely try for a high raft ascent? That would cut out a lot of dirty way.'

'Hnnnm! That would not serve,' said Barundran, adjusting his eye-glasses on his nose and fixing me with that reproachful look he reserved for stupidity. 'The highest mountain yet ascended is Blue-Top in Old Menkinvia, 7000 feet, and from there the world looks not very different. As for rafts. . . . By my calculations, our gas-plants must burst at 8000, or 10,000 feet at the most; and anyone still on board at that time would be running out of air to breathe.'

'That's a pleasant thought,' I said, remembering. Barundran had calculated the height of Khar Durnaran with his Angulable: he made it *30,000* feet above the level of the Great Sea.

Kernin looked at me, guessing my mind. 'Climbing a mountain is not the same as going up in a raft; and that is why we must climb that mountain. One gets used to the thinner air, gradually. . . .'

'Let us leave that evil till we come to it,' I said. 'Things look bad enough already.'

Indeed, to begin with this seemed a fearful flight. The raft was rising—so we guessed: it was black night, and yet we could see no stars. There was a layer of *cloud* overhead—a thing ominous, almost unheard of; and below and ahead of us the black Rath Forest cast up no gleam of water. The poor sheep bleated, Sunhorn whinnied. We were driving through blackness into blackness, and at any moment I feared we would crash horribly into a welter of trees or the bare bleak side of Rathwall.

'Why don't we get off these accursed animals?' yelled Tarsh. 'The Rathvians can't possibly see us, whether we're riding or no!'

'But the gods can see us,' said Kernin, 'and Sinis, and our own consciences. I have sworn to *ride* through the air over Rathwall, with all my company, and ride we will. Hold on, Taras! It cannot be long now.'

'Call me Tarsh!' Then the satyr's mood seemed to lighten somewhat, and he laughed savagely. 'I will hope we are out of Aelvia for good; and so I am Tarsh henceforth for ever. Something has whispered to me that in Rathvia satyrs may have as much honour as humans. . . .' Then a gust caught the raft, and he swayed perilously on his ewe's back. 'Gods! Not long, you

say? Not long before we crash and break our necks. How I wish
sheep had horns to hold on to!'

'In the Seventy-Third Universe they do,' said Wilifern blithely.
'Why, this is nothing. Shall I prophesy? Nay, since we are out of
Aelvia, I hope I may do so. I have *seen*, as you were speaking.
One night we will ride indeed, some of us, on mounts that fly,
and then, Tarsh, you may talk of *holding on*. . . . Tarsh, O
Tarsh-for-ever, will you give us a tune on your reed-pipe to
while away the time? You're not so pretty as a girl-piper, yet
I've heard you play merrily enough in your savage way. Or you,
Orselen, do you give us a classical lay on your lyre . . .'

'No,' I said, 'this is no suitable ride for the peaceful lyre.
Rather does it make me think of the trumpet-call of Sakanek's
Death-Ride, when he defied the ghosts of the princes of Suoran,
and rode at their head over the cliff of sea-girt Suoran into the
Great Sea, and so they all went up together from Pel's flood, still
wrangling into the world of the Sun.'

I should not have mentioned the Death-Ride; for Kernin took
me up at once. 'Play that call,' he said with a laugh, 'that the
Rathvians may *hear* us at least, even if they cannot see.'

So reluctantly I began to blow that terrible call, which is
sometimes played as signal for the charge in a most desperate
battle. And before I was halfway through, we rose smoothly out
of the cloud, and all the stars flashed out, and the red ghost of
the Sun, and the bright oval orange Ring high behind us, and
orange Flickerfly low before us, and under Flickerfly the black
arrowhead of Khar Durnaran in the World-End glow . . . and
under *that*, very near, the black jagged peaks of Rathwall.

'By all gods,' said Kernin softly, as my last note died, 'if our
bulwarks do not burst in the next minute, we are going *over*.'

Our bulwarks did not burst; and in twenty eyeblinks more, we
were above the highest peak, and sailing smoothly into Rathvia.

''Blow that Call again,' said Kernin. 'Let them know that we
are coming.'

I blew and blew, and I shivered and shivered, for the air at
this height and time was becoming very cold. We were still
rising. . . . Below us we saw Rathvia spread out almost forever,
with very few dots of light, and those rather reddish. That is a
lonely, wild tableland, not well watered, for the rocks there are
mostly holestone, which draws down water underground. Only
the River Gan, of ominous name, made one thin blue snaky line,
the line roughly of the way we must go, until it disappeared
more than a hundred miles away. By crossing Rathwall we had

crossed an important line of the world, for the Gan flows not toward the Great Sea but away from it, toward World's End.

By midnight we were some six thousand feet high, and the sheep and Sunhorn were whimpering in distress. Breathing in that cold thin air was a sharp pain. . . . And then suddenly Barundran said: 'The day-wind is done. Friends, we are drifting *back.*'

Kernin leaned forward, and with the point of his sword Trier he pricked a tiny hole in the topmost tube of that bulwark. Immediately the gas came hissing out of it, and we started dipping. That was a sickening fall: not fast but awkward. like a giant leaf fluttering down from some immense tree. We had no safeties, no small tubes for trim, and when that pricked log was empty, we were front-heavy. It was a good thing that all our animals and gear were well tethered.

'Go on playing,' yelled Kernin. I managed to do so somehow, and as I did so I thought that Sakanek's Death-Ride was going to prove extremely appropriate.

And yet in the end we did not crash. Sunkindle found us drifting backward a few feet above the ground, nose-heavy, the high buoyant end of the raft catching the night-wind like the sail of a ship. And as the ground was rising toward Rathwall in the direction we were going, when the Sun pushed us firmly down we hit very neatly, belly flat to the rise of the earth. The landing might have had splendid dignity were it not for the fact that we, on our half-dead mounts, were all *facing the wrong way.* . . . It was a bit like that embarrassing moment in the saga of King Pelenek XI, when at the King's enthronement the Herald's horse had insisted on entering the royal hall tail first, and so *backed up* to the speechless King.

I'm afraid that was a portent of what was to happen to us in Rathvia.

We had come down on a sparsely-grassed upland not far from the thin stream of the Gan. Ahead (that is, tailwards) of us was a small town of houses built somewhat in the Aelvian manner, but all of dark red holestone, and with their blank sides arranged facing outward in a circle like a fleet of beleagured battleships. There was no city wall, but the outer houses themselves made a wall, with few and narrow entrances between. To the right of the town, some three miles distant, rose a dark circular clump of woods. As a backing to all this, dark Rathwall raised its rear side some two thousand feet above the plateau.

But we had little time to examine the far view. Much nearer than the town there came racing toward us a troop of cavalry.

They had somewhat sorry horses, no bigger than Aelvian ponies or our sheep. As they encircled our raft, Sunhorn whinnied; for he was a stallion, and all the Rathvian cavalry horses were mares.

Then the Rathvians were alighting, reaching for our bulwarks, boarding us. They were black-coated folk, perhaps the same we had seen at that Gate, and I thought I recognised the rounded mass of the leader's black hair. But now they wore no masks.

'That was indeed the most amusing feat, O Prince,' said the leader, standing on the floor of the raft and reaching up to embrace Kernin and pull him off Sunhorn's back. 'Ye have passed your test bravely, O most gallant young pricker.'

The Rathvians were all smooth-faced, with slightly snub noses, slant eyes, and skins the colour of honey. Their voices too were like smooth warm honey. We saw their legs now, which were shapely, long-footed, clad in black sandal-buskins. None wore helmets, and none showed any head-peaks.

One of them was helping me off my sheep; and still I did not understand.

But Tarsh did. 'Ahaargh!' he growled, 'I *knew* it!' And he leapt from his mount into the arms of the nearest Rathvian warrior. His flame-gold eyes were alight with excitement, his satyr's mouth was twisted into a leer. 'Ahaaargh, my love!'

'Steady, wood-pricker!' said this Rathvian sharply. 'What, is this Mid-Ring or Ring-ripe with you? Ye shall abide *our* pleasure, slave, not we yours!'

And then I saw, in utter amazement, that every one of the Rathvian soldiers was a woman.

They behaved to us very strangely: in all my twenty-odd years as a virile male, I had known nothing like it. They were neither lewd nor modest, timid nor virago-ish. They were *at ease*, in a way that women in more civilised countries never are with men. They were supremely confident that our masculinity was not the least danger to them: neither our muscle, nor our metal weapons, nor. . . . Well, they seemed never to have heard of the idea of rape.

Not, of course, that any of us, except possibly Tarsh, had any intention of committing rape. We were so entirely in the power of those ladies (if that was the right word for them) that we dared not offer them anything but the utmost politeness. Somehow I felt afraid even to question them—though goddess knows I was bursting with questions. Above all—passion of Prah!—what had happened to their menfolk?

Their leader told us her name: Ulutha, Countess of Namurai, the little Shire-town yonder. She took possession of our raft, and listened indulgently (yes, that *is* the right word) to Kernin's explanations as to how it worked, and how it must be firmly pegged into the ground lest Sunquenching take it soaring up to destruction ten thousand feet high.

'Yes, yes, that understand we,' she said. 'The great Dilly-tree groweth not in Rathvia, but we know of your little games in the lower country. 'Twas not without forethought that I set thee that pass-task, my sweet princeling. To say sooth, ye caught my fancy that time I saw ye at the Black Gate; and I knew you to be ingenious, and trusted well to see you here. Likely lads must be encouraged, if they are to rise to the grace of great ladies.'

'What—how—how do you know so much of the affairs of Aelvia?' said Kernin.

'We have our spies,' said Ulutha calmly. 'D'ye not think now, that one of us might not easily pass disguised through your Aelvian woods, and mayhap mingle among your folk, sometimes as a human woman, sometimes as a forest nymph? 'Twould be but simple policy for us to sit apart up here in our high land, and never know what ye lowlanders might be devising against us.'

Kernin opened his mouth—and then shut it again, and looked grim. I knew he was a little grieved to hear that his Princedom could be so penetrated by mysterious female spies. I looked down at the shapely soldier who was conducting me (for all of us, except Barundran, were being led by the hand). Her buskins came half way up her calves, and between those and the hem of her black tunic her legs showed smooth and hairless and pale amber in colour. Pass as a nymph? Well, she might, just; but she would have to stain her legs darker and stick false hair on them. Her face was strangely beautiful: some human peasant girls of the Aelvian forest-fringes looked a little like that, and then men would laugh and wink and say that their mothers must have companied with satyrs. Our true nymph-maids of the Royal Palace in Eladon had similar but slanter eyes, and their noses were still more snub and broad, their cheeks darker. Yes: I had to admit that this girl, with a little painting, *could* pass as a satyress. But then she would have to strip naked, or nearly naked. The imagination of the thing, I am afraid, began to stir in me.

The girl looked up into my face, and grinned. 'Y'are not so young as your Prince, are you? Six hundred Rings, I guess, if y'are a day; but tolerably well preserved. Well, not being a *U*-lady, I must make do with my winnings; and if you still can, you may amuse me somewhat about Mid-Ring. Don't forget who you belong to, now: Khafuna, knight of Namurai.'

So the black-helmed girl at my side was a knight! Other 'knights' were pegging and weighting down our raft, or herding out our sheep, taking charge of our baggage and weapons and Kernin's great horse. They worked with the utmost efficiency and with no little strength. I thought of the girl pipers of Aelvia, who go boldly into battle; but it is not customary for our girl pipers to handle weapons. Why not, if these girls so clearly could? Well, why should they, when men are available, and are mostly stronger muscled, and also may give their lives for their country with less harm to eggs and hatchlings . . . ?

When men are available.

But as those knight-ladies shepherded our beasts and Barundran, and led the rest of us by the hand to the town of Namurai, I did not see a single man about the countryside. There were fields here of rough-looking wheat, and hedges of rubias canes, and patches of vegetables, and a place by the stream of the Gan where some of the natives came to draw water or to wash clothes; but the fields were being tended and the canes cut for firewood by tough looking women, black-haired and snub-nosed women who wore exactly the sort of belted brown wool tunics that are worn by peasant *men* in Aelvia. Their hair was cut rather short like a compact spherical cap, their shoulders were somewhat burly . . . but they were certainly women. There wasn't a head-peak among them, and several of them, warmed to their work, had opened the necks of their tunics, and I could see the swell of their breasts. One washerwoman, indeed, had stripped to the waist, the better to thump her linen upon a flat holestone rock.

She was perhaps a warming sight, and yet I shivered. There was a coldness, a thinness in the air of that plateau in spite of the bright sun of Second Hour.

Wilifern had been walking quite cheerfully arm-in-arm with his 'knight', and now he turned to me. 'You know where we are, Bard?'

'No,' I said nervously.

'What's become of your lore, then? What about the Third Adventure of Prah?'

'Oh,' I said, staring at the washerwoman. 'Great gods! But I thought that was only a fable.'

'Well, you see it is not. We have reached the Land of Women.' He laughed. 'Let us hope we thrive here as Prah did.'

At the next watering-place, just before the city, I was at first relieved to see a *boy*. He was under ten years of age, with fair-brown hair and blue eyes—whereas every one of our 'knights' was black- or brown-eyed. The lad was naked save for a flimsy wisp of linen cloth about his middle. He was placidly drawing water from the stream; then, having filled his round-bellied jar, he balanced it on his mop of fair curls between his little head-peaks, and began walking with his burden evenly, gracefully toward the town. Only when he saw us did he stop and stare, one hand upon his jar to steady it on his head.

And we all stared back at him. He was barefoot, but round his left ankle he wore a little silver chain, such as palace slave-girls wear in Nakhtos. But this was a *boy*. Kernin looked at that chain, and shuddered.

I asked my knight. 'Oh, him?' she said. 'A little prize carried off by the huntress U-sakhara, fifty Rings ago. Varshu was a little Rindian; he is quite a favourite with us all. Another forty Rings and he should be quite beautiful. . . .'

Then suddenly I saw what this meant. The Night-Hags, the snatchers of boys. . . . As Kernin had once said, *behind all legends there was some truth*. I looked at Khafuna with horror. Was she—would she proceed next night to suck my blood?

She saw my expression, and laughed. 'Nay, Varshu is quite happy. 'A was only a peasant brat anyway, half-starved till he met a certain kind *nymph* on the edge of a wood. We do not work our foreign boys hard—only just enough to keep them healthy till their time comes. Poor things, 'tis sad when they are over-grown, and we must dismiss them to the places of the *old men*. But before then, they have fine sport enough.'

This sounded slightly reassuring; but there was one question I had to ask at once. 'And we—my Prince, and the rest of our fellowship: are we now your slaves, entrapped by deceit—?'

'Oh no,' said Khafuna, indignant. 'We are knights, and therefore women of *honour*. Nay, you will be our honoured guests—for such time as the Countess and the Queen shall determine. No need to hurry on your way. . . .'

'I thought you had a King. At the Gate, Ulutha said—'

'She said *monarch*. I heard her, boy. 'Twas your own mis-mind, to make every monarch a *king*.'

Wilifern interposed. 'You see, Herald, these folk do have a kind of magic, as they claimed.' He chuckled. 'But I think it is a kind we will enjoy.'

'Why do you wear masks at the Black Gate?' I asked.

Khafuna smiled strangely. 'Answer that yourself, lad.'

'So that . . . no man shall know the situation of things in Rathvia.' My mouth was dry with fear.

'Y'are i'the right about that,' she said.

I said nothing more, as we entered the city. The implication was dreadfully clear. If the Rathvian secret must not be known in Aelvia, yet we were now being told it. . . .

Some halls have wide entrances but narrow exits, goes the proverb. As for the ways in and out of Namurai, they were all very narrow lanes under archways; and at every arch stood a female soldier in black armour, with a long black spear.

Namurai bore a strange half-resemblance to a shiretown of Aelvia—which was not really surprising, seeing that Rathvia was first land-taken by settlers from Aelvia—tradition says by Rathlyn, second son of an Earl of Ranelon, in the Palurian year 153. But one main difference was that these streets were arranged on a circle-and-radius plan, like the pattern of a spinner's web.

The other main difference was that there were no men in sight.

No satyrs either; no grown males at all. Just occasionally we saw a young boy's head peeping from a window of one of the better houses. Everything in that country which is done in the Shorelands by men was here being done by women. There were women shopkeepers, women butchers, even women porters . . . hefty wenches, if ever I'd seen any! And so were the women common soldiers, the infantry who guarded the archway into the central Market Circle of the city. These burghers were women of all ages and most degrees of well-favouredness, some stirringly pretty, some plain; not many really ugly. In skin colour they varied from a sweet ivory to a satyr-like darkness. It took me hours to get used to the strangeness of the situation: it was almost like being on another Earth—one of those beyond our Sun, or in that Seventy-Third Universe which Wilifern had invented. But thereafter, I began to be accustomed, and to forget. At times the town would seem perfectly normal; until I realised what I was *not* seeing, what was missing. . . .

The Market Circle was the centre of the spinner's web of streets, with the Countess's curved Palace-front on one side reaching forward its wings like the pincers of the spinner herself. In the middle of the market-place, at the very focus of the city, there rose a great stone statue of a woman in a green-and-brown mottled tunic, carrying a weighted wire or cord in one hand, and reaching down with the other, and giving a sinister smile to a little naked golden boy carved upon the statue's base.

'Ulugana and Hinu,' said Khafuna complacently. She explained that Ulugana the Huntress was the Rathvians' only goddess, and little Hinu her prey (whom I took to be none other than our lord Hinos, the Sun)—he was their only god.

Wilifern laughed. 'The Huntress is surely Aelvia's Green Lady in a new guise, and little Hinu is the Golden Hero in somewhat reduced circumstances. I am not altogether surprised. The Green Lady is a two-faced wench, often in league with the Dark One . . . but let that pass. Handy-dandy! We shall have a fine time of it here. I only wish I were younger and prettier.'

As we marched toward the Palace, Barundran edged closer to me. Our 'knights' had been behaving differently to him: not more respectfully—I'm afraid they regarded him as an amusing curiosity—but at least not pressing near him, so he had more freedom.

'It is amusing, is it not,' said the centaur sagely, 'how little difference it makes, after all.'

'What?' I said, staring.

'With male Two-Legs or with female Two-Legs, the shape of society is much the same. Orders and degrees remain. I have not yet seen a Republic this side of the Great Sea. In Aelvia you had Earls, burghers, yeomen; here you have Countesses, burgheresses, yeowomen. No great change.'

'Yes, by Prah, but there *is* a great change!' I exploded. I turned to Khafuna. 'Well, what did you do to your men? I suppose you murdered them.'

Khafuna looked shocked. 'Oh no! What bugs and goblins d'ye think we are? We are not cruel by nature, as so many males are unless they are handled aright. Our men—they died. Not by our hands, though they may well have deserved that. Rathlyn and Land-Taker was most brutal in his conquest of the poor Woodsfolk, and that was folly, for the invaders were not many, and the Woodspeople fought back. In that war, most of our men died, and therefore we women of Rathvia were constrained to take upon us the government of the survivors. We have managed very well since, as you can see.'

'I see something else,' I said; and then I hesitated.

'Nay, gentle Boy,' she said, 'be not afraid of your mistress. She will not bite thee. Speak up, stripling.' This from Khafuna, who was certainly ten years my junior! But then, young men will sometimes address mature women as 'girl', by way of endearment—or condescension.

'Well,' I said, 'but do not your eggs hatch out as in every other country, about half boys and half girls? *What do you do with your boys?*'

Khafuna gave me a crooked grin. 'We do with them—the

healthy, lusty ones—just what you do with your girls. But our eggs do *not* hatch out half-and-half. We see to that! It was Rathlyn's so-called ''wife'' who first said it at the assembly after the Land-Taking War: ''Now that we are delivered from that servitude, we shall not stoop our necks to that yoke again.'' I will not say what was done in the early Rings; but long time now we have known to tell egg from egg while they are still small and green. We therefore keep only the most promising of the male eggs, to hatch out our lovely little prickers. . . .'

I groaned for shame at such unnatural wickedness; but Barundran said, his old eyes agleam with interest: 'Why, 'tis much like the policy of one of the hordes of Thulor; but since we centaurs bring forth young alive, the means are crueller. Lady, if you cull your males in this fashion, why, in a few generations ye will so have improved your breed that you will be a sort of Heroines, goddesses, and I think need fear no masculine invaders from your *un*selected neighbours. And stealing foreign boys of the healthier sort, that will work well, too: for thereby ye achieve hybrid vigour.'

Khafuna nodded. 'Our huntress spies told us that Centaurs were called Wise; and now I see that to be a true name. Ye shall be a most welcome guest in Rathvia, old Barundran.'

I wondered, though. Perhaps there would be a still more welcome one. . . . As we entered the Palace, I saw Tarsh and his lady-knight walking most closely embraced. He seemed to have learnt the right manners now to please her; and pleasing her he certainly was. The cunning villain! He had guessed the great Rathvian secret—doubtless long ago, at the Black Gate; yet he had not told us others. What quest of his own was he pursuing? And now, he was in great favour. . . .

Astonishing, though, that a human woman could behave so to a *satyr*.

11

Countess Ulutha's palace seemed a queer parody of a lordly house of the Shorelands; and rather of Palur-Nakhtos than of Aelvia. Because slavery was gradually eliminated in Aelvia about the year 300, whereas it persisted in the other Shorelands. It had also persisted in Rathvia, with this little difference: there were no slave women, only slave boys.

The slave boys of the Countess were not very numerous—no more, I think, than the slave girls in the palaces of King Prahelek;

and they were treated about the same, as ornaments and luxuries
for their owner and their owner's friends. I did not see a single
one much older than about twenty years, and they were all
extremely handsome—and rather flimsily dressed, in short clinging loin-cloths by day and long clinging robes by night. They
were about as servile, timid, and provokingly coy as the corresponding slave wenches of King Prahelek: so much is human
'nature' actually a matter of training!

The Rathvian system is this: when a mother discovers that one
of her eggs is a male, she hands it over to the town inspectors. If
these decide it is unpromising, it is exposed on a hill for the
harpy-eagles; otherwise, it is hatched in a large single incubato:
common to the whole town. On hatching, these boys are reared
by females of the lowest class; then, after 40 Rings (the Rathvians
do not count years), they are taken to a different town, and sold
as slaves to gentlewomen. When they are somewhat more than
400 Rings old (twenty years) they are released from slavery—
and banished into certain enclosed forests, or over the inland
frontiers. One and all, the males view this future of freedom with
dread, and when their time comes, they often plead with their
mistresses not to cut the little silver chains from their ankles. But
always in vain. Rathvian ladies like their slave concubines to be
young.

Racially, I thought, the slave youths differed a great deal.
Some were nearly as dark as young satyrs, and the oldest of
them were definitely hirsute, and boasted prominent head-peaks.
I looked at their bare toes—no, they were not clawed; but their
feet were rather long, and the two outer toes on each foot rather
small, which is a satyrish characteristic. I regarded those dark
boys uneasily: yes, they definitely reminded me of Tarsh . .
but how could this be? And there were other lads who looked
perfectly human, either honey-coloured, snub-nosed—in short
Rathvian—or else clearly foreign imports lured by the Huntresses.
With such variety of young lovers, I thought Countess Uluth
must surely have her passions sated; she would not need to
seduce, for instance, her guest Prince Kernin.

But in that I was proved wrong. What I had not realised was
this: Rathvian women regularly grow bored with slaves, and then
look for something *different*.

They gave us two rooms in the Palace, one for Barundran alone
and the other one next door for the rest of us. The view from our
small round window gave only onto the Palace courtyard, which
was enclosed on all sides by outbuildings; in the middle of the

courtyard was a large cage filled with flymonkeys, small harpies, squirrel-rats, and other disconsolate little beasts whom the Rathvian ladies kept to gaze and laugh at; we later found this custom elsewhere in the country. The caged animals quarrelled a lot, and kept up a racket from Kindle to Quenching.

Apart from the noise outside, we were not too uncomfortable, though our room was smallish and our beds were mere coarse straw pallets such as one finds in soldiers' barracks in the Shorelands. The fact was, the Rathvians were quite unused to honouring males as guests. Much the worst feature of our situation was, that our weapons had all been taken from us. Kernin especially had hated to hand over his good sword Trier. But no help. It was not the custom to wear weapons in the Countess's house. More: it was definitely not the custom for males to wear weapons in Rathvia, in any circumstances.

Once we were alone in our room, I said: 'My lord, if you will take my counsel, we will look out for the best moment, and then run for it one night to our great Flier, and try to drift back over Rathwall. This is an ominous beginning to our Quest. If we are not slaves here, we are something very like it, honoured captives, no more—whom they do *not* purpose to let return. We must get out of this accursed Dark Land of Women.'

Kernin smiled grimly. 'Yes, we must get out of it—but not *that* way. Courage, Orselen! What, shall we turn back at the first difficulty? This is merely our first adventure, and one to be faced and overcome on our way to the Last Mountain.'

Wilifern grinned. 'It is also one to be enjoyed. The Land of Women! Why, I have often told lies about it in my tales in the market-place. And now we find the reality. If we got on at this rate, Firafax damn me if we do not end up one day in my very Seventy-Third Universe.'

'All right,' I said; and looked bitterly at Tarsh. 'And what do *you* have to say—traitor?'

'Hahai, good words, good words, Herald,' said Wilifern, and jerked his thumb at the courtyard. 'Are we to start flyting now—like those?'

'I am no traitor,' Tarsh growled. He was looking not at me but at Kernin. 'I follow you, Prince, in hope you will lead me to some honour. Maybe I will find some honour right here. . . . I will see. Maybe yes, maybe no. If not, I go on with you. And I will always tell you what I guess, if it is to your hurt.' He leered. 'But my guess at Black Gate—that was not to your hurt! No, no. By my lifehorn, I go not from here till I make one of those wenches scream for joy. . . .'

*   *   *

The Countess's Great Hall made a beautiful show at that night's dinner feast. By the walls stood slaveboys of great beauty, holding up long-stemmed candelabras of light-berries. There are two species of light-berry in Rathvia, one the usual bluish-white, the other pink: it was the pink kind which the slaveboys held, and this spread a marvellous rosy glow. Also, the walls were of red holestone; and a fire of rubias logs burnt in the hearth. Sunwood does not grow in Rathvia, so rubias is used even for street-torches; with that and the holestone, this makes all their cities rather dark and reddish at night. The effect can be oppressive; but that first night, in the Countess's hall, it was not: not yet. The ladies at the high table wore wreaths of light-berries in their hair, usually one ring of pink berries, but the Countess and a few others, being of high noble rank, wore a double ring, one pink and one blue, most cunningly intertwined like little spinners' webs among their sleek black locks; and the mingled gleams shed such a lustre of beauty on the strange features of the younger women that it was almost painful to contemplate them.

However, we had to contemplate them from afar. 'Poor boys,' said the Countess, 'ye must be quite a-weary and spent with your last night's flight; you must sleep early and sound'; and she led us not to her High Table, but to one at the side of the hall—a place such as might be given in Aelvia to mere yeomen. Kernin recognised the implication, and flushed with anger. But I whispered: 'Patience, my Prince. We must bide our time.'

Wilifern grinned. 'Would you seat a concubine at your own table? And every nation has its prejudices. At Agnai, minstrels and all people with black hair are foddered in the stables; and Rindians will not dine with women in the same room. These ladies are doing us all the honour they can.'

Barundran, though, *was* given a place at the High Table: as an oddity, he evidently did not count as a man. And clearly they knew from their spies how centaurs were entertained in the Shorelands, for they had rigged up the usual long backless stool on which our old philosopher was accustomed to rest his lower body in lieu of a chair; and they fed him only vegetable foods. The lady Usakhara, the Countess's aunt and a notable Huntress, had him on her right hand, and I saw them chatting amiably. The younger ladies, I am afraid, did not behave so well to him; I saw them pointing at his various features and giggling among themselves.

Kernin went on smouldering all through that meal. We were given a rather rough red wine, whereas the ladies had not only red wine but also a different purple drink served in beautiful little glass goblets. I noticed that Barundran did not get any of that either.

At the end of the feast we were going to be dismissed to our chambers, when suddenly a dark-faced young lady came striding over from the High Table. She was the one who had seized Tarsh on the deck of our Flier; and now she took him again firmly by the hand.

'Come, Goldhelm,' she said, her dark eyes all aglow. 'If y'are not too utterly spent with your travails, I would speak with ye. . . .'

Tarsh had a red gleam in his eye. 'Ahaaargh!' he growled; and those two were out of that room in a couple of eyeblinks; and then the light-berry boys drew round the rest of us to escort us, including Barundran, to our chambers.

'I do not understand one point,' I said to Barundran as we stumbled yawning along our corridor. 'Why is it that Tarsh, a satyr, responds so much to these ladies—he didn't like human women much in Aelvia. And they to him: he's the only one they couldn't resist this night. . . .'

'Hnnnm! So you do not understand it? Neither perhaps do I—*entirely*.' He gave me a searching look, and then smiled briefly. 'But I am learning things from the lady U-sakhara. And I think we will all be enlightened—*quite soon*.' After that he would say nothing more, and we went to bed, and slept at once and heavily.

Tarsh half-woke us by stumbling into our common bedchamber about Fourth Toe Hour. He slept from then right through Sunkindle to Fourth Finger Hour; and when he finally woke and we could question him, he simply rolled his red-brown eyes and leered.

'Yes, all right,' I said impatiently, 'but are you sure the wench also enjoyed it?'

It was a long time before he stopped laughing.

The second night's feast went, to begin with, rather like the other. It was the third night of the month, and the Ring had reached full brightness, and the stars outside the hall window were softly blue; blue as the light-berries in the Countess's hair. The ladies at the High Table were taking their purple wine from larger goblets tonight; and they seemed to be in higher spirits. Countess Ulutha proposed a toast to the One-and-only Goddess in her aspect of the Ring, and all had to stand and drink that—we in our red wine, the ladies in their purple.

'All pleasure to the Ring,' chorussed the ladies, 'and long may Hinu flourish!'

Then the ladies came over to our table. Ulutha seized Kernin by the hand, Usakhara took Wilifern, and the 'knight' Khafuna took me. . . .

The scene in Khafuna's bedchamber went like this.

The room was softly lit by a few pink light-berries in their wall-brackets; and my mistress wore a single wreath of the same rosy berries in her black hair. She made me strip down to my loin-cloth; then she threw off her own black-and-silver evening tunic, and sat on the edge of the bed, watching me. She was now stark naked—all but for her high buskins, which still covered her feet and half of her lower legs.

'Kneel,' she said, pointing to the floor at her feet. 'It is customary that the boy unlace his lady's shoes.'

This I now did, trembling slightly—but not with fear, I assure you. Khafuna naked in that dim rosy light, with the little rosy stars in her sleek black hair, was a sight to move a statue of stone. My fingers were clumsy as they unlaced those dainty high boots; but at last I drew them off.

And then I blinked. Her bare feet . . . ! They were long and shapely and symmetrical, the middle toes much longer than the second and fourth, and. . . . But her first and fifth toes on each foot hardly existed, they were nailless little pads; and all up her insteps and half her lower legs—wherever the buskins had hidden, in fact—there were little curly black hairs. More like fur than hair. . . .

'What are you staring at, fool?' Then she understood, and laughed. 'Some girls will shave all the way, but I see no reason why I should. *I* am not ashamed of that side of our ancestry. As for boys, I like both sorts: our own furry, manly little natives, and foreign hairless wonders like you. At least, I *think* I like you. Now, let's put you to the test. . . .'

She stood up then, and pressed herself against me, and. . . . But this is not *that* kind of story. In spite of my inveterate prejudice against satyresses, or anomalous demi-satyresses, Khafuna managed to seduce me—managed very well. She was very aggressive, and I could not help my reactions. I did not even mind it when she rubbed her shaven upper legs against me, and I could feel the prickle of all that stubble.

She let me go at last about midnight. We were all let go, except Tarsh, who slept, if he slept, all night till Sunkindle with his mistress. In the cold hours before dawn, we met in our common chamber to discuss. . . Even Barundran rose from his broad centaur-bed next door to attend our conference.

'You understand now, I take it,' said Barundran, 'the whole truth about Satyrs and Humans.'

Kernin looked rueful. 'I was stupid, old master. I should have seen long ago what you were trying to tell me so diplomatically even in Aelvia. We two kinds are *interfertile*.'

'Hnnnm! I would put it differently. The species Bicornate Biped is very variable—there are several races. The Menkinvian stock, which invaded the Shorelands six or seven hundred years ago, that one has the shortest horns of any known variety, and shorter feet, and five well-developed toes on each foot. The aboriginal Shoreland race—well, Tarsh is a fairly pure specimen. But I would not like to be more precise than that: even Tarsh hath doubtless some seed in him from the first Land-Takers, who were certes also great takers of the local nymphs—not having brought enough of their own females with them from Menkinvia. And in Rathvia, a similar thing happened—but contrariwise, the Rathvian invader-ladies, when they lost so many of their menfolk in that war, they took to coupling with their native slaves, their captive satyrs.' He chuckled. 'I am sorry, my Prince, if you are in some danger of being detained in this country; but if we can continue, and penetrate really far inland, who knows what race we may find? Perhaps one day we may meet a variety, or sub-species, who are more Satyrish than any heretofore known—with longer feet, with only three toes, and furry all over like flymonkeys. . . .'

'Then the Agnaians may be right after all,' muttered Kernin. '*We* may have some satyr blood, we of Nakhtos, we of—Aelvia. . . .'

Wilifern laughed. 'No question: what of it? I have heard tales enough in my wanderings, of nymph-children who were adopted by "human" families, of peasant girls who had satyr lovers. Half of Aelvia knows these facts—only, they are not mentioned in polite society. My own mother, I think, was a half-nymph . . . if these fractions mean anything. They don't mean much: what Barundran has just said is this: we don't *have* some satyr blood, we *are satyrs*.'

'Come now!' I protested, 'that's going too far!'

The minstrel shrugged. 'It's just a matter of words. But the race-strains certainly differ. I wish I were *more* Satyrish; I could do with Tarsh's good keen ears. You know, if that fellow would cultivate his gifts, he might make a perfect musician—a better Bard than you, maybe, Orselen.'

I thought Wilifern was talking nonsense; and changed the subject. 'My lord—how is it with you—I mean, between you and the Lady Ulutha?'

Kernin looked embarrassed. 'Well enough, I suppose. I have been unfaithful to my dear Queen—but I will not be hypocrite enough to pretend I did not enjoy it. The Countess is beautiful. . . . But I am ever mindful of our great Quest. If we please these ladies, will they let us go on our way, or will they only the more detain us?'

'Hnnnm,' Barundran mused. 'This I am certain of: alas, we cannot escape from Rathvia by any main force. U-sakhara has told me that our raft is strongly guarded at all times, and so is every frontier and city gateway. This folk was formed at a time when every settlement had to be a fortress, and now the whole country is still a fortress. May Persuasion be with you, my Prince. . . .'

Wilifern had been staring out of the small window. Suddenly he turned to us. 'I have just *seen*. I saw us riding out of Rathvia, led by a woman. . . .'

'Persuasion, then,' said Barundran. ' 'Tis just as I said. . . .'

Every night the Rathvian ladies seemed to grow more passionate. By Mid-Ring I could no longer cope with Khafuna's demands, and she dismissed me from her bedchamber with some contempt. The next night Wilifern also had to plead inadequacy. Kernin and Tarsh—well, they were younger, but I began to be worried even for them. No question, Ulutha and that dark-faced girl kept casting them, from the High Table, wilder and wilder looks. . . .

The night before Ring-ripe I spoke to Barundran in his room. 'Really, I think these females must be nearly all satyr in their blood-line, if their passions rise so with the phase of the Ring.'

'Nay,' he said, 'that is a slander against your forest-dwelling natives. They do not have rut periods any more than your own women do—and if they did, 'tis not likely it would coincide with the Ring. For according to the traditions of the Middle Plain— which we have taught also to the Menkinvians—there was not always a Ring in the sky. A mere three thousand years ago it burst forth: before that time every night was Ringless, and folk counted neither Rings nor years (which are merely Rings of Rings). Now in three thousand years, species are not apt to change greatly. Certes, we have written records for two thousand years, and since then there is small variance. There are many cycles in Nature, but almost none is of twenty days, or follows the Ring. Your rejoicings at your festivals are a mere matter of custom. . . .'

'Kernin says he is always excited around Last Ring.'

Barundran smiled. 'Last Ring is the night of Sinis, Lady Truth. Mayhap, some suggestion. . . . But to return. No human or satyrish females have adapted their desires to the Ring-month. Not naturally, I mean.'

'Then what is the cause of this outburst of lust . . . ?'

'Their purple wine. They drink more of it, by custom, through Mid-Ring to their great festival of Ring-Ripe; then they stop, and recover themselves. The purple juice cometh of a little plant of this country, which is aphrodisiac to your species. By tomorrow, they will be well flown. . . .'

And they were: flown, almost literally. I expected an orgy, and so there was; but we did not see it. There was no dinner in the Great Hall, the whole palace was in an uproar . . . and then we realised that the place was emptying. The slave boys who gave us our meal grinned and led us to a window looking onto the Market Circle; and in the gold light of Sunquenching, we saw women pouring out of the palace and the other nearby buildings, women of all classes, the common folk on foot, the ladies mounted on their mares. And then the marketplace was emptying, as they went out down the narrow streets, leaving only the echoes and the great statue of the Goddess Ulugana.

'What—' I began; but Barundran stroked his beard and said: 'Come away to my room, and I will tell you.'

And he told us this: that the women were going to that dark wood we had seen at our first arrival, three miles from the city boundary. 'Every town and city of Rathvia hath one of these convenient forests, and each is enclosed with a wall, and a gate, and guards so that the Woodsfolk can never come out. But the women go *in* unto them at Ring-ripe, and there they hold a kind of chase. All night, till Sunkindle. Did you never wonder what the common women did, those who have no slave boys? Well, it is they mostly who pursue the male Woodsfolk, but the great ladies also join the amusement if they have a mind to. It is, I believe, the most free and equal festival they have.'

'Very free, no doubt,' said Kernin, looking grim. 'And I suppose they couple with—satyrs?'

'The Woodsfolk are very mixed by now. They are some of the original inhabitants, males and nymphs and hatchlings. But also the enfranchised male slaves, the better-behaved ones, who have passed twenty years. . . .'

'*Enfranchised*. Good gods!'

'Hnnnm, well. . . . The slaves who have less well pleased their ladies are enfranchised still more, and driven over the inland border into Gagnar. Methinks those will be quite savage, my Prince, and if we are travelling that way, we may have to cope with them.'

'Sinis be my judge,' said Kernin, 'I would like to cope with them this very morrow.'

But on the morrow we awoke in our narrow room on our straw pallets, listening to the cries of the caged animals in the court-yard . . . and the laughter of the ladies of Namurai, who were returning to the Palace, some scratched, some bruised, but all of them happy.

12

Five days later we were out of Ulutha's power, and out of Namurai. Not that that was any great improvement in our situation.

On the second day of No-Ring a great cavalcade appeared riding up the valley of the Gan from the inland direction. News of our great flight over Rathwall had reached the Queen of Rathvia herself; and here she was, riding up with a large force, to demand these new and interesting 'guests' from her vassal, the Countess of Namurai.

Queen U-perakhluna was fair-skinned, but otherwise typically Rathvian in all features. (Kernin confided to me, somewhat later, that she shaved her feet right down to her toes.)

She was also more than thirty years old, and not so pretty as the Countess.

The Queen took us over entirely, persons, weapons, animals—and air-raft. She gave orders to the carpenter-wenches of Namurai, and they fitted axles and great wheels to our Flier, and then sheep were harnessed to the front of the raft and, by day, driven like a wagon-team. Our weapons and other gear were piled like trophies on the raft-wagon. Barundran was most interested to see how the raft trundled fairly smoothly along the road. 'Why, given but a flat enough way, we might have done that ourselves, affixed wheels and driven the Flier to the foot of Mount Durnaran; and then. . . .' He sighed. 'But I fear that notion is now merely academical.'

That whole journey to Luvanash, the capital, was eighty miles, and we covered it leisurely in four days. The road was a dry earth track on the left bank of the River Gan. And every day seemed the same: all morning, and all evening after the storm, the raftcart lumbered at walking pace, and the ladies rode their mares at walking pace, and we—walked, on our feet. Our own animals had been taken from us, and our big sheep were now being driven elsewhere as a herd. The Rathvians greatly admired them, and talked of breeding from them. As for Kernin's great stallion Sunhorn, he was being led by a slave boy, not ridden: he was destined for the Royal stud farm near Luvanash.

And we were still being called 'guests.' But that jest was wearing a little thin.

Rathvia seemed a forlorn land after Aelvia. We stopped at small towns every night, towns with the appearance of red stone forts: Gurun, Nakadush, Hinash. But apart from the towns there were very few settlements. The native Woodsfolk were all penned into those reservations of theirs, the walled forests, and the women lived nearly all in those fort-towns, or in military camps near the hill frontiers. Midway between the towns we seemed to be passing through a desolation. There were no boats on the Gan, and no travellers but ourselves on the road. There were straggly unfenced woods in the distance, but near the road was nothing but yellow savannah and red dust, and we heard no bird sing, nor saw any save high-soaring harpy-vultures. The weather was absolutely regular: cold nights and early mornings, then dry heat in the middle of the day, then a savage storm during Eighth Finger Hour, then a clear evening. As we were gradually descending along the plateau, the midday heats grew gradually worse toward Luvanash. The storms seemed to do nothing for the country but stir up the dust and pour red mud into the narrow stream of the Gan, which swirled it along to goddess-knew what unknown sea.

We were a disconsolate group of foot-travellers among the merry mounted ladies. Even Tarsh seemed to have lost his enthusiasm for the delights of Rathvia: he was no fool, and he had discovered already that pleasuring ladies drew no status along with it. Wilifern seemed to be withdrawn into himself: perhaps he was 'seeing'. Barundran was possibly the calmest of us; well, so far in this country he had not been ill-treated. Kernin said little. On the second night, at Nakadush, he shared the Queen's bed—successfully, if that is the right term. Next morning he remarked: 'Now I know what it is like to be a slave-girl. Well, I should be thankful she doesn't put a silver chain on my ankle.'

Yet he was indomitable. On our last day, as we were approaching Luvanash, he lifted up his eyes past the gap between the city and its inevitable walled forest. 'There it is,' he said softly. 'At least, we are still going the right way.'

'It', of course, was Khar Durnaran, a little lower now in the World-End haze, a little bigger. Eighty miles closer; but still we could not see its base. And long before that, beyond Luvanash, there rose an arc of low dark grey hills. They were some eighty miles further on, about as far ahead as Rathwall was now behind—for Rathvia too was probably once an enormous crater, like Aelvia but wider, older, more barren.

I looked back then the way we had come; and cried out. 'The Sea! Where is the Sea?'

It was a bright clear forenoon, with great visibility—and yet I could see no green shimmer to Ring-ward, no sign of Pelas Magha. Beyond the dark line of Rathwall, as in every other direction, there was nothing but land, land, land, drab plains, dark forests, grey hills, land rising around us for over three hundred miles, or for ever, right up to the haze, an enormous bowl of rock rising to enclose us like the floor inside a tomb. Being a Shorelander, I had never seen that before in all my life.

'Well?' said Kernin, with a kind of grim triumph. 'What did you expect? It is a sign of our progress. We shall not see the Ocean again until we see it from the summit of Khar Durnaran.'

So he had not lost that hope. I turned to Barundran. 'Doesn't it fill *you* with terror to be so hemmed in—not to see that lovely bright green road back to your own dear homeland?'

The centaur smiled sadly. 'Terror? No: it is an interesting new appearance. . . . My dear Orselen, at my age a philosopher knows that his final release from all enclosures cannot be long delayed.'

Luvanash was a larger version of Namurai: the same spider-web of streets, the same circular central place, even the same statue. And the Queen's palace also had an animal-cage in its courtyard, and our two rooms overlooked that again. When we were not required to amuse the Queen and her ladies, we sometimes amused ourselves, rather grimly, by visiting this cage and watching the battles of the flymonkeys and the little harpies. On one visit, Wilifern said: 'I am sure Saeth must have passed this way. When my brother Unvar first joined that order, he used that very emblem to try and persuade me also.' He laughed. 'As if I needed persuading!'

I looked at him curiously. He had neglected his hair-dye recently, and the colour was working out, so that his longish hair looked fantastic, half red and half blue. It seemed to me he was a very half-and-half person, at that: a Liar who told truth. And now he was looking more serious than usual. 'What,' I said, 'are you secretly a Saethman, after all?'

'Why, no. The world is so terrible that one can only make sport of it, not mourn.' He nodded at the cage, where a harpy and a monkey were now locked in what looked like mortal combat, but rather hampered by the spinner-cord mesh of the curved cage wall, into which they kept falling. 'And I suppose all worlds are like that, at bottom—even the Seventy-Third Universe. The Old One and the other gods have arranged that we are always locked like prisoners into *their* cages, *their* dreams. But a man must dream his own dream, in spite of the gods.'

Somehow I did not feel like touching earth. For Wilifern, that seemed not to matter.

'And therefore,' he continued, 'what difference does it make if we are prisoners in Rathvia, or elsewhere?'

'You,' I said, 'why did you come on this Quest? Do you also wish to find Truth on the top of that mountain?'

He laughed. 'Not a bit. I have already enough Truth to last me a lifetime—which, by the way, may not be very long now. The fact is, Orselen, I was a little tired of making up stories about other people. This time I am going to get *into* a story.'

'The tale of our Quest?' I smiled. 'But you can tell that yourself, when we return.'

Slowly he shook his head, and gave me a mocking grin. 'No. That will be a lay for a truthful Bard, not a lying Minstrel. You see, Orselen, I am relying on you.'

The days went by, and the Rings. All the usual things happened. Ladies seduced us, and then grew tired of us; and then there were other ladies. . . . After a couple of Rings, only Tarsh and Kernin were still in request in this way; and then Kernin began to hope that we might soon be dismissed from Rathvia like spent men, over the inland frontier into Gagnar. But when he raised this matter with the Queen, she always put him off. The liberated ex-slave boys were one thing: they had forgotten their original homes. But we—men of enterprise—we might find a way round Rathvia, and so win home to the Shorelands, and reveal the great Rathvian secret. . . .

He mentioned Saeth and Firafax; hadn't they been allowed to pass?

'That business is perhaps a legend,' said the Queen. 'And besides, the saga tells that Saeth was a prince of Ranelon, a far-cousin of our then Queen; and also he found Truth so appall-

ing that he swore not to reveal *anything* that he discovered,
whether about Rathvia or aught else. And again, our polity was
not then so established, there were still some towns of Men in
Rathvia in those days. No, there is no precedent for letting you
go, my dear. Now, do not fret; we will be nice to you, never
fear. I will consider later how to please you.'

Kernin said to me once, furiously: 'I think I have been running
away from women all my life. First my mother, then—even my
dear wife; now—this. By Sinis I swear, if once we get clear of
Rathvia, I'll not lie with another wench till I lie again in my
Niamwy's arms.'

He hoped by this vow to please Sinis, and enlist her aid for
our escape. Perhaps it worked: I do not know. Wilifern told me,
in one of his more serious moments, that the gods do not answer
prayers, but merely enjoy hearing them.

Soon after that, though, our situation took a turn for the
worse. Kernin was trying the tactic of sulking—that is, of *not*
pleasing the Queen, in the hope of dismissal. And then there
occurred the business of Barundran.

Barundran was much worse off in Luvanash than in Namurai.
Here there seemed to be no Huntresses with experience of the
Shorelands, so he was treated much more as a curiosity, and
even as an animal rather than a person. I heard some ladies say
he should be put in the cage along with the flymonkeys; and I
feared that might not be altogether a jest. The younger ladies
teased him, in the way some young people will tease a pet
animal. And in the process, one evening they broke his eye-glasses.

' 'Tis no matter,' said Barundran to Kernin, with a faint
smile. 'True, I can no longer see the stars with great clarity, but
otherwise I can manage well enough. . . .'

Kernin was angrier than I had ever seen him. 'Good gods, my
old Master, what have I brought you to—'

'Nay, I brought myself,' said the centaur. 'My boy, whatever
befalls me, blame not yourself. I too freely chose this Quest.'

'I will see the Queen!' Kernin shouted. He was plucking at his
belt; but now he had no sword there to draw—which may have
been just as well. He asked the Queen to let Barundran at least
leave the country, under a vow of silence about the famous
secret; but she flatly refused. A centaur, she said, was such a
curiosity as Rathvia would not want to lose as long as he lived.

'Well,' said Barundran when he heard this, 'you could go on
without me. . . .'

'Never!' said Kernin; and after that he abandoned the tactic of trying to make the Queen tire of him. That was useless, now. It was far better to keep the Royal favour.

By the Sixth Ring of the Year 631, Kernin was taking his situation very grievously. Six Rings, and we had advanced only some 80 miles upon our Quest, and now no prospect of advancing further! He had reckoned to have climbed that mountain and returned by now. What was happening, what were they thinking of him in Aelvia? When he could, from an upper window of the Palace he would look inland toward Khar Durnaran; or from the Queen's bedchamber, when the Queen was asleep, Ringwards to the grey blur which just might be Aelvia, and Eladon, and another palace. . . .

The Queen began to see how utterly disconsolate most of us were. To amuse us, once she took us along to the Walled Forest, to the Ring-ripe orgy . . . merely as spectators, of course. Kernin did not want to go, but Tarsh said: 'Why not? Ahaaargh, it may be amusing! And besides, Prince, we may learn something useful—to help us escape.' Barundran gravely agreed; and so we all went. It was rather disgusting. . . . But I will now avail myself of the saga-writer's privilege, and say 'nothing important happened that night'—except that we saw the Queen of Rathvia stark naked pursuing frightened satyrs through the bushes. . . .

Rathvia was almost a timeless land. Every day was the same, every afternoon storm lasted exactly through Eighth Finger Hour. The only variation was in the orange oval Ring, ten nights shining, ten nights gone, with the orgy every Ring-ripe night. Kernin once said to me savagely, 'I wonder if Barundran is right, that there was once a time-before-the-Ring, a time before Time itself. That must have been barbarism indeed! But not *much* more barbaric than filthy Rathvia.'

As it happened, the very next day there came a change: the Queen announced that she would be taking us on a royal Progress to Dhanuun, the farthest inland city of Rathvia. The Countess of Dhanuun was her younger sister; she was going to show us off to her relative.

We went in much the same order as for the march from Namurai to Luvanash, except that the Queen graciously let us ride native mares. Our weapons were piled as before on the huge cart that had once been our proud Flier. But now we saw no more of Sunhorn: the stallion remained on the royal stud farm, where I believe he was quite happy; and he is now out of this story.

As we ambled along the rough road by the Gan, Kernin said:

'At least, we are heading in the right direction.' In truth, ahead of us stood the broad floating arrowhead of Khar Durnaran, now grown as wide to the eye as the disc of the Sun. But as we neared Dhanuun, the dark Dragon Hills which are the low inland wall of Rathvia rose up and hid the mountain of our goal.

This further part of Rathvia looked even wilder and more desolate than the country before the capital, and there were fewer towns, and we occasionally had to pitch a camp at night. There were dark straggly woods near the road which might conceal goddess-knew what wild beasts. Tarsh frequently pricked up his ears: there were sphinxes, he said, and wild boars rooting in those copses. But the beasts must have been afraid of our lady knights: as we approached, Tarsh said he could hear the creatures fleeing.

The last evening before we reached Dhanuun, the Countess of that city rode out with all her court to meet us. Her name was Unakuna, and her two daughters were Ukhalua and Uphaiuna—or rather U-nakuña and so forth, for the prefix *U-* is an honorific used for Rathvian high nobility. The Countess was a fair lady nearly as old as the Queen; her elder daughter was also ivory-skinned and rather beautiful; but her younger one, U-phaiuna, was astonishingly dark, with a very snub nose and very long feet, and her ears had definite points. I thought her rather ugly. Tarsh did not.

'Hahai! Easy to guess how *that* happened,' said Wilifern, nodding at U-phaiuna. 'One of those Ring-ripe orgies, no doubt, and the Countess was careless about eating her Maiden-weed.'

This was a No-Ring night, so the newly-arrived ladies showed no more than a chaste and polite interest in us. They were quite as much fascinated by our Flier, and the steel swords and the other gear piled on it. We had therefore more liberty than usual among the tents of that pitched camp. Tarsh was trailing after the dark lady U-phaiuna; I thought he must have amazing stamina. The rest of us kept our distance, and contemplated the scene around the great cart.

Suddenly Wilifern started as if he had been stabbed. 'The weapons! They must not lie on the Flier this night!'

'Why not?' said Kernin. 'By Sinis, they *should*. I have a notion! Suppose we steal onto the Flier in the dead of night, and cut the peg-ropes—throw any guards overboard! Then we might fly directly out of this accursed Rathvia. . . .'

'Hopeless, my Prince,' Barundran murmured regretfully. 'I have been considering that. Have you not noticed, in these parts at night there is almost no wind at all? If the gas has not all leaked out of the Flier by now—a doubtful point—we would merely rise straight up, and either hang so all night or, I think, drift slowly the wrong way. And then Sunkindle would drive us down again in Rathvia, to be taken once more as—hnnnm!— "guests".'

While we were yet talking, Wilifern was running toward the Flier. I saw him gesticulating to the Queen and the Countess. And he convinced them. Soon he saw the women bearing from the deck of the Flier our swords and bows.

'I have told them,' said Wilifern, as he rejoined us, 'that the night air is bad for steel, and even weakens the bows of Aelvia and the Centaurs. Not true, of course: in their scabbards and wrappings, I suppose our weapons would fare as well there as in the tents. But I have a strong *feeling*, and when that comes I am seldom wrong. . . .'

It was now Sunquenching, and the crowd was moving away from the tethered Flier. Suddenly Tarsh emerged from the ruck of women, and came loping toward us. He had his long hairy hands clasped around both his ears.

'What is it, friend?' said Kernin.

'I—don't *know*.' Tarsh stood poised, tense, his curly black beard, indeed all his visible fur bristling. He was sometimes aware of great far-off rhythms of the world, things we would not call sound at all; and indeed there was now a curious hush over the whole countryside. The little bat-monkeys should have been flying overhead now, and the harpy-owls should have been beginning their Sunquenching chorus; but nothing moved, no night bird or handibird sang. Suddenly Tarsh growled, dropped his hands, pricked up his ears, and sprang about, racing Ringleft. 'I hear it—now!'

And then the earth began to shake. Instantly I knew what it was—a 'poem', a crater explosion, as on that New Year at Nakhtos. This one was closer. Yes! There rose the fire-ball, across the stream of the Gan not more than ten miles off. Not a *big* eruption; mercifully, the rising ball of sun-stuff was only a few hundred feet across. But it was enough to shake the earth under our feet, to collapse a couple of tents. . . .

'The Flier!' shouted Kernin, spinning about, running. 'The Flier!'

Sure enough, the earthquake had uprooted all the pegs, and the great raft was sliding up into the twilight air. Kernin rushed, leapt for the bulwark—but fell short, it was already too high. Its buoyancy was great and unbalanced, for our leather armour and shields were still aboard, piled anyhow, and it was now zigzagging upward like a leaf falling the wrong way. In another minute, the Flier was merely a dwindling black rectangle flitting up toward the red ghost of the Sun.

We never saw it again. The gas in the logs must have been remarkably intact. Presumably it rose to some ten thousand feet, and then burst, and the fragments fell among the dark woods and wastes of Rathvia.

'Do not grieve, my Prince,' said Barundran. 'Air-rafts are little more than toys, of no real use for journeying in any determined direction. It is best that we are freed from that false hope. And at least, through our good minstrel's prophetic powers, our essential weapons are saved.'

'Yes,' said Kernin. 'Now all we have to do is to get these women to hand them back to us.'

That night Wilifern asked our female guards for a bowl of water. They made him fetch his own from the stream of the Gan. Once he had it into our tent the water's brightness dimmed, and he proceeded to gaze into it. Five minutes later, his scrying produced a result.

'White earth,' he murmured. 'I see two standing on white earth.' He looked at Kernin with a grim smile. 'Before that, I see us as six riders. But in the end, only two walkers.'

'Who is the sixth?' said Tarsh, and we five all looked at each other.

'I cannot see that one's face,' said Wilifern.

I found my voice. 'Kernin, if we ever escape from this accursed country, I say we should try to win home at once. We have seen that Wili is a true prophet. And so, if you persist in this Quest, three or four people are going to die.'

'I defy prognostication!' Kernin looked bitterly upon the minstrel. 'I wish you would keep these useless—no, I'm sorry, not useless, you saved our swords. But prophecies have a way of fulfilling themselves whatever a man may do; and not always in the way one thinks. And if you all abandon the Quest, nevertheless I will climb that mountain *alone*.'

'You will not be alone,' said Wilifern. 'I have already *seen* that, I think.'

After that, we all said we would go on with Kernin. Even Tarsh had had nearly enough of Rathvia. But how to get out of it?

Dhanuun was very much like Namurai. There were some Huntresses among the Countess's ladies, and so Barundran was treated rather better now. But otherwise, all the usual things happened to us, for a couple of Rings. With the Queen's gracious permission, Kernin became briefly the Countess's lover. Tarsh was seduced by several lady knights, but his heart was no longer in that business.

The satyr seemed now strangely melancholy. His passions were well assuaged, and he evidently did not care any more for the ladies of Rathvia. Except one: the young dark Princess U-phaiuna. But U-phaiuna was curiously elusive. She did not seem to be taking part in the purple wine feasts or the Ring-ripe orgies. She had not been to bed with any of us—which caused no pain to any of us, except possibly Tarsh.

On the second Ring-ripe night we were left to our own devices in the Countess's palace while most of the town rushed out to the local Walled Forest. Barundran was asleep in his room; the rest of us sat about disconsolately on our pallets. Wilifern was trying to cheer up Kernin with some impossible tale of the Seventy-Third Universe, alleging that the Suns there never quenched, for light in that world had no natural rhythm of its own; and I was playing Sulani's Lullaby, that most soothing piece, upon my lyre. But Kernin was neither amused nor soothed.

'We must make a run for it,' he said. 'It's not far from here, and there's no other way.'

'Hopeless,' I objected. 'There are still some guards at the town gates, and whole armies in the Dragon Hills, and we know nothing of the paths there.'

At that moment the door of the room creaked open, and a dark figure stood in the entrance, black-cloaked and hooded. When she pushed back her hood, we saw that she was the Princess U-phaiuna.

Kernin started up, tense with hatred. 'Well, mistress, which of us have you chosen to serve your pleasure this night?'

'None of you,' said the dark girl, and abruptly wrinkled her snub nose—'made a face', as we say in the Aelvian dialect—which made her face comically uglier than before. 'May I sit down with you? I have something important to discuss.'

We all stared. This was the first time in Rathvia that any woman had asked our permission to do anything. Tarsh leaped to his feet, overcome with emotion, and took the princess gently by the hand, and led her to a place on the pallet beside him. She laughed, and gave him a friendly squeeze on the shoulder.

'I know you like me, Tarshu. I like the look of you also, to be honest. We may well become lovers some time, if our friendship ripens in the proper way. But see here, all of you! I'm not going to treat you like slaves and concubines. I've had enough of that already, I'm sick of it. I'm sick of a good number of things here. Do you know, just because I'm unfashionably dark-skinned for the U-nobility—also because I ask too many questions—my mother has arranged to make me a Huntress? Oh, I've been in training for that for twenty Rings already. My career will be to slip across the mountains, dodging the dragons and the big harpies and maybe the odd prowling ex-slave, to see if I can steal some little boy from Rindos or Agnai, and bring him back here to be reared for their pleasure. Or so *they* think. I'd rather be a spy, I guess, not a child-stealer, and go into your Aelvia. . . .' She paused. 'Tell me, what's it really like in the Shorelands? Is it true that in Aelvia and so forth, men treat women like slaves, not the other way around?'

'It is *not* true,' said Kernin. 'Not in Aelvia, anyway. There, men and women are most nearly *equal* of any of the Shorelands.'

Abruptly Wilifern laughed. 'Princess U-phaiuna—'

'Call me Phai,' she said. 'I am that to my friends, or such as call themselves my friends; though I think few here would care if I was killed upon the Huntress paths.'

'Well then, Princess Phai,' said Wilifern, 'if we are to play the honesty game, I have travelled more lands than any of our company except old Barundran, and I do not find that in any human land women and men are truly equals. My own Aelvia is the best of lands in this respect, but even so. . . . Moreover, if you are thinking of making a bolt for it. . . .'

Phai started, but she said no word. Wili continued:

'. . . I would counsel you not to try Aelvia. There you might not suffer for being female; but you would certainly suffer for not being what most of us call "human". They would take you for a nymph, quite certainly, and treat you as a servant-wench, only fit to tend goats or the children of your masters.'

'By Sinis!' cried Kernin, his eyes flashing green in the glow of the light-berries, 'it shall not be so any longer, when I return to my Princedom! Lady Phai, by all gods I swear that if you will aid us now, I will make all satyrs and nymphs full freefolk of Aelvia—and you yourself shall be an honoured guest if ever you will visit us. And not a "guest" in the way we are guests *here*.'

Tarsh grimaced. 'That was well thought of, friend Kernin, if somewhat belatedly. But I doubt if you have that much power to change the Aelvians, *Queen's Consort*.' He turned to Phai, and caressed her cloaked shoulder. 'Lady, you have heard of our Prince's quest? Well, I have my own quest also. I am seeking a land where our *own* people, we satyrs, can dwell in peace and in freedom from hornless overlords. There are tales in the woods of Aelvia of such a land, far inland, the Happy Valley. And there shath and shani, satyr and satyress, also dwell side by side like equals. That is the kind of land I would seek, not Rathvia or Aelvia.'

'I have heard of that legend too,' said Phai frankly. 'I have wandered in our Walled Forests, but not on orgy nights; I have been by day, and have spoken with my father's people there. If there is such a land, it lies beyond Gagnar near the Great Mountain; and I am willing to seek it with you, if you accept me. That is, if you will accept me as a *friend*, not a mistress—in any sense.'

This speech of Phai's caused a sensation among us. I looked at Wili: here was our Sixth Rider. I hurried to Barundran's room, and woke the old centaur, and brought him to our council. And there, in the dead of Ring-ripe night, we swore great oaths to Princess Phai, making her a member of our Quest, and vowing to treat her as a sister-warrior.

'Well now,' she said briskly, 'now that's settled, we must escape at *once*. This is our only chance, while most of *them* are out of town and drunk with purple wine. And I know the ways, and how to get horses, and I know where your weapons are stored. . . .'

13

We trotted out of Dhanuun on the mares which Phai had 'borrowed' on her own authority from the Countess's stables. That girl was a miracle: we could have done nothing without her. She procured us black night-cloaks, such as the Rathvian ladies sometimes wore, and we kept the hoods drawn down over our faces, and so passed the sentries as women, the Princess U-phaiuna's girl-friends in fact, riding belatedly to the orgy. Barundran passed as himself, the well-known centaur philosopher going along with the 'girls' to observe their amusements. It was only when we were a mile out of town that we swung off the Walled Forest road, and began to gallop toward the Dragon Hills.

We took all the precious possessions that we could carry under our disguises, or in the large pockets of the blanket that Barundran was wearing: no shields or armour now, unfortunately, but our swords, two short Centaurish bows, Tarsh's golden helm—and I took my trumpet and lyre slung round my neck. Kernin was stroking the basket-hilt of Trier as if that sword was a long-lost

friend. Wilifern did not bring his zithar: he had a foreboding that
he would have little chance to play it in future. Phai was armed
with the weapons of a Rathvian Huntress: short-bow, dagger,
weighted cord for throwing or strangling. Tarsh offered her his
own steel sword, which he did not much favour, but she bade
him keep that till she asked for it—'Which may be never,' she
said. In the event, she was proved right in a sense; for when she
might have found a sword useful, long afterward, Tarsh did not
then have one to give her.

We rode through barren foothills under the glorious stars of
Heaven, the Ring high over our backs like a red-gold sky crown,
sharp on its inner edge, vague on its outer side; but our faces
were set toward the lovely Sea of Angels and low dim Flickerfly.
At last the hills loomed up and eclipsed that little orange star.
There was no road, only a rough path; and then we came to what
seemed like a sheer cliff.

'Follow!' said Phai, and dismounted, and led her mare through
a screen of bushes seemingly into the cliff itself. We did follow,
amazed. It was a tight squeeze for old Barundran in that rough
tunnel through the holestone, and the horses whinnied with fear
as we pressed on into blackness. But soon their hooves began to
ring more hollowly, the metal shoes echoing like bells in the
dome of a temple, and we saw lights above us. At first I thought
we had emerged, and that was the sky; but the sky-map was
utterly strange, there were no wide patches of light, only little
blue-white points—and every one of those 'stars' was winking!

'By Firafax!' laughed Wilifern. 'We've fallen through into the
Seventy-Third Universe!'

But his voice echoed back from that 'sky', and Phai said:
'This is Flickerfly Cave. *Real* flickerflies, I mean, on the cave
roof. This is the riskiest place, it is a known beauty-spot, but
there shouldn't be anyone about now. Come on!'

She led us on through yet another narrow tunnel that rose
steeply . . . and then we were out under the blessed true stars,
with a cool breeze in our faces like a breath of freedom. We
were still in Rathvia, there were more hills ahead, forested, high,
difficult—but this was the place Phai had scouted before, and
knew to be unguarded. We mounted and climbed a thousand
feet. I was afraid that at any moment one of our mares would
stumble and throw her rider, but in the end we got over the worst
place without accident; and then we were clear and rushing
downhill over a bare grassy slope.

'Out of Rathvia at last!' shouted Kernin, as we galloped down
into Gagnar. 'O Princess Phai, I love you!'

Tarsh growled at that, but Kernin laughed. 'Like a sister, I mean. Nay, Sinis knows what oath I swore back yonder, in that country of foul lust.'

And now we could see the black arrowhead of Khar Durnaran again, and the orange Flickerfly star of heaven over it; but the Ring was beginning to fade, and in rhythm with that, Flickerfly was turning very dim. For that matter, it had looked dimmer as we moved through Rathvia, even on full Ring nights; and after this night, as we went through Gagnar, we never saw it again. From now on, whenever we could not see Khar Durnaran for looming trees, we steered by high Pelas Velnul, the Sea of Angels.

Not that there were many trees ahead of us for the first hour past the frontiers. The soldiers of Rathvia burn this plain bare so as to give enemies and ex-slaves no cover. But at last we saw a long tree-row on our right, and Phai yelled to us that this marked the stream of the Gan, which had issued out of Rathvia by a strongly-guarded gorge. 'We'd better cross it,' she said. 'The land on the right bank has the worst reputation—for dragons, springers, and such-like—so we'll be safer there from pursuit.'

We swam our horses, and Barundran swam himself, into the blue-glowing waters of that river which seems to be named for the Goddess of Death. But the river proved less sinister than its name: no flying-mouths rose to attack our feet or our horses' bellies, and we drifted down with the current quite a way before Phai led us out between the trailing queen-trees of the further bank. After that we made our way, somewhat slowly, through the edges of the river's forest fringe, and so pressed on till Sunkindle.

By the time the Sun turned gold and heavy, we were forty miles beyond Rathvia, and our mounts and we too were exhausted. It was time to camp.

We chose a grove where we could lie fairly well concealed in a tangle of heart-leaves and swordbushes, but could see out over a wide arc of the open plain Ringleft and downriver. There was a spreading harpy-oak in the middle of our grove, and this the person on watch climbed while the others slept. But Barundran was so obviously exhausted (and, besides, he was no tree climber) that Kernin insisted he should stand no watch, and we others all agreed to that. He lay on his side within the perimeter of sword-bushes close by the mares; at a casual glance you might have mistaken him for a horse like them. As for Phai, she climbed the tree when Tarsh did, and shared part of his watch with him. She was nearly as good a climber as Tarsh: though she did not of course have claws on her three middle toes, when she discarded her buskins to climb we saw that she had five well-developed toes on feet which were long but otherwise almost 'human' and quite shapely, not furred; and with the spread of her five toes she went up the tree nearly as nimbly as a wingless monkey. She and Tarsh kept a good, alert watch. I heard them murmuring together in low tones as I fell asleep.

We roused about midday, after at most four hours' sleep each; but it was still vital to put more distance between us and Rathvia. Kernin and Phai were getting the mares on their feet and helping up old Barundran. These two, the Prince and the half-nymph lady, had become the joint leaders of our expedition: Kernin of course, since his blazing spirit was the reason why we were in this wilderness in the first place; Phai because of her Huntress training. She did not exactly know this country—the Rathvians did not venture very far into it—but she knew more about it, from rumour and distant view, than any of us others. 'One more day's march,' she said, 'and we will be in the Great Forest of Gagnar—and certainly none of my aunt's people will follow us there. Then we will have only the native denizens and the wandering ex-slaves to worry about.'

We rode out onto the plain, keeping near the edge of the river-woods. Almost any direction might be equally dangerous; but Kernin placed Barundran in the middle of our cavalcade, partly to render us less strangely singular to any watching eyes, partly because he was now showing a sort of guilty protectiveness toward his tired old tutor. Kernin and Phai rode in the lead, with Tarsh as rearguard frequently turning round in the saddle to pick up any signs of pursuit with his keen senses. I asked Wilifern, half joking, if *his* special powers might not be as good a defence.

He laughed. 'Not to be relied upon. My hunches come and go—and sometimes they don't come just when I most need them.'

'The gods are merciful, then,' said Kernin over his shoulder. 'If you always knew what was ahead of you, your life would not be worth living.'

'Nor my death worth dying,' said Wilifern, with a strange smile.

It was hot now under the blazing afternoon sun. We had taken off our cloaks and packed them behind our saddles, and still we sweated in our Aelvian wool tunics. As we went on this journey, the plateau still descended gradually to warmer lands; it seemed likely to me that Khar Durnaran must rise abruptly from a hot country very near to sea level. Barundran was better off than most of us, having rolled up his blanket and reverted to near-nakedness. And Phai looked cool enough in her green-and-brown mottled tunic, the short-skirted garb of a Huntress which blended excellently with the background of waving long grasses or tree-trunks. She wore her tunic very open at the neck, showing much of her brown skin, which was nearly the same colour as the mare she rode. We were all getting used to her appearance now; and to me this day she seemed much less ugly. In fact, she wasn't ugly at all: there was a strange beauty about her form and her dark, nymph-like features, the beauty of a healthy, trained body and a tough young spirit.

Kernin's mood was changed: he had altogether thrown off the depression of the last few Ring-months in Rathvia. 'At last we are on our way!' he cried, pointing ahead with his sword. 'To Khar Durnaran! And it can't be more than three hundred more miles to the foot of the mountain. We might be there in another half Ring.'

'I would place all my fingers on the earth,' I said, 'if I didn't have to dismount. So far it has taken us nine Rings to cover two hundred miles. If we do not better that rate, if more pitfalls lie in store for us. . . . And how ever are to get *back*? Not through Rathvia, certainly.'

Phai turned in her saddle. 'There are ways round Rathvia, Orsu, as we Huntresses know. Courage, minstrel! I will tell you all I know of them.'

I ignored her inaccuracy in calling me 'minstrel'. I said: 'Kernin, once again I ask you, if there are ways round and back home, I think we should consider taking them, and fairly soon at that. Our dear friends in the Shorelands will be giving us up for dead.'

'I have sworn to climb the Last Mountain and find the Ring of Truth,' said Kernin, 'and having come this far, climb it and find it I will. Besides, would you have me break my new-sworn faith with Princess Phai—to find a better country for her than the Shorelands?'

At that I was silenced. Barundran sighed, and then smiled. 'Let us not repine, dear friends. I am come to think like Wilifern, that this journey of ours is fated. I do not think I will climb the Last Mountain—but at least, I am travelling beyond the ends of the Known World. All things here are *new*. And travelling so, I could die happy. Now here, for instance, is a half-new thing. What has happened to the afternoon storm?'

Indeed, the storm that day seemed long delayed. It was evident that this was drier country than Rathvia: on our right, beyond the riverside trees, a vast savannah stretched into the distance, a sea of yellowish grass. Overhead the sky had turned from blue to that curious white glare one sees in the lower nomes of Palur whenever the storm fails. White sky is a terrible strain on the eyes and nerves; in Palur in this sort of weather prudent people stay at home in darkened rooms.

'White sky is a curious problem in natural philosophy,' said Barundran, shading his eyes with his hand and squinting up at the glare. 'Sirirendran hath speculated that it is due to very high clouds. But since the Sun is not dimmed in any way, and its disc remains hard and clear, it would follow that the clouds in question are higher than the Sun. Which is surely absurd.'

The rest of us preferred not to trouble ourselves with the abstract scientific problem at the moment, but rode on doggedly, heads down to shield our eyes from the glare. Luckily, the sky at last darkened, and low clouds drifted across the Sun. The storm was coming, though late. And before the first rain fell, we had reached the dark green wall we had been approaching all day: the Great Forest of Gagnar.

'Goodbye, Rathvia,' said Phai, turning her mare about under the first tree and looking back over the now rain-swept savannah. There was, I thought, a tear in her eye: understandably. For all its faults, Rathvia had been her home, which she had now abandoned for ever by coming with us. She was trying to gaze over the seventy miles to the Dragon Hills, but the grey rain hid all the far view. Tarsh came up to her and silently gripped her slim brown hand. Then she brightened, and leaned over and kissed him.

'Good Tarshu,' she said, 'nice Tarshu! If I am ever a Princess again, I will make you my Prince!'

Tarsh laughed. 'I see y'have still some ideas to unlearn, mistress. In most lands of men or satyrs, folk put the matter the other way round. Nay, I meant no offence: if ever we rule, it will be as joint monarchs. But first we must find a tribe to rule.'

Certainly we had seen no signs of people so far, neither men, satyrs, nor anything in between. The savannah had been empty country; but the Great Forest might be different. Phai reckoned it was another seventy or eighty miles wide, and very much more to left and right; beyond it would be a dimly known barren upland or plain also straddling the Gan. The forest surely would be a place of danger; here if anywhere we might meet the wandering ex-slaves of Rathvia, not to mention pit-dragons, springer-dragons, big sphinxes, gryphons. . . . So this night once more we had to keep a sharp watch. We found a clearing a short way into the forest, a place dominated by a great tall angel-tree, and made this our base, fortifying our perimeter as Phai showed us by gathering spinner-cords and stretching them between the smaller trees of the clearing edge.

Angel-trees are difficult to climb for lack of low branches, but both Phai and Tarsh managed to do it, Phai using a loop of dry-scraped spinner cord to help her, while Tarsh relied on his foot-claws in the low gravity of late Quenching. Then they sat up above the great fan-leaves, between the huge stalks and the main trunk, keeping a look-out for flying monsters—but no winged dragons or gryphons appeared. Indeed, we began to think that the dangers of Gagnar had been much overrated. A greater problem would soon be provisions, especially for our mares and for Barundran. We had brought supplies with us from Dhanuun, but they would not last more than four or five days, and then we must forage and hunt.

In the event, it took us three days to traverse the forest. It was very tough going at times, and once or twice we had to use our swords to hack our paths; also, we did not lack moments of drama. Once we nearly stumbled into a dragon-pit—but Tarsh felt the echoes in the little concealed crater just in time, and we crept around that place. Another time we were attacked by a flock of large harpies—those birds nearly as big as men, with almost human arms, but with claws on both hands and feet. But we had the victory, and came out of that battle with no loss; unfortunately the two harpies we shot with our bows were quite inedible. So was one large gryphon which flew out of a bush, and savaged Tarsh's mare before we killed it. That was a fine beast, all red and tawny feathers, the biggest four-footed bird I have ever seen. Tarsh's poor horse was never the same after. She could still move, but not swiftly.

'No matter,' said Tarsh, 'if we have to kill her, I can run nearly as fast on my own legs.'

Then on the last day of our forest crossing, suddenly Tarsh said: 'We are being followed. By folk on two feet.'

Well, we set an ambush for that band. We guessed what they wanted, and used Phai as our bait. As she rode seemingly alone through a clearing, they jumped out of the heartleaf bushes, half a dozen shaggy naked men, some as satyr-like as Tarsh, one perfectly 'human' with greying blond hair: none of them young. These were outcasts from Rathvia. We were determined to destroy this band, since Man is the most dangerous animal in any wilderness, and we could not afford to leave these fellows on our trail, possibly to gather more bands against us. We shot three with arrows, and smote two with the sword, but hoped to take one alive to give us news of the further country.

Unfortunately, at the last moment Tarsh's zeal or instincts overcame him, and he kicked in the belly the fair-haired man who had run closest to Phai—kicked him straight-footed with all three murderous claws, and then raked downwards.

As the man lay in the midst of the clearing, with the blood gushing from his entrails, Kernin tried to question him. 'What lies beyond this forest?'

Our victim grimaced horribly. 'Dragon-men,' he mumbled.

'What?' I said. 'Speak up, man, or I cut your throat.'

He looked up at me in cold hatred. His eyes were blue, and his accent had a faint trace of the Rindian. 'Strike at once, if you will,' he said. 'Nay—there is nothing beyond this forest. Open country—nothing to fear.'

'You mentioned dragon-men,' I said. 'What did you mean?'

'I meant—you were as bad as dragons.' Then he choked, and died; and his ghost came out of him. It was an ugly ghost with shredding edges.

Kernin immediately felt remorse. 'I was too ruthless. My old sin, in the wars. We should have parleyed with them.'

'No,' said Phai, looking down at the ghastly dead body of the one-time Rindian. 'This one had a most miserable life; so did the others. But they were *ruined* men. If you had spared them, tried to recruit them to help our journey, they would only have waited their chance to slay you while you slept, and then would have tried to make me their slave-boyess. Cruelty breeds cruelty; and we Huntresses know what the Outcasts of Gagnar are like. They are better dead.'

We fled that accursed spot as quickly as we could, the ghosts of the dead dissipating overhead into a white mist among the fans of the angel-trees.

That night we came to the far fringe of the thick forest, and camped at a place where we could see a tree-dotted valley, a ridge of cliffs on the right, and the blue glow of the River Gan on the left. Looking up, we could also see the stars, very bright and sharp and blue-white, for it was the eve of Prah's Day and there was no Ring.

'I shall be interested to see the Ring next time it appears,' said Barundran cheerfully. 'Perhaps, from the foot of the Last Mountain: and if I cannot see it clear for want of eyeglasses, you can tell me. So far, every "degree" of Sun-movement I have travelled from my own country, the Ring has seemed less of a thin ellipse, and more like a circle. It is as though Heaven were a hollow globe, and the Ring a true circle on its surface. As we move away from it, and it mounts higher in the sky, we see it more nearly as it really is. So far the change is quite regular. I have calculated that if it continues to change evenly, the Ring will appear a perfect circle when it mounts into the zenith, behind the Sun.'

'Refraction permitting,' said Kernin with a laugh.

'Yes, refraction permitting, or not interfering. . . . Hnnnm! There is another curious thing, my boy. As we are moving farther from the Ring, more opposite, as it were, its inner diameter is contracting; but not in a linear fashion. I mean, the contraction of the Ring is tending to a limit. At a guess, I would say that inner limit might be the same as the apparent diameter of the Sun.'

'That will be curious, if it's true,' said Kernin. 'Old tutor, when we return you must send off another monograph to the Middle Plain.'

Barundran coughed. '*You* also can write good Centaurish, my boy. If for any reason I am unable to write up our discoveries for the great Academies, I trust you will not omit to do so.'

That same night we observed two Winking Stars, one a familiar one close to the edge of the Sea of Angels, another very low down over Pelas Ranol which had not been observed to wink before. In fact, said Barundran, there was no star at all known in that position; which was directly over his own old home, Kintobara.

'There are such curious changes in Heaven of late. Hnnnm! If only we knew what they meant. If only we could read the language of the Winking Stars.'

Slow, slow, quick, slow, winked those yellowish stars, definitely taking it in turns.

'The Angels on the shore of their Sea are speaking to their friends at the New Low Star,' said Kernin, with a smile. Then he grew more serious. 'I wonder what we shall see from the top of Khar Durnaran. Heaven should look so much clearer from there. Oh, to be winged like a gryphon or a great harpy! I would like to fly off Earth altogether, up to that beautiful starry Heaven that we see up there.'

Barundran sighed. 'A philosopher must learn moderation, my boy, and to contain his desires within what is possible. . . .'

*   *   *

The next day we moved slowly out into the open river-valley. Over the forest the afternoon rains had been regular; but now we were coming into dry country again. The valley was narrowing, as the line of reddish cliffs on the right drew in; there was a corresponding cliff on the other side of the river. We seemed, in fact, to be heading into a narrow gorge. Luckily this was a good place for finding food, both animal and vegetable. There were wild loaf-nut trees growing along the banks of the river, which supplied Barundran with pleasant nourishment; there were reeds and grasses for our horses; and there were many little game animals. Phai snared a small spring-deer with her throwing-cord, and Tarsh cut its throat: we would have fresh meat for our midday meal.

We moved along the valley that morning in high spirits. It was a bright blue day, not too hot, and the riverside trees would supply us with shade when we needed it. It was also very clear: we could not see Khar Durnaran for the looming gorge ahead, but at least behind us we could see an enormous expanse of the world rising up until it faded into haze three hundred miles away. We could see, for instance, all the mass of the Great Forest we had just passed, and beyond that nearly all of Rathvia even to grey Rathwall, which in that direction was now our Farthest Mountain; and behind that, we knew, false-high in a false World's End, stood dear Aelvia and all the Shorelands, seemingly climbing toward the blue of Heaven. The world was enormous, and there was still no sign of any of Gormarendran's 'singularities', no edge of an overhanging Sky, no shadow-land beyond sight of the Sun. But still, we reckoned we were now less than two hundred miles from our chosen goal, the place where our Prince hoped to find the Ring of Truth.

Laughingly, Phai once pointed back and half Ring-right. 'And that way is the trail I've told you about—which will lead you at last back to Aelvia *round* the hills of Rathvia. Oh, the gods are good, after all! I do believe we shall all be happy at last.'

'This is how one should journey, this is how one should go Questing,' said Kernin, smiling. 'And with such talented friends, how can we fail, Orselen? Saeth had no such company with him, and yet he achieved his goal.'

This time my superstition overcame me, and I leapt off my mare and touched the earth. It seemed to me that we were at all times at the mercy of Nami, Mother Earth, maker of earthquakes and craters, who hatches her children and receives them again at last into her bosom; who is the greatest of all gods, in spite of the *high* notions of Barundran and Kernin; the source of all poems, of all life, and whose mere daughters are Suori and Sinis and Ganthis. Was not Kernin's journey a great piece of presumption, an attempt to question the shape of Her, who ends all questions in silence and dust? And now his optimism made me tremble, and I clutched the red soil and muttered a prayer.

All the others laughed—for glee, I think. It was that kind of morning, with most of us feeling fresh and joyful; even old Barundran had a young twinkle in his eye. We did not worry about what the afternoon or evening might bring. Human life is very much like that. At any rate, that day remains with me now, always, like an emblem.

By midday it was getting hotter, and we guessed that there might be no storm. It would not be pleasant to press on into the gorge under white sky. And then suddenly Tarsh's mare collapsed under him, and died. Poor beast, the wounds inflicted by that gryphon had completed their work at last.

We decided to camp just where we were, and to butcher the mare's carcass for meat. There was a huge queen-tree by the bank of the Gan, with trailing green skirts making almost a shade-house for weary travellers, and another line of loaf-nut trees near by. Once we had dealt with the mare, and picketed the other horses under the loaf-nut trees, I was strolling with Kernin toward the big queen-tree, when Phai turned to face us with arms outstretched. She had Tarsh beside her.

'Could you make do with the other trees for a while?' she said. 'And also keep watch. Tarsh and I have decided that we would like to make love.'

Well, there was nothing we could say against that: she and Tarsh had had no opportunity before, yet their feelings for each other were obvious. 'I have a supply of Maiden-weed,' said Phai frankly, 'so there will be no consequence; which might be an awkward thing upon a march like this.'

She and Tarsh went down to the river bank, and stripped, and bathed, pouring water gently, gravely upon each other. Apparently this was a ritual Phai had learnt on one of her daytime visits to a Walled Forest: among the Woodsfolk it signified something very like marriage. Then our two friends moved naked, hand in hand, into the green skirts of the Queen-tree, where they stayed while the sky turned white and then blue again. After that, they emerged and bathed once more, and we resumed our journey.

We could reckon on one more hour of light. Kernin said: 'I do not like the look of that river-gorge. It would be a bad place to spend the night, hemmed in so narrowly by those cliffs. Tarsh, do you *hear* anything in the cliffs?'

Various dragons, of course, including the Springer kind, like to build their dens in cliffs or the sides of abrupt craters. Tarsh paused in his march, yawned, and cocked his ears. He was beginning to show signs of lack of sleep: he had often been staying awake not only for his own watch every night, but also through Phai's, and even on the march the strain of alertness fell mostly on him. Wearily now he listened; then shook his head.

'Nothing stirring. And if there are any holes in the cliffs, they must be small ones.'

We moved on slowly now, since our mares and Barundran and Tarsh were all tired. The cliffs closed in on us. Kernin said: 'I still do not like this place. If we camp for the night in this gorge, we will have no view; whereas anything coming from the higher land could peer over the cliffs at *us*. I suggest we look for the next easy way up the cliff, and then climb it, and camp out on the open tableland above.'

We agreed to that; but we did not see any easy ways up the cliff. Instead, the gorge grew narrower, and we plodded on, hemmed in on a narrow path between the vertical cliff on the right and the Gan on the left. The Sun began to die, and the river to glow blue in the twilight; its waters pouring over its stony bed made a rather monotonous murmur. On and on we marched, and the cliffs and the river marched beside us. The cliffs were of a kind of soft holestone, but we saw no caves. The orange cliffs, the blue water, the red dying Sun in the zenith, the first patches of stars. It is possible that the peaceful beauty of the scene, our weariness, and the lullaby of the murmuring river combined to dull our alertness, as we plodded along in single file. Tarsh was in the lead now, but the river-noise must have made his hearing less efficient.

Suddenly Wilifern cried out 'Stop!'—but his hunch had come too late.

The next moment I felt a sharp pain in my bare right knee, as though I had been stung by an invisible serpent. Then another piercing bite in my right shoulder, through the wool of my tunic. I clutched at that place with my left hand—and found a sliver of hard wood, a dart as long as a finger sticking up through my tunic out of my flesh.

Ahead of me, Barundran toppled with a great splash onto the shallow margin of the river. All the rest of us were crying out, clutching at dart-stings. The cliffside: nothing was visible there except some dark patches of bushes, not much wider than a man's body, about waist high above the path.

And then one of the bushes stirred, and a figure slipped out. At first I thought it was a man. But then, in the dark gold light of the dying sun, I noticed the stance—the naked greyish body thrust forward, balanced by the stubby tail; I also saw the hideous ugliness of those skull-like features, that hairless head.

The thing confronting us was first cousin to a Springer; but smaller, with a relatively bigger skull; and it carried a rod like a long flute in its two hands. Now there were more stirrings of bushes, and more of these Springer-men dropped out of their holes onto the path.

It was like a nightmare: I tried to draw my sword . . . and found that I could not. There was a numbness in all my limbs. The others were in like case: they were dropping limply from their horses, as the poor beasts took fright and bolted, some ahead, some into the river.

When my horse threw me, I must have fallen soft, because I was still conscious. I was lying twisted against something soft that moved: probably the hands of a Springer-man. I was facing toward the river and the place where Barundran lay, and I could still see and hear, though I could not move.

Barundran raised his head out of the shallows and addressed Kernin. 'My boy—I think I am achieving my Quest now. But do you go on. . . .' And then he looked up into the zenith, and whispered: 'Karondru dumetha, theranandru kraan. . . .' It is the prayer of dying centaurs, which means, in its beginning, 'Hail holy Sun, life-giving Lord. . . .'

Barundran never finished his prayer. The poison which paralysed us bipeds worked differently on his body-stuff. The next moment I saw his dark head fall into the bright water—and then his spirit, brighter than the water, began to rise. It came out cleanly, intact in every limb. I have no doubt that Barundran's soul went up entire to the Sun, and in that place of light learnt every necessary truth about all worlds.

His body, I think, was taken by the river. But I could not be sure, because my eyesight failed, and now for me there was only darkness, and obscure movements as the Springer-men dragged us into their holes.

14

We came to ourselves in what at first seemed a tomb. It was a hollow in the rock like an egg some thirty feet in diameter, or rather half an egg, for it had a flattened floor. It was dimly lit by blue-white smears on the roof, rather like star-patches: a nasty parody of Flickerfly Cave in Rathvia. Later we discovered that these star-like patches were smears of lightberry juice.

We were laying side by side in an orderly row, all naked and of course weaponless. The power of movement returned to our bodies only gradually, starting at the head, so that at first the Springer-men did not need to restrain us with bonds; and afterward we saw that it was useless to offer violence or attempt escape. Nor were the reptile folk offering us violence. A great many of them were surrounding us, dark hideous forms like goblins in that blue shadowy space, and one of them was talking. He/she/it seemed to have been talking for some time, talking monotonously, *lecturing*. It was all like some dull unpleasant dream, from which there could be no awakening.

'All two-leg be sibling. Folk-of-Kopa take other two-leg for own good, make all two-leg think good. Folk of other round think wrong, think some two-leg more high than other two-leg. That be evil, not-equal be evil. Evil must be destroyed, Folk-of-Kopa will destroy. All two-leg sibling, all two-leg equal, all number equal-high. You now five more number for Folk-of-Kopa. More number for Kopa, Kopa more strong against evil round. Evil must be destroyed, Folk-of-Kopa will destroy. All two-leg sibling. . . .'

I fell really asleep after that. When I awoke, it was to find myself physically more or less normal, only very cold and stiff. We were in another, smaller rock-chamber, and through a hole in the rock on one side there was coming in real *light*, the blue-bright light of the sky. It was day out there. . . . I almost cried out with relief.

But there were half a dozen goblins standing over us again. And the Speaker was lecturing once more. It was amazing that this creature spoke a human tongue at all, until later on we discovered the explanation. Its language was more or less Rathvian Shorelandish, but simplified, and distorted by an inhuman vocal apparatus. The Speaker was now pointing to us in turn with its little clawless hands: it was *naming* us (if that is the right term).

'Ki-mo-tapa-pei. Repeat! Ki-mo-tapa-pei.'

'Ki-mo-tapa-pei,' said Phai blankly. 'That's me?'

'Correct. *Ki* in your language be "one", *mo* be "zero", *tapa* be "nine", *pei* be "three". You will learn the language of the Folk quick. Now, you male sibling: you be Ki-mo-tapa-pa. . . .'

This was Tarsh, looking truculent, feeling his head. They had taken away his helmet, revealing his odd equipment of one and a half horns. And they were naming him Sibling 1094.

Kernin touched him on the arm. 'Keep quiet,' he whispered in the Aelvian dialect, 'we're altogether in their power. Later. . . .'

'Not will speak unknown tongue!' the Speaker reproved. 'Sibling 1095, you may need more correction.'

'Fault acknowledged by this sibling,' said Kernin expressionlessly. 'Sibling 1095 was telling 1094 to pay attention to Sibling 323 her discourse. Sibling 323 her discourse very good, very interesting. Nevertheless, Sibling 1095 at fault.'

Evidently Kernin had been awake and alert much longer than I. I listened dumbly while the Speaker—the female goblin named 323—gave Wilifern his name-number (1096) and me mine (1097).

'Now will have duties assigned,' said 323. 'Outside, all new siblings.'

We crawled through the narrow hole, and so into the blinding light of full day. When our eyes adjusted, we saw that we were standing on the floor of a crater about one mile in diameter. But such a crater! The floor was dead flat, and bounded on all sides by a circular vertical cliff. The hole from which we had just emerged was near the base of this cliff, and there were similar holes all round the cliff-base, evidently the cave-dwellings of the Folk of Kopa. There were no buildings on the valley floor except a few wooden sheds, like the sheds Shoreland farmers use to keep their tools in. The flat round valley was intensely cultivated, divided into sectors and concentric circles by paths and tiny irrigation streams; the fields between were small, some mere garden-patches, all full of a great variety of vegetables, some kinds of which we could not recognise. And everywhere the fields were being tended by industrious goblins: there must have been nearly a thousand workers, including some quite small hatchlings, in that confined space. Only in the middle of the crater-valley, half a mile away, was the monotonous scene relieved by a clump of higher-growing vegetation, something which nodded and waved in an oddly familiar way.

My attention was held at first, though, by the foreground: Sibling 323 and her friends. They were all quite naked, except for a few pouches and belts of vegetable fibre which they used as object-carriers. I could not for a long time tell males from females, for in that respect these people were rather like birds, and rape must have been physically impossible among them: Tarsh was staring at the place between their legs, horrified. But then he realised the truth, that these reptiles were an intelligent species of Springer, and so he should have expected that anatomy. In this species, the males were only slightly smaller than the females—hence my initial bafflement. Physically, the main differences from the deadly Springers were these: the tail was much shorter, so that these folk could waddle in almost human fashion as well as hop; and their five-fingered hands were clawless and as sensitive as our own. Being reptiles, they would become cool and somewhat torpid at night, but low night gravity compensated for that, and so they could get around well enough after Quenching.

I thought: Poor Barundran, he would have been so interested to verify his theory that there could be many different intelligent species spread through the unknown regions of this great Earth. Intelligent Springers. . . . They still seemed to me hideously ugly; but I soon had to admit that this was mere human prejudice. *We* must have seemed equally repulsive to them—hot-blooded, hairy, tailless monsters—yet they pretended otherwise: *on principle!*

That was the most human thing about these reptiles: they were hypocrites. If they were not, we would surely all have been dead by now, instead of being *numbered* among their own citizens.

They put us to work. I will not describe our tasks in detail, since I have always found practical agriculture deadly boring, as well as beneath the dignity of a Bard, let alone a Prince. And we had to work naked, since all Siblings went so. During the course of that day, I found an opportunity to talk to Kernin in a pause of our work among the vegetable patches. He said:

'Orselen, I owe these folk a grudge for murdering poor old Barundran; but otherwise, by their lights, they are acting very well toward us. One can even admire them. The Kopans hold that *all intelligent bipeds* should have equal rights, they are a republic, and they are having to defend themselves against other crater-cities of Springer-folk who have other ideas. We should not judge them too harshly, we should not condemn them. . . .'

'Except for having waylaid us travellers who were doing them no harm, and for probably ruining our Quest. Good Goddess, how are we to get clear again?'

He put his finger to his lips. 'I don't know. But not by showing any resistance just yet. Let us learn all we can, pretend to become good "siblings"; then we will see.'

We saw a lot, even that very first day. Obviously this crater

was a hollow in the plateau not far from the River Gan, and the
Kopans had tunnelled through the rock to the point above the
river path. The rock indeed was fairly soft, and some of the
tunnels may have been natural ones when this area, at some
time, had more rainfall; but still, they must have put in a lot of
effort, especially on the main canal through the largest tunnel to
the river. Well, that was like them: in everything they did they
were methodical and patient, and fairly well equipped with
wooden and flint tools, though they did not use metal. Our
swords and other gear puzzled them considerably. When Sibling
323 questioned us about them, Kernin told her that the swords
were cutting tools used for hacking paths through forests. Since
the only real weapons used by the Springer-folk were anaesthetic
blowpipes, 323 seemed to believe the explanation.

'But not are very useful size,' she said. 'We break up for use
as hand-cutters, perhaps. . . . And what be these?'

She was pointing to my trumpet and lyre. I tried to explain
about music; but it was hopeless. The Springers did not sing or
play, in fact they were tone-deaf. Their only ceremony which
involved anything like a song was a sort of hideous chant which
they performed at Sunkindle in the centre of the crater, holding
hands in a ring about the focal clump of vegetation. The words
of the chant were quite devoid of poetry, consisting in fact of
slogans. The following is a fair translation:

> Long flourish Kopa—long flourish all equal
>   siblings
> All two-legs good—but some two-legs be in
>   error
> Error must be destroyed!—may the craters of
>   evil perish
> Work is good—work for the siblings

And so on. They had no music, no poetry; and Sibling 323 told
me that my lyre would be taken apart, the strings to be used for
tying up bundles of Kopan cabbages; and the gold casing of my
trumpet would be beaten into working knives.

The work they put us to was not, I suppose, very terrible, at
least by their standards, but to me it was the greatest indignity I
had ever suffered, worse than anything in Rathvia. (Kernin said
the opposite: in his opinion, almost *nothing* could be worse than
Rathvia.) We had to carry baskets of vegetables, to work on the
earth with wooden hoes, to assist our reptilian 'siblings' to
improve or alter irrigation channels—and all under the blazing
sun, and always stark naked. Phai was treated a little better than

the rest of us: I am afraid the Kopans were hypocrites also in this, that while all siblings were equal in theory, in practice their females had higher status than their males. Kopa was managed basically by a little group of elder females called the Mothers, of whom 323 was one. And the Mothers soon took Phai out of the fields, and put her to the lighter task of caring for eggs.

The Kopans' eggs were stored at night in little chambers stuffed with straw at the base of the perimeter cliff, and were taken out for sunning during the day. The females who were allotted to this light task had plenty of time for gossip. And in this way, Phai began to learn quickly the Kopan language—and much else.

The first night she returned to us from this task, she said: 'I've found out how 323 can speak Rathvian. They caught one of those outcast slaves some time back, and made him a Sibling, and 323 learnt the language from him.' She shuddered. 'I've seen his skeleton!'

'What!' said Kernin.

'Yes. He didn't last all that long, I think, the food and the work disagreed with him—but they are vague about time. They have his bones stored in that big wooden hut near the Centre—it's a place that Mothers use as a sort of museum. 323 says that when he died they *tried* to use his flesh as fertiliser, but it didn't do the crops much good. . . .'

'Is that what they do with their own "siblings"?' I asked. 'Don't they give them decent burial, in tombs?'

Phai laughed. 'Oh no. Nothing is ever wasted here. Not even dead bodies; not even names—I mean, numbers! When a Sibling dies or gets captured by an enemy crater, his number is given to the next sibling hatched or—"recruited". We have been given the numbers of five soldiers who were lost in a skirmish with Tota last Ring.' She shivered, and clasped her hands over her bare shoulders. 'I am cold.'

So were we all, after Sunquenching. They would not give us back our clothes because they themselves did not use them, and all siblings had to be treated equally. It was in vain to plead that we were mammals, that we did not go comfortably torpid at night. Naked we had to remain. They gave us a small cave-chamber to sleep in, a hole whose only exit was into the main crater, and that exit watched by blow-pipe-wielding guards. When we were definitely siblings in good standing, those guards might possibly go away. But till then, we had to survive.

We survived the cold of night by all huddling together. And that way we did survive, but it was hard to sleep in that bare rock hovel. When we were wakeful, Wilifern would sometimes try to amuse us by telling us lying tales of Firafax, of the Keelless Sea of Dreams, of the Seventy-Third Universe. One night he announced to us that in the Seventy-Third Universe there were no Springer-folk: the physical laws of that universe, being different from ours, did not permit the existence of intelligent reptiles. At this, most of us cheered.

'O that we were there!' said Phai.

'Aren't you ashamed, Wili, of such blatant escapism?' I said.

'Not a bit!' Wilifern laughed. 'Don't you think, in our situation, *escapism* is just what we need?'

'We certainly have a situation worth escaping *from*,' groaned Tarsh.

It was worst for him, of course, and Phai. Phai once said frankly that if it would comfort us, she would make love with any of us, since she liked us all. And then a point struck her, and she cried 'Oh!' She had forgotten that she had lost her store of Maiden-weed. The Siblings did not use that; therefore. . . . Indeed, a few days later she told us what 323 had said to her: the Mothers hoped she would breed. They had never raised a human egg before, but according to their principles, they now ought to. As the Kopan Mothers were or had been themselves polyandrous, they assumed that Phai was mated with all four of us.

Tarsh swore. 'By my horns, no child of mine or my lady's will be hatched in this filthy pit.' And we all agreed. We had none of us ever made any move toward accepting Phai's kind offer. Kernin was in any case now sworn to celibacy during the Quest; and Wilifern and I loved Phai too much in another way, and respected both her and our other comrade Tarsh. Still, it was a grievous trial of our inner strength. Phai slept in Tarsh's arms, and they dared not make love; and sometimes we heard her weeping.

There was another trial in store for Tarsh. About a Ring after our arrival in Kopa, he was summoned to the Mothers. We did not see him for half a day. When the guards brought him back at Sunquenching, he was staggering. And his outline was strangely different; no longer uneven.

Then I realised. They had cut off his remaining head-horn. Their own males were not horned, and they could not bear the oddity of that one long projection on Tarsh's head.

He was humiliated and bitter. Phai flung her arms around him sobbing, then comforting him. Wilifern laughed sardonically. 'Come, friend, it might have been worse. They might have removed your *other* projection, to make you *still more* like their males. . . .'

'Well, they cut my toe-claws,' said Tarsh. 'Look.'

It was true. He was now no more weaponed on the feet than we were; and that was why he was limping.

'It is time we got out of here,' said Kernin. 'Courage, my friends! I am beginning to have an idea.'

He showed me what he meant the next day. It never seemed to rain in this place—hence the need for irrigation, with water brought through a tunnel from the Gan; and during the afternoon period of white sky the workers had a meal-time rest. Our food was all vegetable stuff, and nearly tasteless; but we ate all we could to keep up our strength. That afternoon Kernin met me during the meal-break, and led me, as if casually, toward the centre of the crater-valley.

'What do you think those are?' he asked, pointing to the clump of great plants which rose above the fields into the horrible white dazzle.

I cupped my hands around my eyes. 'Why, they look like giant gas-plants.' They were not exactly the same species as in Aelvia, though: these ones were greatly constricted at the base, in fact they grew from very narrow stems. The great greenish-white plump fingers were also somewhat more erect than the Aelvian type would have been during full daylight.

'If one were cut off,' said Kernin, 'say, by a sword slash, I wonder how long it would take for the gas to leak out of that narrow stem? Long enough to fly right out of the crater, perhaps?'

'That would be a desperate method,' I said. 'What, clinging to a leaking gas-trunk? If we failed, we would be finished.'

'What other way is there?' said Kernin, and I had to agree with him. The Kopans kept soldiers on watch at all times in the tunnels and in posts above the perimeter cliff; only the centre of the crater was weakly guarded.

We got to see those giant gas-plants more often, starting the very next morning; for now we knew enough of the Kopan language to join in the Sunkindle Chant, and we were driven out of our cave at dawn to join the other Siblings at the ceremony. All holding hands around the big gas-plant clump (Goddess! I had to hold the hand of a cold scaly reptile), we chanted our hideous nonsense. The gas-plants were the nearest thing Kopa had to a flag or communal symbol: the reptile-folk had no religion as far as we could discover, but as the sunlight pushed the waving gas-fingers down toward the circle of Siblings, it was supposed to mean something edifying about Siblinghood. When the Sun had reached full strength, and the big fingers were nearly horizontal, we stopped our squawling, and dispersed to our dung-laying and burden-carrying.

All that day, as we went about our work, we watched the movements of the blowpipe-carrying guards. There *were* a few patrolling the middle of the crater, gazing not at the workers (who seemed never to think of rebelling) but up at the sky, on the lookout for marauding flying beasts: there were indeed some harpies circling up there, but we never saw one attack. There was also a single guard at the door of the Museum shed, where we knew the Mothers had cached the weapons and other gear they had stolen from us—whatever they had not already destroyed.

'If there were an attack,' said Kernin, whispering to me, 'that would be a good time. May Prah inspire the Pokans with aggression.' Poka was the nearest enemy crater, directly across the Gan gorge. I forget if it was an evil place because dedicated to open Inequality, or an evil place because dedicated to a rival brand of Equality. No matter. Each crater was liable to launch raids on the others, either through the tunnels or over the cliff edges, mainly to try and seize eggs and younglings, so as to bring these up as right-thinking citizens of Poka or Kopa.

The first night that the guard was removed from the exit of our 'bedchamber', Kernin waited till the night was old and cold; then he crawled out, alone, into the valley. He refused utterly to let anyone else come with him. 'We need to make this experiment; and it needs only one pair of hands to do it. That pair shall be mine. If I am caught, I will say you knew nothing of it; and you must do the same. They may even believe us.'

We waited anxiously, cold and awake, for what seemed like hours; and then we saw a body blocking the stars that shone through our cave-mouth.

'It is I,' said Kernin, 'and—*it works*. . . .'

He had crept to the middle of the crater, avoiding the half-torpid guards who prowled in small groups near the wooden tool-sheds and the Museum; he had slipped into a tool-shed, and stolen a flint knife. And with that he had crawled into the very heart of the gas-plant clump, and sawn through a stem. . . .

'It went up like a dream. And it did not fall again inside Kopa. When I could last see it, it was still rising. None of *them* noticed. *I think we can do it*. . . .'

Next morning, the sawn-off gas-plant stem was not noticed by the Siblings. And even if it had been, it might not have mattered. Gas-plants sometimes break from their stems naturally: that is one method by which they propagate themselves. We chanted our nonsense around the still abundant clump, and then dispersed to our work.

The next night was brighter, for it was New Ring; but we could not bear to wait any longer. More than two Ring-months we had been prisoners of the Siblings, and the thought of freedom was irresistible. It was all we could do to wait till about midnight—not that we knew it *was* midnight, we could only guess roughly.

'Now!' said Wilifern suddenly. 'I feel—it will be now or never!'

'Come,' said Kernin; and we all crawled out. We made our way along the well-known paths—not directly to the gas-plants, but to the Museum. Phai had told us that two of our swords were still intact in there—one of them being Trier; and we needed swords above all things.

Wilifern's hunch served us well, at least most of the way. There was one guard as usual at the Museum door, but we saw him before he was aware of us. If Tarsh had been still equipped with footclaws, he would have known what to do; but even so, there were five of us to one of him, and we jumped him before he could use his blowpipe, and then Phai strangled him with her bare hands. The wooden lock of the Museum door did not keep us out for long.

It was dark in that shed, with just a few thin rays of Ring-light coming through chinks in the wooden walls, and we had to grope our way. I fell into something cold that rattled.

"Sibling 579—his skeleton,' whispered Phai. 'The swords should be just beyond him.'

And—praised be all the gods—they were! Kernin knew Trier by feel, and snatched it up and kissed its hilt; then I grabbed the other sword, and we all got out of there fast and trekked off toward the gas-plants. Wilifern thoughtfully picked up the dead guard's blowpipe and supply of darts.

'I think I could manage this,' he said. 'It can't be too different from playing a ten-pipe, and I've sometimes borrowed those from my girls.'

But our luck ran out just before we reached the gas-plants. A noise of reptilian croaks and hisses burst out from the perimeter-cliff on the riverward side, the side from which we had come: Poka was indeed staging a raid. And that did *not* help us. One accursed squad of soldiers, over a dozen siblings strong, came hopping across the crater, I suppose as reinforcements for the attacked cliff. They came round the side of the gas-plant clump

just as Kernin slashed with Trier, and launched Tarsh into the
air, clinging desperately to that severed trunk.

The soldiers halted abruptly. 'Siblings!' croaked their leader.
'What is this? It is not yet time for the Siblinghood Ceremony.'

The next moment the reptiles noticed the strange shape flying
upward, the huge gas-trunk with Tarsh hugging its underside.
And then they knew that something was badly wrong. Meanwhile I had slashed the second stem, and launched Phai.

'Wili, you now—' yelled Kernin.

Wilifern paused before mounting his plant, and blew lustily on
his stolen pipe. His dart took the squad-leader in the naked flesh
of her throat. She keeled over instantly.

'One!' chanted Wilifern. 'Orsu, see you make a good lay of
this.' At once he blew again—and shot another of our enemies.

'Wili!' shouted Kernin. 'I will not go till you do.'

At this the minstrel shrugged, and leapt nimbly to his gas-plant
stem, riding it like a horse between his legs. Then Kernin
slashed the lower neck of the stem, and that plant was free.

The squad was shooting back at us now; wooden darts were
burying themselves among the gas-plants. Kernin and I leapt onto
our own chosen plants, and slashed behind us. Oh, the blissful
feeling, as at last we rose clear into the air! We two rode the way
Wili did—it was difficult to do anything else without dropping
our swords. Within a few eyeblinks we were floating up, higher
and higher, our legs pressing into the soft and half-yielding skin
of the plant, holding on for dear life—upside down.

We could not see anything of Tarsh or Phai; presumably they
had got clear away, and as they each had four free limbs to cling
on with, they should be quite safe. The rest of us were within
sight of each other, rising now fairly evenly—O joy!—much
higher than the circling cliff of that accursed crater.

The motion of my plant swung me suddenly quite close to
Wilifern. In the orange light of the Ring I could see, just, that he
was smiling. His hair hung down away from his head like
flames, red flames with blue tips. In one hand he was still
holding that blowpipe, holding it elegantly as though it were a
flute.

'I wish I could play one more merry tune, in honour of
Firafax,' he said, 'but those who made this little pipe are
unmusical. Well, Orselen, set it down in your lay, that I would
not have mounted unless compelled by my Prince. Even so, I
struck down two, and that with an unaccustomed weapon.'

The blowpipe now slipped from his grasp and sailed downwards.
Then I saw, to my horror, that his knees were relaxing; and as he

turned, the Ring-light showed a tiny wooden dart sticking into the skin of his naked shoulder.

He laughed. 'Remember me to the Keelless Sea. I am about to dive into it, I think. . . .'

And then he was gone.

We saw his body sailing down, then picking up speed, and finally hurtling: we were already so high that even in night gravity that must be a deadly fall. In the end he struck, horribly, on the edge of the cliff, his head against a boulder; and a little while later as we drifted across the landscape, we saw his spirit rising. But we were now so far away that we could not verify the fate of his soul.

15

The gas leaked out of our plants long before Kindle, and we fell gently to the surface of the plateau. Kernin came down half a minute after and two hundred yards away from me; luckily, in the last moments before our landing we saw two drifting dots sinking to the ground far to our right. We both made good landings, leaping clear and alighting on our feet. As our plants, released from the weight of our bodies, went whooshing temporarily up into the air again, Kernin waved his sword, and pointed.

'Come on, Orselen! We must get to the others—fast!'

That was an unpleasant journey, running naked over the chill sand and rock of that desert; and at first we were very cold from our ride through the air. We had very little idea how far off Phai and Tarsh were; and we might stumble into another crater-town of the Springer-folk at any moment. We had been drifting Ringback and a little away from the river; and that way, we knew, lay the crater of Tota. Our friends might indeed have fallen into it, and be already prisoners. Then all of a sudden we saw two long gleaming shapes shoot up into the air a mere four hundred yards ahead. 'There they are!' Kernin shouted; and in another minute we were overjoyed to meet up with Tarsh and Phai, who were running toward us.

'Where is Wili?' exclaimed Phai, after we had exchanged the first glad greetings.

'Dead,' I said; and told the manner of it. 'And even before we rose, he was fey and aware that his end was upon him.' My voice broke. 'He—he was worthy to be a Bard; or a great warrior.'

'He was a very gallant comrade,' said Kernin, curt and grim, 'and we will miss him for ever. But now is no time to weep, nor would he wish that. We must press on: Sunkindle must not catch us on this accursed bare tableland. We are almost safe here at night; but by day, the Sibling patrol may begin to prowl.'

We began to run again then, Kernin leading; and I noted with a certain wry amusement that we were running still Ringbackward, toward Khar Durnaran. Naked, without food, with no resources but our bare bodies and two sheathless swords, our Prince was still pursuing his Quest and taking us with him. But in truth his way was as good a way to run as any other. Over to the left, somewhere, must be the stream of the Gan, which might water a better country; or it might not—was it still pent in that perilous gorge? Ahead of us, and now brightening in the first rays of Sunkindle, the Last Mountain looked very big, a great truncated cone with a whitish rim, rising now in all its revealed majesty from a vast ridge and range. We had never been able to see it while we were prisoners in Kopa; and now we were seeing it for the first time as no ghost floating in haze, but a real palpable peak rising from solid earth.

'It must be less than 200 miles,' Kernin panted as we ran side by side. 'By Sinis' Sword, but I will not fail of that place now!' And he swung up Trier at every stride, as though menacing the mountain with it.

But we certainly weren't going to make it to the Last Mountain this night. As the light grew, we were searching for a hiding place; and at last Tarsh found one.

'Over to the left,' he said hoarsely. 'Trees. . . .'

It was a tiny oasis, just a few half-dry thorn-trees growing out of a little hollow, perhaps a small decayed crater. We approached cautiously; but there were no dangerous animals or Springer soldiers in the place, just a few small handibirds who squawked and rose fluttering at our approach. Tarsh promptly scaled two of the trees—his feet were healed now, though his claws had not yet grown back—and he robbed the nests there. Bad luck for the handibirds, good luck for us; such is life. The raw eggs with the half-developed embryos in them were not pleasant eating; but we were starving, and needed that nourishment. Tarsh relished the food more than the rest of us. 'At last, *animal* food,' he growled. ' 'Tis not much, but—wait till I get my hands on a deer—or a rat—or a Springer soldier. . . .'

Then we settled down, hiding ourselves in the small shade of the trees, to take it in turns to sleep and wait out that day.

Kernin took first watch, I the second. It was a nuisance that having no clock with us there was no way of measuring time

accurately. The normal practice on Shoreland army campaigns is
for the man on watch to mutter to himself the long set passage in
Sakanek, the March to Suoran—over and over again. Ten repetitions give one hour. But I was too tired to keep up my reciting,
and in fact the repetitions were putting me to sleep, and I faltered
and lost count. Then I remembered with a pang one of Wilifern's
stories of the Seventy-Third Universe—how on those imaginary
worlds, the folk can tell the time quite accurately without clocks
or poems by simply *watching the motion of the Sun or stars.* . . .
I now tried to imagine a world where the Sun and the stars
moved across the sky—this fancy was a way of passing the hot
hours; but I must confess my imagination failed. I might be a
brilliant musician, but as a poet—in his odd way, poor Wilifern
had been far my superior. I sat in my lookout post in the
thorn-tree, and watched the dazzling sands of the desert. Nothing
moved there. I looked down at Phai, sleeping naked in the
hollow with one arm round Tarsh's waist. Poor princess, I
was supposed to wake her next, some time before the sky turned
white. I am afraid I half nodded to sleep, and then there was
Phai clambering up the tree toward me.

'We are trained, among the Huntresses, to wake at a given
time,' she smiled. 'Get down to sleep now, Orsu.'

It seemed only a few minutes that I slept in the hollow; and
then the others were rousing me, and I saw that the Sun was
already dark gold.

This next night we loped along, very hungry, but with a
certain confidence. And before Fourth Toe Hour, at a rough
guess, we came down from the plateau by a gradual descent into
a vegetated valley; and through trees we saw blue glowing water;
and this was the River Gan. We hailed it like a friend, but Phai
wept to think of the last time we had seen it, that day when she
had consummated her love with Tarsh, and Barundran and Wilifern
had been still with us. At least now we were clearly past that
terrible gorge, and the air in this forested valley was mild and
moist, and we felt that all about us there was life. We had to
walk warily now, of course, because where there is life there is
danger; but also food.

Tarsh became temporarily our leader, and for the next few
hours we were hunter-gatherers. By Sunkindle we were well fed
and feeling much better. Tarsh had stalked and strangled with his
bare hands a young jump-deer; and Phai had shown us swordsmen
how to harvest and start drying part of a spinner's web, whose
cords could serve all sorts of uses.

We spent the next day fairly securely in the great swaying fans of an angel-tree; and then moved off again at Sunquenching, down the river valley. I thought of protesting once more to Kernin about the direction of our travels; but soon gave up the idea, as I knew nothing would move our fanatical Prince now that Khar Durnaran was so close; and besides, Tarsh and Phai were all for pressing on. And so we proceeded for several days, or rather nights; for we were night wanderers now, and night hunters. Travelling by night has a wonderful lightness about it, since gravity is so much lower. Satyrs are quite used to night journeys, but I think it is something even civilised men should practise more, and not merely rowing up rivers to take advantage of the more sluggish flow, as we do on Sinolis in Palur-Nakhtos.

At the end of one of our marches, Kernin said to me: 'Do you know, Orselen, I think that old dream of mine is being fulfilled bit by bit. As we were rising out of Kopa, before poor Wili fell, I suddenly felt that I was re-living something. And then I remembered my dream. There were the ''envious'' creatures below me, in the garden-like crater . . . only they were not insects, after all, they were reptiles, that squad of Sibling Springers. And perhaps they had a certain beauty of their own sort, after all. . . .'

I shuddered. 'I will prefer to forget that sort of beauty,' I said.

By the fifth night of that Ring-month we felt sure that we had left the country of the Springer-folk well behind. This was a broad, lush valley, with no sign of craters; nor for that matter of any two-legged inhabitants. It was full of game, which we hunted successfully, and the only dangerous beasts we met, such as gryphons or large harpies, we managed to scare off without an actual battle. We were no longer naked: Phai had improvised thorn-needles and with small spinner-threads she had sewn us kilts of heart-leaves which were almost handsome. For weapons— she had a throwing-cord weighted with stones, and Tarsh had a fearsome-looking club very like the one pictured for Prah on his conquest of the Elder Gods; and of course Kernin and I had our good steel swords, now dangling by our sides in vegetable sheaths attached to rope belts.

'Why,' Kernin laughed once, 'we are quite presentable; all we want now is for Phai to make us shoulder-vests, and we could appear at the court of any king, as an embassy.'

'All very well,' I said, 'but I do not see how we are to climb *that*.'

'That' was Khar Durnaran, now looming a mere sixty miles away. We could see the base of the mountain even more clearly, a long ridge stretching seemingly for ever to left and right. Pretty soon the River Gan must do something about that mountain

barrier; was it going to end in a lake before it, or tunnel under
that enormous ridge, or fling itself through another and higher
gorge?

'Gorge' seemed to be the answer, for the next night we saw
the valley drawing in once more. Kernin was excited and restless;
he said we should not stop at dawn where we were, but climb the
higher ground on the right. I was dubious about that, but this
was much better watered country than among the Springer-folk,
there was a welcome storm every afternoon, and there was
plenty of cover even on the higher hills. So we climbed out of
the valley onto a rolling country of scattered trees and grass, all
green-gold in the lovely light of early Kindle; and we were going
to find a day-camp site, when suddenly Tarsh said: 'There is a
big, big hollow ahead. Maybe a crater, maybe another valley.'

'If we keep to the right of it,' said Kernin, 'we will come in
thirty miles to the base of Khar Durnaran itself.'

'And what then?' I said. 'Does it look climbable, on this side?
Would that be an easy trot up for people who are barefoot and
half naked?'

He had to admit that it would not. The Last Mountain was
now quite awesome—a huge bulk rising some five miles into the
air and cutting off all further views of the world; with a high
shoulder to our left, and above that the final peak with that
strange whiteness like a collar round its blunt head. The side of
the mountain facing us looked like a sheer precipice.

'Well,' said Kernin, 'perhaps we should investigate Tarsh's
valley. There may be a better way up from there.'

We moved on through the bright freshness of the morning,
tired but unwilling to stop now. Cool breaths of air were blowing
in our faces; perhaps they had come down from the enormous
cliffs of Khar Durnaran. Kernin seemed strangely excited; so did
Tarsh. The satyr lifted his nostrils, and snuffed the air, then
pointed ahead. 'There is good country. I smell good grass, and
sheep, and—perhaps—'

And then, as we descended that slope, we saw a great dark
green hollow before us, a roundish valley some twenty or thirty
miles wide, with blue gleams of water in places between woods
near the middle. It made me think, with a sudden pang, of dear
distant Aelvia—but a much smaller and wilder Aelvia, with no
roads, cities, or other traces of human habitation. At its far end
was a tremendous reddish cliff, obviously the base of the ridge
of Khar Durnaran; with a narrow gap in it, very deep—a gorge
indeed, if that was the gorge of the River Gan! Perhaps this
valley too had once been a crater; but if so, the land must have

risen around it, for it had no wall-mountains except on the far side the huge wall of Khar Durnaran itself. There was no barrier between ourselves and the green valley, only a gentle slope of grass dotted with small heart-leaf trees.

Then—it happened. From around one of the nearby trees there came into view a couple of figures. We saw them before they saw us; and then they started, and stood stock still, gazing at us in amazement, as we at them.

They were satyrs—or rather, a satyr and a satyress. The male had little curly horns, not very much longer than a man's head-peaks; and both of them were reddish-brown of skin, not so dark as Tarsh or Phai. Their body-hair too had a reddish tinge. But the most striking thing about them was not their colouring, but their *feet*. I thought instantly: Poor Barundran is vindicated. Three-toed satyrs. Not only were they three-toed, but their feet were very long, and their heels did not at any time touch the ground: they were hocks rather than heels. And their little toes made a rough pad, almost a hoof, and they went nimbly on these tip-toes like a goat or a sheep.

They were quite naked, and carried no weapons. I thought they were afraid of us, and so perhaps at first they were. But then the male satyr's odd features lit up with an expression of radiant joy.

'Wirawas! Wirawas!' he exclaimed; and then he pulled his female by the hand, and both of them tripped up to us on those dainty goat-feet, and—they worshipped Tarsh!

When they had ceased grovelling, they bounded up again, and looked at the rest of us more doubtfully. The female pointed to the feet of myself and Kernin, and she eyed Phai up and down with amazement; and then jabbered to her mate in some unknown tongue.

'Saya?' said the male dubiously, pointing in an odd fashion, two-handed, at me. 'Saya?' Then he turned back to Tarsh, and beamed again happily. 'Wirawas!'

Suddenly I had an inspiration. 'Could he be saying *Firafax*?'

The satyr danced up and down with joy, nodding vigorously. 'Wirawas! Wirawas!'

'You had better say you *are* Firafax, Tarsh,' Kernin advised with a smile. 'That is the way to some prosperity for us, I think.'

Tarsh grinned, flourished his huge club, and struck an impressive attitude. He beat himself on the chest with his free hand. 'Ay—I am *Wirawas*, come back to you, good people!' he roared. 'I Wirawas! I Wirawas!' Then he leered at us. 'Well, at least I

am a big enough liar. Just to be on the safe side, shall I claim to
be Firafax's son?'

The satyr and the satyress now began to conduct us down the
hillside, crying continually 'Wirewas', and making little leaps of
joy.

'I know what this place is,' said Phai softly, 'it is the Happy
Valley. It is the place we have been seeking, Tarsh, my love.'

She was right: it was.

As we came loping down the slope, the air grew warmer and
moister, and the trees clustered more closely. They were trees of
nearly every kind that we knew in Aelvia; only the occasional
gas-plant was of the Kopan species, with very constricted stems.
There were plenty of animals, too: mostly wild deer and wild
sheep, which fled at our approach. And then, as our satyr-guides
led us on, hallooing, more satyrs emerged from behind trees and
out of bushes, satyrs of both sexes and all ages except the oldest;
and when they saw us, they also shouted 'Wirawas!' and flocked
about us till we were leading a sort of triumphal procession—but
so much pleasanter than a King's triumph after a war, since we
had no chained prisoners with us, nor bloody swords, but all our
faunish followers were unarmed and naked and dancing upon
their little goat-feet. Phai exclaimed with joy at the chubby little
satyr-children: it was so long since she, or any of us, had seen
anything like human children.

Then, after a long, long downhill run—but we did not now feel
tired—we came to the bank of the River Gan, in the centre of the
valley, all clumped about in this place with big queen-trees. No
stopping even here! Our guides led us to a ford, a place set with
big stepping-stones, and here we waded and splashed across,
while the little satyr-children threw themselves into the blue
water on either side of the ford, and swam. Clearly there were no
flying-mouths or other dangerous fish in this valley. The river
glided tranquilly as rivers do in the first hours of morning, with
its waves flattened by the strong sun, but it had not yet picked up
its midday speed of flow.

On the other side of the river, the ground rose abruptly to a
low green hill, under which there was a vast dark cave. Some of
our satyrs had sped ahead, to give news of our approach, so that
when we reached the Sacred Cave, we were met. The Old Ones
emerged from the dark cave-mouth, shaggy, grizzled, goat-footed
males, blowing enormous straight wooden flutes. Well, they
were not exactly flutes, more like Luzelish bassoons—but there
is nothing quite like these instruments in our Shorelands. They
were cut from giant reeds, and painted about the front end in

imitation of huge phalloi; and they had little reeds in the mouthpieces; and they came in several sizes, from the length of an average sword almost to the length of a thrusting-spear. The sounds they made were indescribable: I have never heard so barbaric an uproar, not even from the wild bards of the Luzelish during the last Rindian war. But this was done in our honour, and so we had to stand there while those dreadful horns were blown almost in our ears, and smile with pretended pleasure. Well, pretended on my part; from Tarsh's broad grin I think it possible he actually enjoyed that racket. More probably, he enjoyed what it implied for him.

The 'concert' ceased very abruptly. Then one of the old satyrs, he who had been blowing the longest and most devastating of the phallos-flutes, lowered his instrument and addressed Tarsh:

'Wirawas! Sasa wena, ai wina ni naga niana! Wirawas, u wina be wena Saya?'

I thank the Goddess, I was truly inspired by Her that day. As he spoke, I was making rapid transpositions, guesses. I whispered to Tarsh: 'Shall I be your herald? I think I follow this language.'

'Go ahead,' he grunted. 'It's all gibberish to me.'

I said in a loud voice: 'Wirawas, sasa wena, wina-i ni kuras-lu, Taras! Wina-i be wena-lu—u wina-i Saya.'

It worked—it worked marvellously! They put down their monstrous instruments; and came forward, and adored Tarsh.

'How on earth did you know their lingo?' said Kernin, highly impressed.

'Easy.' I smiled. 'It's simply *decayed Old Shorelandish*!'

'What did they say, and what did you reply?'

'They were welcoming Firafax, Friend of Satyrs, to their valley, and asking if Saeth were not come also. I told them that Firafax had returned to them in the person of his son Tarsh, and said we were his friends; but that this time, Saeth had not come. In this dialect "Saeth" is pronounced "Saya", and "Tarsh"— ironic, isn't it?—has to be "Taras", like in Aelvia.'

'So it is all true,' said Kernin slowly. Then he turned, and looked at the white crown of Khar Durnaran, just visible over the queen-trees. 'Do you remember Wili's prophecy about "standing on white earth"? Well, Saeth and Firafax did it—and we also shall stand on that fellow's head yet!'

The Old Ones now took us into their cave. It was very dark in there, for the satyrs did not know the use of light-berries; but as our eyes grew accustomed to the dimness, we saw that the Old

Ones were proudly pointing out scratched carvings and paintings on the walls. Most of these must have been their own work, or the work of their ancestors; they were rude representations of satyrs and sheep, and in one place an animal with a horn on its forehead—surely a horse. Beside the horse stood a line of more-or-less human figures, distinguishable from the local satyrs by their long flat-planted feet. Two of these were carved much larger than the others.

'Wirawas be Saya,' said the eldest Old One with great awe, bowing low before Tarsh. Then he beckoned to us, and pointed out another carving, high up at the back of the cave, the place of greatest honour.

'I can't make out those figures,' said Kernin.

'Not figures, not pictures,' I said. 'It's writing! Old Shorelandish runes!'

'By Sinis!' exclaimed Kernin. 'You're right!'

The huge runes spelt out just one word:

:S.A.E.T.H.:

The Old Ones confirmed our guess: 'Saya' had carved that with his own hand. So their ancestors had told them.

'Now if only,' I said, 'if only he had had the sense to write a bit more, he might have spared us a dreadful ascent. Merely carving his name, like a burgher on holiday out of Eladon!'

'Saeth was always the one without imagination,' said Kernin smiling. 'If Firafax had thought to write, now. . . . But of course if he had, we wouldn't have been able to believe him. And in a way I am glad. I do not want to be *spared that ascent*, as you put it, Orselen. . . .'

'It will be some time before you can climb that mountain,' said Tarsh. 'Kernin, I suspect I have come into a kingdom here: you see how they worship me? Well, this is the end of *my* Quest, and of Phai's too: we have no intention of going up that hideous grandfather of all hills. If you wish to, *you* may . . . but do not try it yet for a while. You will doubtless need Orselen to accompany you, but for several Rings *I* am going to need Orselen to be my interpreter. You see, I do not speak any kind of Old Shorelandish; yet I must immediately organise my new kingdom.'

Kernin looked outraged. 'Tarsh, you—'

'Call me Taras, damn you! I take back that name. Or King Taras, if you will.'

'Passion of Prah!' Kernin swore. 'Why, you twice-hornless—'

Phai interposed. 'No, Kernu! Do not insult your old companions. Tarshu is quite right: this at last is a good country, and he is going to be its King and I its Queen. We can teach these simple people a few useful arts—such as, to defend themselves if they are ever attacked by Springer-folk or by Men. As for *your* strange ambition, it must take second place to the purposes of life.'

Kernin's hand went automatically to his swordhilt—the habitual gesture of a thwarted Prince; but I placed my hand on my own hilt, and said: 'No, brother! Phai and Taras are in the right. I have never in my life drawn upon *you*, my Prince, but if you will now disturb the peace of King Taras the First of Happy Valley, you will imperil us all; and that I cannot allow. What! already you are making the natives stare. . . .'

His hand dropped from his sword. Swiftly, I continued. 'In any case, it will take us much time to prepare the ascent of that mountain. What, are we going to climb it in our present state, dressed only in kilts of leaves? We will have to catch sheep, make ourselves garments of wool, and boots of leather. We will have to learn more about the mountain from these natives, for instance which path Saeth and Firafax took. All this will require time. And by the way, it will not be all *that* easy to talk to these folk. I have only been able to work out a few sentences; and at that, this garbled Old Shorelandish is not their common tongue. It seems to be a sacred language known only to their Old Ones. So: all this means several Rings of work—whether Taras hinders us or no.'

'I suppose you are right,' said Kernin slowly. Then he laughed, and went down on one knee before Tarsh and Phai. 'Forgive me, your Majesties. I am now your guest, it seems.'

Phai smiled. 'Well, you will not be a "guest" as you were in Rathvia. If you must do this mad thing, Kernu, we will help you—all in good time.'

And so the reign of Taras and Phai, in the Happy Valley, began. Their first regal act was to go that afternoon into the curtaining shade of one of the queen-trees by the river. Phai had not yet found any supply of Maiden-weed, but that did not matter now. The royal couple stayed in their green bower all through the afternoon storm, while the Old Ones, dripping rain from their shaggy fur but none the less joyful, played a hymeneal serenade on their phallos-horns.

Three Rings later, Phai brought forth; and with her Rathvian lore she was immediately able to say that the egg was male. The dynasty of King Taras the First was going to be quickly confirmed with a Prince.

PART FOUR

The Elder Gods

16

Nearly a year we have been away, I said to myself as I viewed that amazing arrangement of gas-plant tubes. Nearly a year; and if we succeed, how many Rings to get back; and still, to save a few days, and risk our necks the worse—he has to resort to *this*!

We were all standing, that late afternoon, on a high lawn of the valley about ten miles from the Wooden Cove, as Taras-and-Phai's new little palace was called. Almost over our heads loomed the dreadful bulk of Khar Durnaran, like a cliff five and a half miles high. A great troop of satyrs panted as they tugged on the ropes, holding our contraption steady. It was not a raft this time, but a bunch of gas-tubes all tightly sealed at the cut stem-ends, and connected by strong spinner-cords to the basket underneath—a basket just big enough to hold two men and their gear. Kernin had convinced himself that this arrangement would give maximum lightness, lift, and stability. And a net of spinner-cords strengthened each tube. We might reach twenty thousand feet without exploding; in which case, we might stop breathing first instead.

'You should go up by Saeth's path,' said King Taras, disapproving, turning from a last consultation with one of his Elders. We all spoke the local satyr language fairly well now, and the natives had pointed out to us the steep path up which, according to their legends, there had once marched Wirawas the Half-Satyr, and Saya the Cloth-Wearer, and all their train of half-satyr followers to the conquest of Gara Sinisa, Mount Truth. Oh yes, there had been followers: they sounded like satyrs from Aelvia, companions of Firafax, bold ones who had climbed, and come down again, and had mostly stayed in the Happy Valley and become ancestors. The more we heard, the more obvious it became that Firafax and Saeth had led a very real expedition, and they surely must have achieved some success up that mountainside; so why couldn't we follow in their footsteps?

Kernin grinned. After all our travels and travails, he was looking almost youthful once more, and his green eyes were bright. Like me, he was well clothed in a grey wool tunic and cloak and sheep-leather boots, and his sword Trier dangled in a leather sheath by his side. We were leaving the other sword as a precious tool for Taras's kingdom; but Kernin needed to keep his so as to puncture a gas-tube or two at a critical moment; also, he was determined to flourish that sword, dedicated as it was to Sinis, upon the summit of Mount Truth. Now he drew Trier, and raised it to his lips, and so saluted King Taras and Queen Phai.

'Your Majesties,' he said, with a green twinkle in his eyes, 'I have no mind to plod up that steep cliff path for ten nights; nor would that be easy, since your satyrs are afraid to accompany us, and so we have not so many porters as Firafax and Saeth. And besides, we are not really sure where that path leads. One at least of those heroes was a notorious liar; who knows if they ever got to the top? As we mean to do.'

'All right, all right,' growled Taras. 'But my satyrs do well to be afraid. They say that fire-demons live at the top of that mountain, and I believe them. I saw what I saw. Well, it is no use, is it? You will do this thing, no matter what we say. But I am sorry about Orselen. *There* is a useful man lost.' He turned to me. 'You will not change your mind? My offer to make you my Chief Bard-Herald is still open.'

'Thank you, Taras,' I said, bowing, 'but you know whose Chief Herald I am. Where he goes, there must I—or be shamed forever among the Bard-Heralds of the Shorelands.'

'I will refrain from saying that they will never know,' said Taras with a cynical grin. And then Phai ran forward, and embraced us both most heartily.

'Old comrades,' she said, 'I partly understand, and partly do not. But go now, with the blessing of all the gods, to your royal hunt for Truth!'

Then we two jumped into that flimsy basket, and I checked that all our stores and gear were aboard. And a minute later the light began to mellow. The Sun was quenching.

'Cast off!' cried Kernin; and the Elders blew their terrible horns, and at the last blast we were released—and drifted smoothly up from the lawn. The last face I saw upturned was Queen Phai's. And then we were too high for faces. We were going up very fast into the grey-green evening sky.

Kernin, holding onto one of the ropes, leaned out of the basket, looking up at the orange-gold sun. The wind blew his hair out like flames: he seemed transfigured. He was praying—

but not petitions, his cries were exultations. 'O holy Sun! O Ring! O stars! O Sinis, Lady of Truth, we come!'

Since Sinis receives the soul at death, I thought this last an ill-omened speech; but we were too far above the Earth now for me to reach my ten fingers into it. I touched my belly, and the next best thing, since the body of Man is also in a sense Earth; and hoped that we would not be troubling Sinis too soon.

Our vessel moved at first somewhat away from the mountain; but Kernin was expecting that; it was the path taken by all his experimental launchings of gas-tubes. Up-and-out, then the high circling back—then the disappearance somewhere near the Lower Summit, that high shoulder of the mountain twenty-two, twenty-three thousand feet up. . . . And now we were following the same dreadful path through the thinning air. We were opposite the Gan Gorge now, that terrible narrow dragon-haunted gap past which the local satyrs never ventured. Great red layered cliffs. . . . We were already level with the canyon's apparent top—nine thousand, ten thousand feet. . . . I seemed to catch sight of a blue-white sparkle beyond, but I could not be sure if my vision was normal. Certainly I felt dazed. Breathing was becoming difficult.

Luckily our ascent turned less steep now. We were swerving back toward the great mountain itself, and the blue-white gleam disappeared behind a dark wall of rock. It was Ringripe night, so now as the Sun died Khar Durnaran showed up obscurely, a great dark-gold bulk in the light of the Ring.

'I told you there'd be light enough,' shouted Kernin, against the whining of the wind.

'Save your breath,' I groaned, 'you'll soon need it.'

He leaned against me, and pressed my shoulder. 'Poor old Orsu. What I've led you into! But Wilifern had *the sight,* and he saw two figures standing on the white earth on top of the mountain—else I would not have brought you.' He looked down over the edge of the basket. 'And now, the utmost of that dream of mine is fulfilled. I am rising up through the air from a valley like a garden indeed—and up a *much higher hill.'*

The view was now awesome; and puzzling. We were so high, and the air was so thin and clear, that we could see probably every country we had traversed in our journey, and maybe even the Pelas Magha; but we could not tell one place from another, or even Earth from Sky. It was all one confusion of light—orange light from the Ring, and blue-white light from rivers or little lakes or the Great Sea . . . or the stars. The Ring was very definitely more circular now than it was in the Shorelands; it looked very beautiful and more like a royal crown than ever, its inner edge utterly sharp, its outer side fading gradually into blackness. And Barundran had surely been right: the inner edge of the Ring looked as if it would fit neatly around the dull red disc of the Night Sun.

Kernin said suddenly: 'I cannot see the World End fires! Look, Pelas Magha makes all one sea of light with Pelas Ranol, the Sky-Sea of the Edge beyond the land of the Centaurs! Orselen, what is this?'

I was so dazed and confused that I could not orient myself properly. The only way I could really tell Earth from Sky was by the mild tug of night gravity; 'down' was toward Earth, 'up' toward those other lights of the Sky. Finally I thought I saw what Kernin meant. Yes, the long low Sky-Sea of Pelas Ranol was now higher in the sky, since through all our Quest we had been travelling steadily away from it; its upper edge was slightly distorted by that greater altitude, but I still recognised it; but now it had no lower limit. Instead, it joined smoothly onto the outline of the nearer shores of Pelas Magha. For that matter, the world had altogether lost that ring of hazy night-light which the Learned Centaurs call the 'horizon'—that raised band which corresponds to the day-haze and separates the view of Earth from the view of Sky. I stared, and shook my head to get rid of the fantastic appearance; but in that I failed.

'All is one,' I said mechanically. I laughed weakly. 'As below, so above.'

'What?' shouted Kernin.

'I was quoting. A couple of proverbs of the Sons of Saeth.'

'We should have listened more to them before we started.'

'That's a nice thing to say *now*,' I told him.

'But what does it *mean*?' said Kernin, looking out at that impossible view.

'Don't ask me. Perhaps it is another triumph of the powers of almighty Refraction. Or else, our sight is disorganised. I feel dazed enough for that to be true.'

But within a few seconds, our sight seemed to be working well enough at short range. The basket was slowly rotating, and now the blaze of the Great (Combined) Sea spun away from us, and we saw ahead a long dark jagged ridge like the spine of a dragon. We were approaching it rapidly. Over to our right the ridge rose to a sharp peak. It seemed we were not going to clear that.

'The Lower Summit!' yelled Kernin. 'Orsu, prepare to disembark! Your rope!'

My heart fluttered, not only with the strain of the altitude. This was probably the most dangerous moment of our whole mad ascent: we had somehow to moor our vessel, then lose buoyancy, and then unload our stores, all on a steep mountainside, buffeted by mighty winds, gasping in thin air, pierced with deadly cold. It occurred to me once more that Kernin was actually insane. That did not matter now. I also was insane to be following him. And if we were not very skilful and very lucky, there would soon be two madmen dead.

Our gas-tubes struck first, against the sheer side of a cliff. I thought for a moment that at least one must be pierced, in which case we would start plunging down that terrible mountain face. We had bounced, and were now rising again. I saw a huge patch of blue-white light revolving before my eyes, and thought wildly that it must be a bush of light-berries. Light-berries, growing at 22,000 feet on Khar Durnaran! But no, it was Pelas Magha a thousand miles away. Then we spun once more, and were confronting the dragon-back of that ridge.

And in the next eyeblink, I saw a tree!

It was one leafless thorn-tree, that hardiest of all woody plants, growing just under the Lower Summit; it probably derived its nourishment from the afternoon storm clouds. Kernin yelled, and I yelled 'Yes, I see' . . . and I waited for the best moment, and flung my noose.

It was an excellent cast, though I say so myself. The noose caught hard on one of the stubby, knobbly branches; and immediately Kernin swung up Trier and pierced the smallest of our gas-tubes. As we began to lose buoyancy, we both took to casting more nooses. The wind on the ridge was terrible; we had several bad failures and moments of extreme peril; but after ten minutes we had our craft securely tied several ways to that tree, and Kernin pierced two more gas-tubes, so that we could really begin to think about disembarking. However, we decided to eat first, while we were still in a stable lodging, so we took out our supply of roast and smoked mutton, and forced some down our jaws. We did not feel hungry, only light-headed and weak, but we were on a night schedule now, and this was supper-time, and it was important to eat regularly.

That done, Kernin pierced all the remaining gas-tubes, and we disembarked. To my great relief, the wind was dropping, and no sooner had we shouldered all our bundles, than the Sun began to glow orange and then flame-gold. That terrible night was over!

'Goodbye, Flier Two!' said Kernin, and stooped and kissed the dried-rush basket of our craft, that had been so neatly plaited for us by Phai and her goat-foot nymph ladies. We left our vessel drooping horribly, snagged in that thorn-tree till perhaps some storm would uproot vessel, tree and all, and hurl them down the mountain. As for ourselves, we now had to set up a secure day-camp—preferably before gravity became too grave in our present burdened condition.

'That way,' said Kernin, pointing Ringback down the farther slope of the ridge. 'A little down, and we'll be out of the wind.' So we plodded on, very cautiously, using the stout hardwood sticks we had prepared for this purpose to steady us. I was glad that we were not actually climbing: my breath was coming in painful gasps. Kernin had reckoned that humans could breathe even at this height, since Saeth almost certainly had done so; but still, I thought, Saeth had accustomed his lungs to this thin air gradually. The surface was rocky, but not slippery, or we would surely have slipped.

We came to a little flat ledge, with what looked like actual patches of soil in places. '*Here,*' said Kernin; and thankfully I dropped my bundle. But *he* did not. He was gazing ahead at the view down the slope, the view of the country beyond Khar Durnaran.

In the clear gold glow of that high dawn, we saw a plain, and in the near middle of the plain an oval of pale blue-white light. I did not at first understand what it was. Then Kernin drew his sword, and pointed with it, and cried out:

'The Keelless Sea! The Keelless Sea!'

I stood beside him then, and stared also. Yes, as the sunlight grew, that rounded patch lost its own light and became plainly revealed as a blue-green sea of ordinary, homely water. Or a great lake. It was only sixty or seventy miles across, with a flat dark green curving shoreline, and no signs of habitation or ships; and beyond, the unknown land rose and rose into a distance of a thousand miles or so, rose indeed seemingly for ever, a tangle of forests and hills and more forests and more hills; and all of that land was country unknown to men or centaurs, country beyond the Known World and the Farthest Mountain and that Keelless Sea which we had thought to be the Edge-Sea of all things.

'The world goes on *for ever*,' Kernin whispered. 'Gormarendran was right. In a way. . . . But there is no Shadow Land, no World Beyond Our Sky. It is all infinite Earth, our same Earth, and as far as you can see, it is surely in full vertical sunlight. Where is the Edge? There is no Edge. *Where is the World's End haze?*'

'I don't know.' My head was swimming. For the Earth seemed

to *rise for ever*, and it was at least *ten degrees high* when it became so blue with distance that you could see no more details, and could not tell Earth from Sky. 'Kernin,' I said, 'I think we are going insane. You'd better drop your bundle at once, and we'll set up our tent and get some sleep. I don't know what this view means, and I don't think I very much care. We are at the end of our strength, and if we are to climb to the top we need to spare ourselves now. If the world still looks the same way tomorrow, then we can begin to think. But now I don't think our views—or our eyesight—are worth a Firafax tale out of the Seventy-Third Universe.'

He laughed then, and said I was right, and we camped. The patches of soil held our hardwood pegs, and we slept comfortably in our tent till about mid-afternoon. Then we woke to find ourselves involved in a miserable grey wet mist.

'Of course!' Kernin waved his arms about in the ghostly stuff as if delighted. 'It's the afternoon storm—at least, it's that in the world down below. We're in a cloud! This ridge is in the cloud layer.'

It was windy while the storm lasted, with damp gusts blowing through every crevice into our sheepskin tent. I feared at any moment the pegs would be torn from the soil, and then. . . . But the gods Gorlun of storm and Nami of earth were merciful, the pegs held, and at last there came a great calm, and the air cleared.

'Come on,' said Kernin. 'Time to march!'

We were on our way before Sunquenching, moving just under the ridge of the Lower Summit. On our left, the Keelless Sea was beginning to glimmer with its own light—and that strange view was altogether unchanged! We felt physically more normal now, not very strong, but not light-headed. The view seemed to be no illusion. Kernin pointed out a trickle of pale light almost under our feet, joining the Sea.

'That's most likely the mouth of the River Gan. We must tell Taras and Phai about that when we get down. If they can conquer Dragon Canyon from the dragons, or go around it, they can build their kingdom a sea-port, and the Keelless Sea will no longer be keelless. Who says exploration is useless to humanity?'

But he soon forgot about utility as our march proceeded. We were climbing very gradually now along the col which joined the Lower Summit to the main mountain; but that night we did not gain more than about five hundred feet, which was a good thing for our unacclimated lungs. And always on our left we had that enigmatic view—which transformed itself quickly from a mys-

tery of the twilight to an equally strange mystery of the night.
The Far Country beyond the Sea marched up until somewhere,
thousands of miles away, it seemed to turn into Sky and known
stars. . . .

After a while I had to tell Kernin not to look at all that, or he
would miss his footing and kill himself. There was very little of
the Ring left on this Sinis' or Last Ring night, so marching was
not easy. We were really in a dilemma: if we marched by day we
could see our way, but gravity would be a terrible handicap.
Kernin should really have waited for New Ring to make his
assault on the mountain—but of course that would have meant
waiting another eleven days, which was too much for his patience.
We had bunches of light-berries tied to our woolen caps, but
they would soon be dying on us.

During this night's march I sometimes heard Kernin muttering
to himself. I caught some words: 'As above, so below . . . as
below, so above. O, good goddess! No getting away from
her. . . .' And then again, brokenly, bitter: 'O, sweet Sinis!' But
when I asked him what was the matter he said: 'Nothing. Let us
go on.' Once he said to me with an abrupt laugh: 'The Ring of
Truth! What do you make of *that* phrase, Orselen? I presume
Wilifern had it from his Saethman brother; indeed, it *does* have a
certain ring of truth to it!'

I said: 'It surely won't be an actual magic ring like in the
Myth-Poems. My guess is, it's a crater. The top of the mountain
looks flat from below, like a crater's rim. And a small crater did
burst there on the morning of your hatching. But that didn't
visibly alter the summit's rim—so there must have been a bigger,
older crater there before.'

'So the Ring of Truth is merely a crater,' he said. Again that
abrupt laugh. 'Well, we shall see.'

We had trouble finding a camp-site at the end of this night's
march; in the end, we had to cross the main ridge and find a
ledge a little way down the Ringward face. Here, when we went
to bed at Kindle, we were looking toward Pelas Magha and the
Shorelands and dear Aelvia. Kernin said nothing about that; but I
could not help wondering what his feelings were. How were
things in the Triple Kingdom? Did they still have peace there?
How were Queen Niamwy and my own dear Hafren? I ought to
have a child by now, that egg should have hatched. . . . I
wondered if Hafren was still faithful to me, or if she had another
man. If so, I could not blame her.

I wondered above all how long it would take us to get back. If
we ever did get back.

The next night's march was harrowing. We were climbing in earnest now, and we made some three thousand feet in a confusion of blackness and stars. We were feeling rather than seeing our way; by the end of the night I was preferring to shut my eyes, the view (such as it was) was so confusing. There seemed to be stars and sky-seas and sky-rivers through a whole hemisphere from zenith nearly to nadir—yes, even *down*. At one time I had the illusion that I was crawling along a flat plain with the stars over my back—whereas in fact at that moment we were going up a near-vertical cliff. Then a little later, for an insane half-hour I wondered if all this 'climb' was a mere illusion; perhaps we only *thought* we survived that first night's gas-vessel ascent, perhaps we died at the thorn-tree, and the world looked strange to us now, it all looked like *sky* because we really were in the sky: we were ghosts. It is held by some Centaur philosophers that ghosts do not know they are dead. Or, as the Sons of Saeth put it, 'As below, no above.'

I did not tell Kernin about this fancy of mine. Instead, when we found a horrible little ledge on the mountain's face, late into Sunkindle, I said: 'We can't go on like this. It can't be more than another 5000 feet—but if we try it in darkness, we shall fall. We must make the final climb *by day*. A long rest now—a whole twenty hours—and then we'll be in the best possible condition.'

He chafed at that. 'I love night climbing. It's the next best thing to night flying. And what about the afternoon storm? I wouldn't want to be caught in high gravity, climbing in *that*.'

'We may be *above* the storm-clouds by now. Why don't we observe, this afternoon?'

He agreed to that; and we were awake by the right time in the afternoon, and when we sensed the light changing, we got up from our sheepskin beds and walked cautiously to the tent's doorway.

At once we both cried out, clutched our eyes, and staggered back into our shelter.

It was like white sky—but much, much worse. For now the *whole world* except the nearby rocks we stood on, the *whole universe* was white sky. As above, so below. . . . From zenith to nadir was dazzling whiteness, almost unbroken, with the Sun shining white in the midst of that whiteness, as blinding and pitiless as a ball of incandescent white-hot steel. The white clouds reflected the white sun from all angles. Only in a few places were there little dark rifts—and those could occur seemingly anywhere, below, or level with our eyes, or upwards as near to

the Sun as we could bear to look. There was just one difference—
the dark areas below or level with our eyes were long streaks,
whereas the high ones were wider, rounder patches. The ones
halfway up were intermediate in shape.

Kernin was the first to recover. He crawled to the doorway,
and gazed outward at the insane spectacle, shading his eyes with
his hands. Then he began to laugh. 'Well, Orsu, we are definitely *above the storms*. What we are seeing is the *tops of
clouds*. And I think I know what those dark patches are. They
are the places where the storms fail. Come, look.' When I joined
him he pointed to one of the nearest low ones. 'That long streak
must be the desert of the Springer-folk, where it never rained
. . . foreshortened, of course. And maybe that further streak, the
slightly wider-looking one, is the lower nomes of Palur and part
of Pelas Magha.'

'Then, what about. . . .' I pointed upwards.

'As below, so above,' he said mockingly.

'What do you mean?' I did not like his expression now: there
seemed to be something dreadful haunting his eyes, a sheer
misery or heartbreak worse than anything I had seen in him even
in Rathvia.

'I am not *absolutely* sure,' he said slowly. 'But—I think
another's day's climb will make all certain.' Under his breath I
think he muttered: 'Dreadfully certain.'

As we watched, the whiteness of the world gradually dissolved,
and we saw once more like a map Gagnar, Rathvia, the Shorelands,
Pelas Magha. Kernin had been quite right about those two dark
rifts, one certainly had been over Gagnar, the other over Palur.
'And there,' said Kernin, pointing thirty degrees up *into the sky*,
'there stands the Middle Plain, home of the Wise Centaurs.'

I did not then understand his meaning; but certainly the sky—or
whatever it was—from the far shore of Pelas Magha to the zenith
looked strange, unlike any sky I had ever observed from the
level of the plains. For we were now above most of the air which
clings like a skin to Earth, and makes sky and distance blue. At
really high angles, I now saw that the sky was not an even blue,
but right up to the height of the Sun it was mottled, wrinkled, in
some places darker, in some places much lighter. And many of
these irregularities seemed to correspond, obscurely, with the
larger star-patches of the night sky. One dark greenish patch, just
appearing over the next cliff we had to climb, was surely in the
place of the Pelas Velnul, the Sea of Angels. But this was not
the night sky, it was the *day* sky.

Then we had Sunquenching. Sunquenching, from twenty-five

thousand feet, meant that the mottled day sky transformed smoothly into stars. Yes, that dark green patch *did* turn into the blue-white Pelas Velnul; and other little green patches became the various medium-sized stars, the Lake of Harpies, the Sea of Hummingbirds, and so on. And the greatest of all the star-seas was the combined Pelas Ranol-Pelas Magha—a blazing blue-white ocean which united Sky and Earth.

'As above, so below; as below, so above,' Kernin chanted sardonically. And he would not explain his speech any further. But during that night, which we spent dozing fitfully in our tent, I heard him muttering such things as 'Refraction! Hah!' or 'Infinite worlds!' Once I heard him say very quietly to himself: 'Better the Seventy-Third Universe of black space.'

Next morning we struck camp at the first light of Kindle. I felt physically almost normal now, and confident of climbing even in full gravity: the long rest had done me good. I besought Kernin to tell me what he thought our strange views meant. He said:

'Work it out for yourself. And when you do, you'll understand, I think, why Saeth buried his discoveries in obscure sayings, and why Firafax preferred lies ever after. O gods, I am heir to the King of Infinite Space—and I find myself bounced in a—a sort of tomb! An egg from which I can never hatch!'

I said: 'If you have found out some great truth—*the* great truth—why go up any further?'

He had been looking wretched, but that brought the green fire to his eyes again. 'Because we are men,' he said.

I think I have not yet made it clear how cold it was on that mountain. I have not made it clear because I cannot—the cold was *indescribably* bitter, especially at night, especially just before Kindle at 25,000 feet and over; and you of Shorelands cannot form any adequate idea of it. It was certainly much colder than our cold hovel-cave in the desert rim of Kopa, and felt colder, even though we were now well clothed, not naked. We had sheepskin groundsheets and wool tunics and cloaks, and a tent—and still we were cold in bed, even lying huddled side by side for warmth. And we were cold even after Sunkindle, when we began that first daytime climb from 25,000 feet.

But we ceased noticing the cold after the first five minutes of this climb, because we had other and worse problems to attend to. This also was/is like nothing in your experience—climbing slopes sometimes of one-in-one, with our tent and bedding on our backs, in full day gravity, at over 25,000 feet. At that height, I do not know how much air was left—we would have needed the subtle wisdom of Barundran to tell us, and Barundran, alas, was now a blessed spirit looking down on our sufferings from his eternal home in the Sun. But there was not much air—perhaps a third of what you enjoy in bright Palur or Agnai or Menkinvia at the level of the Great Sea. With that little air, even when one is acclimatised, one cannot climb very strongly. Our burdens seemed heavy, and our muscles weak. But Kernin's spirit was strong; so up we went, all morning and through the middle of the day.

Well, we climbed, somehow, and the view of the world remained what it had been—namely, incredible—only, the higher we went the more clearly incredible it looked. All that forenoon the sky grew more obviously mottled: it was no longer a sky, but an upside-down map. We were coming up the Ringward face of the Last Mountain, and then about Seventh Finger Hour, just before mid-afternoon at 28,000 feet, we reached the level where the ground turned white. Luckily the slope here was not difficult, or else we would surely have slipped to our deaths. For this white stuff was not chalk, as we had surmised. It was loose and very slippery. Kernin picked some up in his hand, and then swore. 'Passion of Prah! It's so cold, it *burns*!'

I stared at the white stuff on his palm. As I watched it, it ceased to be white; it dissolved away and turned transparent; it became *water*. Kernin flung it down, and wrung his hand. A few more experiments proved the curious, the absolutely novel phenomenon: the white 'soil' about the crown of Khar Durnaran was *solidified water*. A grim thought: since a man's body is largely water, if he were to lie naked on the heights of Khar Durnaran, *he* would turn solid presently like a statue. Luckily, there was not very much of this solid water on the ground, and we were able to scrape much of it away and make camp just before the afternoon storm. Not that we had any storm up here. Instead, the chill air was marvellously still; but the whole universe assumed a blinding whiteness, in which any further climbing would have been terribly dangerous. Once more, we saw some dark streaks and patches—in the same places as yesterday, streaks below and rounder patches above, up to all heights.

Looking up at the high patches, I said: 'Then Heaven also has its deserts.'

Kernin laughed shortly. 'Now, are you seeing it?'

And it was just then, as the afternoon storms dissolved over all the hollow globe of the universe, that I *did* see it. The image of the world's shape kindled within me, bright and irresistible as the white-bright sun of Second Finger Hour.

'Oh goddess!' I cried. 'It cannot be!'

'But it is,' said Kernin relentlessly. 'It all makes sense now, doesn't it? Why the Sun is always vertical, in every land: because it is in the centre of our *hollow Earth*. Why distant lands and distant seas look raised. And the seas of Heaven, such as the Sea of Angels—they are real seas of water, just like Pelas Magha, and if we were to travel far enough *over the Earth*, we would come to them!'

I cried out in fear. 'All that rock and water over our heads—why, it may fall on us!'

'Not likely.' Kernin laughed, half bitter, but also half in wonder at this marvel of natural philosophy. 'Have you forgotten the Sun? Gravity must be *wholly* due to the Sun's rays. Perhaps Barundran was wrong, and Earth is merely inert, the stuff which always resists spirit and light, and fills most of the universe with hard solidity, the mere enemy of bright living forms. You know how light-stuff and dark-stuff seem to repel each other? Well, it is the sun's rays which drive the walls of Earth apart. It must be so.'

He paused, and looked up at the heights of the mountain above us. 'But perhaps there is some water-stuff, some light-seeds mixed in some parts of the Earth. Well, we know there is—hence the bursting out of craters from time to time. And if there is light-stuff mixed in this mountain, maybe it was the blessed Sun which drew up Khar Durnaran to be a witness to the Truth. And there is still more Truth—the Ring of Truth—perhaps to be had on the very top. The Ring of Heaven, for instance—I mean Olari who waxes and wanes every twenty days—that is one of the things I still do not understand; a good reason in itself for climbing on.' He looked at me bitterly. 'But here and now we have the main answers, Orselen. I have been seeking infinite worlds all my life, and now I find they do not exist. This whole universe is finite. There is no escape from it—unless downwards!'

'Why, yes,' I said, misunderstanding his last remark. 'The only escape from life and life's duties is by death. I have always believed that.'

'Well, you are proved right, brother,' said Kernin sardonically. 'No, there surely cannot be any way through. Well, let us now do our duty, such as it is. Let us sleep, and then arise tomorrow, and go on this futile journey—which is still no more futile than *any* journey, since all journeys are equally limited.'

But before we retired to our tent that night we saw something which raised Kernin's spirits a little and improved his mood, since it gave him a new mystery to wonder about. Just after

Quenching, we looked Ringback as far as we could round the shoulder of the mountain—and saw tiny lights moving across the sky like a procession of little stars. It was impossible to say how far away they were—they could have been luminous dragons (if such existed) at a few miles, or they could have been thousands of miles away on the other side of the world. There seemed to be at least three sets of lights, but we did not have time to verify that, for they disappeared quickly round the shoulder of the mountain, apparently ascending.

'Those fire demons!' cried Kernin. 'You remember, the ones Taras and the other satyrs claimed they saw near the top of Khar Durnaran? When was that, ten nights ago?'

'Fifteen,' I said, staring at the black edge of the mountain where the lights had disappeared. 'Yes. The appearance matches. What, do you think we will find a nest of demons on the top?'

'That would be something!' He laughed, and went to bed fairly cheerful. I myself was now getting used to the idea that the world was a hollow sphere. It was, after all, sufficiently large for all practical purposes! If, as Barundran had long since ascertained, 63 miles made the Sun shift one degree, then the whole circuit must be 63 times 400, or 25,200 miles. And it was mostly land; we reckoned the two big oceans and the smaller seas did not cover a quarter of the whole surface. That was an awful lot of universe! And it seemed to have held apart for many thousands of years, so it surely wouldn't fall in and crush us in a hurry. Kernin's gloom about the finiteness of space struck me as metaphysical nonsense. After all, whether the universe is bounded or unbounded in space makes no difference to a man's life. That is bounded in any case . . . to a space of some sixty years.

17

We slept badly that night. At 28,000 feet the cold was still more intense than at 25,000, and I kept wondering if we were going to turn solid. The last time we nodded awake, Kernin said, 'Let's start,' and I did not gainsay him. So we struck camp in the black night only two thousand feet below the summit of Khar Durnaran. Luckily there was almost no wind: it was all bitter cold silence, as in that famous passage of the Creation Myth-Poem, when the gods had just made the universe, but Hinos had not yet given the Word, the command for Time to start moving. We seemed to see the whole hollow universe burning about us, from Pelas Velnul, the Sea of Angels above the black summit, to Pelas

Magha, the Sea of the Shorelands at our backs. I wondered briefly if Niamwy or Hafren were awake in that hour before dawn, looking across more than six hundred miles to the grey-black arrowhead of Khar Durnaran from Eladon. Niamwy, perhaps; but Hafren doubtless slept sound in the arms of some warrior or Bard, and thought no more of me.

We began to climb; and for once I thanked the gods that we were beginning in darkness with its low gravity. There was just enough light reflected by that strange solid water underfoot to enable us to see our way; and all around us burnt the stars, sharper than I had ever seen them: in that thin air I could even pick out the white serpent-threads of rivers in Heaven, for instance one falling into Pelas Velnul—falling upwards, as it seemed, for its mouth was in the lower shore. There was no Ring, for this was the night before Prah's Day.

It was terribly, unbelievably cold—I have never known it worse than in that hour before that dawn; if there had been any wind I am sure we would have fallen. But Kernin was now, somehow, once more in a mood of exultation. 'I—I feel freer at night,' he gasped, 'especially black night, like now, with no Ring. Darkness makes lightness . . . like flying. If only we had some tamable great birds or gryphons to hitch to our rafts . . .' He paused, panting for breath, then continued: '. . . we could travel all about the world in the air. In the black air, by night, guided by the stars. . . .'

'Oh, shut up, shut *up!*' I muttered, choking (Kernin did not hear me). Truly, this was no time for romantic ravings. Every breath was like a swordthrust in the lungs—so cold, so thin. I wondered whether humans really *could* breathe at 30,000 feet. Perhaps Saeth and Firafax had not needed to climb this far; or perhaps the mountain had risen higher since their time—as our sagas indicate that lands and seas move considerably over the centuries with the breathings and the 'poems' of the Earth. Whatever the truth of that, I now started to feel sure I would never make it to the summit.

I must confess that at this point in our climb I began to hate my Prince. And yet I could not help admiring him too. He was climbing slopes of one-in-one which were powdered with slippery solid water, and he was bounding up them as if it were mere pleasure—*and* he was carrying the heavier bundle on his back, the sheepskin cover of our tent.

It's all very well for you, I thought, but you are younger than me. Much younger.

Then the Sun kindled, and things became not better but *worse*.

We could see—oh, yes, we could see *too much* The reflection of the yellow-white sun off that solid water was nearly blinding; and of course the gravity. . . . But it was useless to suggest a halt; I saw that nothing would stop Kernin short of the summit this day. Except his death. Not *my* death: if I had fallen, I am sure he would have shrugged, and gone on. As he went on after Barundran, after Wilifern. . . . And then the second figure with him on the summit would not be mine. Perhaps it would be a fire-demon; or the goddess Sinis, winged, stern, and beautiful, his only real love.

Toward midday the slopes grew steeper, and the climb directly up the Ringward face became impossible. 'Over to the right,' gasped Kernin, waving his stick. We found a sort of path, and pressed on, climbing much less up now, but making more distance, edging our way slowly up the wall of the ultimate crater which tops Khar Durnaran.

White sky—the afternoon storm over all the universe—caught us still on the move, still under the lip of the crater; but Kernin would not even pause. 'Another two hundred feet, and we're there,' he gasped.

I never want to climb another 200 feet like those. Too much light is just as bad as no light at all—in fact worse, for the brightness assaults your brain in a way darkness does not. My eyes were beginning to hurt horribly. Whiteness from the clouds, from Earth, from Sky, from Earth-Sky, from the solid water. . . . Surely the gods must have saved our lives in spite of our madness; they say that the great Mother admires boldness in her boys. And at one time I thought I saw a great winged figure, all white and grey, hovering over Kernin's shoulder. That may have been truly Sinis, goddess of Truth and Death; or it may have been only a trick of the cloud-pattern half-way across the universe.

And then suddenly, it was all over. The blinding whiteness greyed and shredded, the storms were past. And a few minutes later, in the last hour of evening, we topped the last rise, and stood on the crest of Khar Durnaran. And the Ring of Truth lay before us, on Prah's Evening of the last Ring-month of the year 631, conquered.

Kernin laughed for joy, and drew his sword Trier, and flourished it in token of victory. And I hugged my brother about the waist, speechless.

We were so full of our achievement that it was a few seconds before we really saw them.

The summit crater of Khar Durnaran is a round plateau half a mile in diameter; the wall of the crater is missing on part of the

far side, the side of the Keelless Sea. Perhaps that gap was
blown out by the eruption at Kernin's hatching; certainly there is
a small depression near that end, a little crater within the big
one. Anyhow, the main crater is half protected from bitter
winds, it is a hidden little plain with no solid water in it, 30,000
feet above the world; and as we stood on the highest point of the
crater and looked down, we saw that the circular plain was
occupied. Inhabited.

But not by men.

They stood in groups near the centre and the depression
toward the far end, but also much nearer to us in twos and threes
around the perimeter, where they were busying themselves with
what looked like piles of sunwood—piles such as Aelvian peasants arrange at Mid-Ring for celebratory bonfires. There was
indeed a peaceful, almost homely air to these people's activities.
But the people themselves were winged, gigantic harpies. Harpies a little taller than men, wearing what looked very much like
short swords in slim scabbards at their waist-belts.

In the far-side depression they seemed to have built some kind
of hut. Also, near the centre they were milling about certain
large vehicles or vessels, which faintly resembled our air-rafts,
but were much slimmer, with gracefully curving lines. Hitched
to these sled-like vessels were enormous, fiery-feathered gryphons—gryphons of some unknown species bigger than horses.

I seized Kernin by the arm, thinking to drag him back from
the crater; but it was too late. Those harpy-folk had marvellously
keen eyesight, and already they had seen us. They raised a
cry—but a cry nothing like a harpy's screech. It was melodious,
tinkling, articulate.

Kernin stood in place, his sword Trier still raised, his eyes
aglow. 'The Elder Gods return!' he breathed; and then shook his
head, and laughed. 'But they look solid. Harpy-people? Why
not? If there are clever Springers, why not clever harpies? But
they deserve a better name—how beautiful they look! Are these
Tarsh's Fire-demons? No, surely—bright *angels*!'

He stood his ground, and therefore I had to stand mine, while
half a dozen of these Elder Gods or Angels came fluttering up to
us from the crater plain. They were good fliers, even in that thin
air. And of course they were a rational species, to judge from all
their gear—and no mere animals would have done what they
clearly had done, flown up to the crown of Khar Durnaran—
from what unknown, distant country?

Once they had alighted on the crater wall a few yards before
us, we saw every detail of them clearly enough in the golden

light of the first few minutes of Quenching. They really were very like large harpies. Like harpies they had three forward-pointing toes on the feet, and three long fingers opposed to a short thumb. But their fingers ended in delicate nails, not claws. All their exposed flesh on feet, hands, and faces was pale blue; their great slanting eyes were golden; their lips and head-crests flame-gold; and their wing and tail feathers white but tipped with a delicate rose colour. They were really very handsome bird-people. In spite of the great cold, they wore nothing but swords and sword-belts; their feathers must have been a marvellous covering. It was also obvious that their lungs were more efficient than ours, for they seemed to be moving with ease, and not panting.

What endeared them to me at once was this, that they did not attack us. They did not even draw their little swords, though Kernin still held Trier unsheathed. The leading Angel, a very pale-blue-faced person with a three-peaked head-crest of orange feathers, said to us in a bell-like voice—rather like a song-phoenix, if you can imagine a song-phoenix talking—

'Kobotar avinen, domeno dohanon; avo-ey!' And he spread his blue hands in a gesture which looked reassuring.

Kernin smiled and bowed and sheathed his sword; and then we were involved in a sort of helpless parley. For neither we nor the Angels knew a word of the other party's language. But good will makes up for a lot of difficulty. For we too soon made them see that we were no threat to them; they gazed with astonishment over the outer edge of the crater wall, looking down the terrible Ringward face of Khar Durnaran. We had come up *that*? —Evidently that was what the angels' chief was saying; and we were not winged creatures. Yes, said Kernin, nodding vigorously, we two alone, on our feet. . . .

This news filled the angels with the utmost admiration for us. They immediately invited us down into their stronghold, the crater, and we were very glad to go with them. We had indeed no choice: dark night was coming on apace, and we needed to camp, and the angels seemed well settled in here. The encircling walls of that little crater made me think for a moment of infernal Kopa; but the Angels proved to be a much pleasanter species than the Springers.

For one thing, they immediately saw to our comfort—took our bundles from us, warmed us at a bonfire in front of their hut, and gave us to eat. It was all vegetarian fare—nuts, cakes, and so forth—but a welcome change after so many days of smoked mutton. And there was one long brown berry as big as a man's thumb which had a startling effect. When we bit through its rind, it released thick air—the trick after that was not to swallow, but to breathe. The angels did not use this air-berry much themselves, but they gave it largely to their gryphon-steeds to help their performance at high altitudes.

Now that we were fed, warm and comfortable, we were able to take in another point of the Angels' nobility. Like us, they were engaged upon some sort of *exploit*. This was not a town, this exalted crater, but a temporary camp. It was frustrating that we could not speak to them, but we could get many ideas just by looking; and they were glad to show us everything, under the direction of the triple-crested angel who had first accosted us. His name seemed to be 'Daelir', and his rank one of importance.

In the first place, Daelir made signs that they had not flown up to this crater on their own wings. Those sled-like vehicles were true air-chariots. They had fantastic upper-works, picked out in many colours of paint like royal galleys, but their bulwarks swelled out in a manner we understood. Gas-plants. . . . On the other hand, there was not quite enough gas in those bulwarks to make the chariotships rise, not even at night. They were slightly *heavier than air*, at least with a crew on board. Daelir showed us by gestures that, when the huge tame gryphons flew up and pulled, the vessels were so shaped that they would plane neatly through the air—and rise so, and move easily. Kernin showed that he found this incredible; whereupon Daelir laughed (his laugh was like a tinkle of small bells); and proceeded to demonstrate. He jumped into a small air-boat, and shook the harness, and the team of four gryphons leaped up and forward— and within eyeblinks, they were carrying him and his little chariot on a triumphal tour above and round the crater.

When Daelir landed again and jumped to the crater floor a few yards from us, Kernin made him a profound bow. 'I see you have truly mastered the art of air travel, O ingenious winged men. What I and my friends were groping towards with our clumsy rafts, these last few years, I see that you accomplished a great many years ago.'

Daelir and his henchmen seemed pleased at our reactions. They certainly went out of their way to entertain us. They had begun to light a great many of those bonfires round the perimeter of the crater, and they took us now to warm ourselves again at one of these. The sunwood blazed up, giving a glorious yellow-white glow, and as much heat as we needed. I might add that the angels also used light-berries, especially tucking some into the harness of their gryphons and tying some to various points on their air-chariots; so with one thing and another, we now had a lot of light in that crater. And from time to time we chewed air-berries, and in spite of our long climb felt invigorated rather than tired. We certainly did not want to go to sleep now. It was like being guests at some fantastic feast among the gods. And if I had been just a little more superstitious, I think I would have believed our winged friends to be the Elder Gods indeed. But I doubt if even Prah could have conquered them, at least before his apotheosis.

And now Kernin was burning with curiosity. He recalled those tales of flying chariots in Thulor a few years back. That surely pointed to our new winged friends. Now, where exactly had the Angels come from?

Daelir made a curious circling motion with his slim blue arm, pointing to the sky. The beginning of his sweep seemed to be the lower edge of Pelas Velnul. What, could it be that that name, 'Sea of Angels', represented some old true knowledge? We had had our star-names from the Menkinvians, who had them in the first place from the Centaurs. But if Daelir was saying what he seemed to be saying, then the Angels had flown in their air-chariots a whole third of the way round the universe—but not via Thulor at all, rather the other way, across the unknown Far Lands and the Keelless Sea. . . .

And then we heard loud musical cries from the far lip of the crater, the edge we had scaled, the one facing the Shorelands. A couple of angels stationed there were fluttering from their posts, and everywhere their friends were now uttering cries of joy. All their faces were turned to that high point of the crater wall.

And then, about five minutes later, there flew over the edge three large gryphon ships, ablaze with light-berries on harness, stern-post and prow. The newcomers circled low, and landed.

And Daelir half flew, half ran to meet them. The leader of the newcomers jumped down and embraced him. Then swarms of angels who had been stationed in the crater leapt aboard, and embraced all the newly-arrived crews. It was all a tremendous flutter, and a symphony of bell-like voices crying out for joy.

Kernin laughed. 'If this is how they always welcome their friends, they must be a most loving people, indeed!' Then he started, and he looked at me suddenly with a kind of awe. 'Why, Orselen: these ones flew in *from the direction of the Shorelands*!'

He was right, of course. And another thing: the newly-arrived bird-folk were mostly darker of skin than their 'hosts', the welcomers. The leader of the new arrivals had a dark blue-green face, and an almost purple single-peaked head-crest. Daelir was now speaking to this one, pointing us out.

The dark leader paced towards us, then stopped, facing us. And bowed—exactly in the fashion of Palur, left arm behind, right arm advanced! It was utterly strange, uncanny, to see a giant handibird bow so. And then that Angel spoke.

'I am Manur of Taluz, noble men-travellers. Do I guess right, am I addressing the Prince of Aelvia and his faithful Bard-Herald?'

We were both speechless for a moment. Those words: they were bell-like, in a voice like a song-bird's, but the syllables were very precise Modern-Classical Shorelandish, with just a tinge of Menkinvian vowels. I was reminded slightly of poor Barundran's speech. Then I remembered my duty.

'I am the Herald,' I said, 'and this is Prince Kernin. Have you flown here from Aelvia, noble Angel?'

'The name of our Kind is Flirhan, in the plural Flirhanar,' said Munar. 'Yes, I have flown from Aelvia, and from many other places besides. But if you will excuse me, noble humans, for a few moments—there is an urgent matter I must attend to, a message to our Ancients. After that, I will be at your service.'

We were left staring at each other, full of surmise; and then our attention was attracted by what the Angels—the Flirhanar—were doing. Munar had got up on the high prow of a chariot-ship in the middle of the crater, and from there was directing operations. All the sunwood bonfires were now lit. At Munar's signals with a waved sword, the angels at each bonfire were covering their fire with a huge blanket and then disclosing it again. Every movement was quite precise, and timed. So many eyeblinks closed, then smartly opened. Some closures were twice as long as others. And then Munar made a sweeping sword-cut, and the interruptions of the bonfire lights stopped.

Then every face was turned upward to one direction, high in the sky. And a yellow-white star, a star the colour of a sunwood flame, near the lower edge of the Sea of Angels, began to wink; long winks and short winks.

'They are replying,' cried Kernin. 'O mighty gods! Do you see it, Orselen—*we* are now standing in a Winking Star!'

'Yes,' I said, 'as above, so below. I wonder what message Munar has sent?'

One of the dark-faced newcomers was standing close beside us. He turned, and said in good precise Shorelandish:

'Munar has just told the Ancients of Amatu: "The circle is closed between the Ring and the Throat." And the Ancients of

Amatu have replied: "Munar of Taluz is henceforth surnamed Munar the Circumnavigator." '

'Circum—' I began. The Flirhan had used an old classical word for 'one who sails all round the Great Sea.'

'I mean,' said the Flirhan, 'that our two expeditions have now met, in circling the world in opposite directions. This high mountain was chosen, many Rings back, as being a good and likely spot for our two forces to meet. And when we fly on with Munar to Amatu, we will be the first of our kind to put an airish girdle round the hollow world.'

Then Manur stood again before us in person. Kernin went down on one knee before the Angel. 'Sir, I must hail you as the greatest—'

Munar smiled—yes, Flirhanar *can* smile, though on those pointed, flame-like lips the effect is strange. 'Call me not Sir, noble Prince; "Madam" or "Lady" would be more correct in your tongue, for I am a female.'

We stared at the dark-faced Circumnavigator. A female? Well, certainly, why not; there was no way of telling.

'Daelir is a Sir, I am a Lady,' said Munar, 'not that it matters, among our kind. Daelir and I are also of different Flirhan Provinces, and different colour-races, and that matters not either. Little differences of body form, or even big ones, should not make enmities between Knowing Peoples—that is the message we have been taking from the Ancients of Amatu right through the lands of the Centaurs, and now more recently of Men. A new age is beginning for the world, O Prince of Aelvia; an age in which the two sides of Earth, and the two great Oceans, will know each other. Air-chariots will fly from Amatu to Kintobara and Palur and Eladon—'

'Excuse my rudeness, Lady,' said Kernin, 'but have you passed Palur and Eladon in your travels?'

'Indeed, yes. And in those lands there was much anxiety for your safety, Prince. Much wonder also, at your remarkable and daring attempt on this far and high mountain. I promised Queen Niamwy that I would look out for you, and aid you if I could. . . .'

'Queen Niamwy—is she well?' cried Kernin.

'Very well, and her three children also,' smiled Munar.

'You don't,' I said, 'happen to know a lady of the Queen's court—the lady Hafren?'

'Oh yes.' The dark face, the flame-coloured lips smiled. 'Hafren and her son Omren are also well. She told me to tell you, Orselen—if you hurry back, she will forgive you for so long neglecting her.'

I might have questioned Munar further about the state of the Triple Kingdom, but now Kernin seized upon our strange messenger's words, as hungrily as a hunting sphinx on its prey. 'You have circled the world—by the direction of the Ring?'

'Yes,' said Munar, smiling enigmatically. 'By the Ring, by Thulor, by Kintobara, Kherindorna, Menkinvia, and your Shorelands. This last part of our journey took us ten Rings—'

'What *is* the Ring?' cried Kernin. 'We learnt the hollow-globe shape of the universe as we climbed the height of this mountain. But if Heaven and Earth are all one hollow sphere, the Ring must be a *country*. A circular country which shines orange during ten nights! Did you pass by that marvel?'

'We did more—we passed through it. Yes, it is a country, not too different from many others; except that it is hot from double daylight, and the afternoon storms there are violent indeed. In the Bright Nights of that land the other Sun, the little one, shines orange from the Throat during the Little Sun's day, which is as long as ten of our days. . . .'

'Pardon, Lady,' said Kernin, 'but I do not understand this at all. What is the Throat? What is the Little Sun?'

'The Throat,' said Munar, 'is what you call the Flickerfly Star. In your country it is very dim; it is brighter among the Centaurs, who are more opposite to it; and at the Ring country, *directly* opposite, it is a real blaze of orange light, a point as bright as our Sun when that is only a few minutes into Quenching. Now we Flirhanar call Flickerfly the Throat with good reason, for many of us have peered into that great hole. Do you know, Prince, that some three thousand years ago there was no Throat, and consequently no Ring? All days were the same, all nights Ringless. . . .'

'Yes, my old Tutor told me. Wait a moment, Lady.' Kernin had seized the chance of a brief natural pause to break into Munar's lecture; I could see that a fire of some new and terrible excitement was blazing in his eyes. 'You say the Throat, opposite the Ring, is a great *hole*. What, a hole *through the Earth*? Sweet Sinis, may it be so, that Earth has an outer side, that we may hatch out of this egg into freedom—'

'What are you saying?' Munar's golden slanting eyes narrowed. 'Is this some Aelvian minstrel's tale, some absurd fiction? The Earth has no "outer side", how could it? It is like a tomb, not an egg. We Flirhanar know that for certain.'

Kernin seemed to slump, to shrink. For the first time that night he looked tired. 'I—I hoped,' he murmured. 'I was indeed thinking of a tale once told me by an old friend. But he is dead; alas, poor Wilifern. Go on, Lady.'

'As I was saying,' Munar resumed, 'the Throat did not always exist. When it did burst open, it was a blessing of God, though at the time it did not seem so to those who caused it. Know then, O Prince, that in those Ringless days there were no civilised peoples anywhere in the round of Earth; even we Flirhanar lived little better than the birds, without calculation of times or names for directions. Only in one place on the hollow globe there dwelt a race of *kobotar*—Men, you might call them, or satyrs—who greatly coveted gold and precious stones, the way some birds collect pretty bright trifles; and although these men were ignorant barbarians, they became miners. Their country was rich in precious ores, and they drove their shafts into it, deep, deep. . . .' She paused; but this time Kernin did not interrupt.

'Now I must tell you our whole philosophy of the Universe. Most of the Universe, we think, is dark stuff, solid matter; but light stuff, sun-stuff, has a natural enmity with such, a love for itself, and from time to time it collects in little holes—which, if they be small, we call craters, when they explode—or if they be great, we call them Suns. The Suns have so much force of light that they push away the dark stuff from them, and so clear spherical spaces—worlds, Earths. These worlds would be uninhabitable but for one thing. There is a rhythm in all light-stuff, as in all life: it burns more brightly at certain intervals, depending on the precise species or compound of the stuff, and above all the amount. In any given compound, the bigger the amount, the greater the frequency and amplitude of variation. Little lightberries have just a tiny slow flicker, barely perceptible; with the bigger species you see it more; similarly with flickerflies. Suns have the greatest flicker of all, and we call that Day and Night.'

'You keep on mentioning Suns,' I protested. 'But surely there is only one Sun.' I pointed up to the dull red disc in the zenith. 'That one: in the centre of the world.'

'There are certainly *two* Suns,' said Munar, 'and probably very many, infinitely many, scattered at random through the fullness of Infinite Rock; and each sun clears a world-hollow with its rays. There must equally be an infinity of worlds. . . .'

'Infinite worlds!' Kernin started: in the now-dying flames of the nearby bonfire I saw his eyes flash again with renewed vigour and hope. 'Infinite worlds, under our feet . . . !'

'But most will be at enormous distances.' Munar's strange dark face seemed sad. 'And nearly all, except now ours, will be worlds of utter barbarism, without distinguishable Quarters, and

with every night and day the same—so with no stimulus to
thought or counting—as was our case till the explosion of the
Throat, till the shining forth of the Ring. Those worlds are
unreachable, and surely not worth reaching. We are the one
privileged Hollow World, O Prince; because it happened, by
chance or the will of God, that another Hollow World lay or had
approached close to ours. *Very* close at one point, though the
Mad Miners knew it not . . . until the rock gave way under their
feet, and the gaping hole of the Throat opened three thousand
years ago, and the light of the orange Little Sun shone out of
the Little World through the opening, and cast the appearance of
the Ring on the opposite side of our world. Look, it is like this.'
And Munar drew with the point of her sword a diagram-map in
the soil near the bonfire:

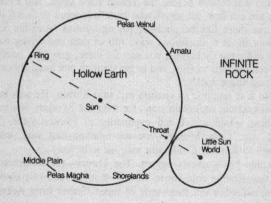

'The black centre of the Ring,' said Munar, 'is simply the
shadow of our darkened Sun at night; the outer edge of the Ring
fades away as the Little Sun is no longer visible through the
Throat. The Little Sun is smaller and cooler than our sun, and
never brighter in colour than orange; and so it has a longer
rhythm: its day-and-night are twenty-and-one-tenth times longer
than ours: hence the cycle of the Sky-Ring.'

Kernin was joyful again. 'Then there *is* at least *one* other
Earth, and we *can reach it*—through this hole which we call
Flickerfly, and you the Throat. A world whose days are twenty
days long, and whose nights are twenty nights! Have *you* peered
into that world, Lady Munar?'

'Yes,' said the Angel. She looked at Daelir, her paler friend, who had drawn near. The night was growing very cold, and the bonfires were going out, and the Flirhanar were covering their gryphon-steeds with something very like horse-blankets, and were at last putting on cloaks themselves. I shivered, and hoped that Kernin would not keep us here talking cosmology indefinitely, and I looked longingly at that hut in the smaller hollow. But Flirhanar do resist cold well, and Munar seemed as indefatigable as my Prince. She too, after an epic journey, seemed willing to talk the whole night through, on a mountain at 30,000 feet. She continued:

'Sir Prince, I have peered into that Other Earth, and Daelir has even ventured into it. It is a small world, only one quarter the size of ours, and colder, and more barren, and in its long nights water solidifies *everywhere*, even on the lowest plains. It had no rational inhabitants before the Throat burst open, and even now there are but few, all satyrs who have wandered or fallen into it, and live there like brigands or roving hunters. And the Throat, the way in, is a dangerous way, full of dust and flying rocks—those make the flickerings you see; for there, gravity is neutralised between the two worlds, and to get through one must fly or float, avoiding those rocks.'

'But it *is* possible to venture *in*,' said Kernin. He was looking far beyond our mountain now, far over the Keelless Sea into the trackless waste which led eventually to Flickerfly-the-Throat. 'And you, Lady Munar—you are heading that way, on your voyage to Amatu? *Could you take me with you?*'

At this I was utterly aghast. The Throat—the dangerous way into that strange cold Little World—it must surely lie *thousands* of miles further on; thousands of miles further from Aelvia and our families.

'It is some 2500 miles from here,' said Munar, 'and as I say, Prince, when you see it, it is but a cold desolation. But yes, I could take you there. You are a great adventurer—I know of none greater among wingless peoples, no, not in all our records. It would be a great delight for me to take you in my aerial chariot to the Throat of the Little World, or even beyond, to beautiful Amatu itself, the place of the Ancients, and the pleasant shores of our Sea of Angels, and the tree-tower homes of the Flirhanar. Our land of the three united provinces of the Knowing Flighted Ones, that would surely delight such a venturer as you. But there is one matter which I have not yet mentioned. You did not give me time to mention it, you were so concerned with the shape of the universe. I have more messages for you, O King of Infinite Space, from your people in the Shorelands.'

'King of Infinite Space!' Kernin laughed sourly. 'That is my father's title, not mine. And I know now what a mockery it is. But why do you, who are so courtly, and clearly so well versed in our usages—why do you give me a title that is not yet mine?'

'But it is yours, now.' Suddenly Munar's dark face in the dying firelight looked ominous, terrible. She seemed a messenger from a world beyond life. There is a statue of Ganthis, the dark aspect of Death, in her temple at Nakhtos which also has slanting yellow eyes; and Munar's face now reminded me of that one. 'Lord Kernin: I have called you till now Prince, because you are indeed still Prince of Aelvia; but you are also, by the death of King Prahelek three Rings past, Lord of the Four Quarters, King of Palur. And the Queen Mother, Kandiri of Nakhtos, has given me a message for you, a private message which I am yet to deliver. It is this: "Let Omren's son and his brother return at once and succour the Kingdom, or all is lost." '

Now, I will not explain Queen Kandiri's phrases here in full: reason of state forbids, and will do, I think, all my lifetime. But it was well known to Queen Kandiri why Kernin and I called each other 'brother'. It had also been arranged between us two and the Queen of Nakhtos that this form of words should be used as a kind of signet-ring—a Ring of Truth, if you will—to authenticate important messages of great urgency. And so, when we heard those words now, in the dead of night on the summit of Khar Durnaran from the lips of that dark angel—well, it was like a sword piercing both our hearts.

And—still Kernin rebelled! 'My mother calls me back! Why? What is wrong with the Kingdom, that I cannot leave it a little longer?'

'It would not be just a *little* longer, Prince-and-King, if you came with me,' said Munar. 'We have staging posts from here all the way to Amatu, but even so, it would take many Rings. You ask about the state of your Kingdom? I will tell you. There is a new young King of Rindos, and he has denounced the great Truce. He has called in the Luzelish barbarians, and given his sister in marriage to the High Chief of that horde. Agnai has joined him in alliance also. By all indications, those allies are about to launch a great war against the River Kingdoms. The young King of Rindos has sworn to put Palur to a greater and bloodier sack than Suoran, and the King of Agnai has sworn to lead Queen Niamwy of Aelvia in chains in his triumph. Judge now, O Prince and King, where your duty lies. Indeed, we

Flirhanar hate all war; and I would be delighted to have you as my fellow-traveller to the Throat and Amatu; but it is possible that you may now think differently.'

I started forward. 'Now, Kernin, there cannot be any question. . . .'

'I won't!' shouted Kernin. 'These women—they are always trying to stop me! But now, no! I won't go back!'

I said: 'Kernin; brother; if you go not back now, you are shamed for ever. By Sinis whom you worship, the Trier of hearts—will you see your wife led captive, and your children slaves, and the shorelands under the yoke of the Luzelish—just to gratify your thirst for new worlds?'

He was standing with one shoulder toward the dying fire; the Flirhanar were roving nearby with little sprigs of light-berries tucked into their headcrests; Munar had just accepted one from Daelir. There was just enough light, with those artificial ones and the steely stars and the dead Sun for me to see Kernin's face. I was standing nearly between him and Munar now, both literally and otherwise. His hand hovered over his sword-hilt . . . and then I think he remembered the name of his sword, which I had just invoked—and his hand dropped to his side. And I saw the flame quench in his eyes like a dying Sun; and his shoulders drooped, and he shrank back from me.

'You caught me once before,' he whispered, so softly that only I heard him. Yes, he had heard that tale; or remembered the event, for he had a keen memory, going right back to his hatchling days.

Then he stepped sideways, and turned from me to the wing-folk leaders, and laughed. A bitter laugh, and short.

'My princeling days are over, it seems. I have found the Ring of Truth, and it is a hollow thing, and at the end of every journey a man finds himself hemmed in by the limited Earth. She is a jealous Goddess. Well, Munar, I cannot go with you on your great journey. If any of you winged ones could help me on a shorter one, namely back to Aelvia, I would be very grateful.'

'I had thought of that,' said Munar. 'Daelir and his crews have had a more tedious journey than my people, over dull barbaric wilds, and then they have had a long wait on this cold mountain-top. There is no reason now why one or two shiploads of them should not fly on to Aelvia, to see the beautiful Shorelands. And there is no reason why they could not take two Men with them. You can be back in Aelvia in five or six nights, O King.'

'I thank you heartily, and will accept your offer,' said Kernin.

I caught him about the shoulders, and kissed him on the cheek.

'Brother,' I said, 'you are now a King indeed.'

18

There remains but a little to tell now. The Epic of Suoran ends with the funeral games for the dead hero Sakanek; thus my stumbling prose history has at least a slightly happier epilogue.

We glided down from Khar Durnaran at Second Finger Hour the next morning after our eventful night; and spent that day among the astonished satyrs of the Happy Valley, and with King Taras and Queen Phai. We told them about our discoveries; and the cosmic ones did not disturb the King or Queen at all. But Taras was overjoyed to hear that the Keelless Sea was so near, with a waste empire on its shores for the taking. He has since driven the cliff-dragons altogether out of Dragon Canyon, and has built a seaport at the mouth of the Gan; and his three-toed satyrs are becoming a people of consequence and even politeness; but their faces are set the other way from the Shorelands, they are making journeys out into the wild toward Flickerfly-the-Throat. Taras' son Katiras will be a great King of satyrs; perhaps in some far country.

Our journey home from the Valley was easy and uneventful, as we knew the land well, and could point out to Daelir the safest places for day-camps. Our voyage might have been quicker, but that Daelin had given his fresh gryphons to Munar in exchange for her tired ones, and therefore we made only little journeys for the first few nights, resting our steeds well and letting them browse on their favourite loafnuts in the lush Gan valley. But we mended our pace later. Thus, we did not set foot on land at all in Rathvia, but flew over it in the course of one night. And then—homecoming, early on New Year's morning of the Year 632, with our gryphon-chariots landing on the meads between Haf and Sinel just outside Eladon.

We caused less stir, at first sight, than I and Kernin had expected. But then, the Flirhanar had already visited Aelvia; and moreover, the country was in a warlike turmoil anyway, with the people's minds on other matters. The real news for Aelvia that day was not one more visit of the winged folk, but the return of their Prince.

Niamwy met him in that golden dawn, at the head of a

cavalcade, for she was just riding out from her capital to the war in the lower lands. She seemed older; but then, so did Kernin. When she saw him standing there on the meadow in front of the winged folk, she leapt from her horse; and their gladness as they embraced was a glorious thing to see.

And then another lady was jumping from her horse, too. Hafren had a set of tenpipes slung around her shoulders; she was in her rough battlegear, but I am happy to say she was somewhat more covered than the first time I ever set eye on her. She tossed her locks that glinted redly in the light of that Kindling sun, and laughed.

'Well, Bard, I see you came quick enough in answer to my message. Flying, look you! As it happens, I have no lover this Ring; my last Earl cast me off for a Countess, and my last knight I discarded myself; so, if you care to sue for my favours again. . . .'

I embraced her; and then she said: 'At least, I have used Maiden-weed ever since your departure. Our little son is my only one; and he is well; but he is with the nymph-nurses back at the Palace, and I think this war will not wait.'

No, the war could not wait: Kernin was in saddle already, on a great yellow horse beside the Queen, and flourishing Trier in the direction of Agnai; and I am afraid we were able to afford poor Daelir and his crews but scant hospitality for the most part of that day. Still, they were more mobile than the army of Aelvia, and we gave them better cheer that night at Dythlorn, the Shire town near the Aelvian Wall. Dythlorn is dear in my memory now, for in the Earl's little palace there we celebrated our homecoming indeed, Kernin with Niamwy, I with Hafren. 'Been away a year and a day, just like the heroes of the lying minstrel tales,' Hafren laughed, when we were at last in our bedchamber, 'but let it happen never again, Orsu, never again.'

I agreed fervently. 'The best Ring of Truth is here, my love, in your encircling arms.'

Well, it is not my purpose to relate the Last Rindian War. It was a bitter struggle, lasting all of ten Rings; but in the end we had the victory on every front, and after that we made a peace indeed. The young King of Rindos was killed, and then we made a pact with the Luzelish, and allowed them to settle on certain conditions in Rindian territory, with their new capital at Luvilion, and they are now in a fair way to become a civilised people. As for Agnai, we could certainly have taken that city; but Kernin would not. He had already insulted their little Princess once, he said, if unintentionally; and besides, he had no wish to be an Emperor of all the Shorelands.

'Being a King is bad enough,' he remarked ruefully.

And indeed, I think he is not yet truly reconciled to being a King. He has made his mother Kandiri his regent in Palur as well as Nakhtos, and spends most of his time in dear cool Aelvia—where he prefers to be called Prince. Yet he has kept all his promises most faithfully: both the Disputed Nomes are now Aelvian (which will soon hardly matter); and satyrs in Aelvia are now permitted to dress like other people, and to vote for knights and burghers in the folk-moot; and all slaves in Palur-Nakhtos have been freed.

Kernin and Niamwy have a little manor with a wide sunken garden near the Sinel upstream from Eladon; and here we often keep our small court, and welcome visitors—sometimes human, sometimes satyrs, sometimes centaurs, and sometimes the winged Flirhanar. It is a certain truth that the world is changing. Aelvia and all the Shorelands are now in touch with the opposite ends of the Earth. Yet as far as I am concerned, the opposite ends of the Earth can stay where they are, or come and visit *us* if they are so minded; I prefer our manor with the sunken garden, which we call Little Happy Valley, and my dear Hafren, and our children. Our eldest son Omren looks to be a very promising young musician; and I trust to see him Chief Bard of the Triple Kingdom before I die.

Kernin, I fear, may have other thoughts. I have seen him look speculatively at his son Aelenek, who is now a sturdy boy of ten years. Once, when I had made all this story, and showed it to him in the manor garden, he muttered:

'Brother, in five years Aelenek will be fit to rule. When one is old, as Barundran said, one is free. . . .'

I looked at him aghast. 'What now? Where would you go this time? Is it to be Amatu, or the Throat?'

He laughed drily. 'I think not. I have heard so much about them now, from all our flying travellers. The hollow world is becoming a small place.'

'Well,' I said, 'beside the Ten Thousand Things of reality, there are also the Million Things of dream. There is Firafax as well as Sinis. That way, you can enter the Seventy-Third Universe any time you like, and become indeed a King of Infinite Space. . . .'

Kernin frowned, then smiled. Once more I saw the green lights in his eyes. 'But Sinis was always my goddess. Orselen, there must be a way out.'

I saw him gazing down at the grass in the lowest part of the sunken garden. 'As above, so below? Or *not* above, *but* below. Orselen, all my life I tried to escape upwards, by flight. But the true way out of this egg is to *dig*.'

And then I remembered the history of the Mad Miners, who tunnelled their way into another world. *An* other world? Perhaps there are others. . . .

So far, Kernin has done nothing more. I only hope that he will not; that we do not, one night, see a second Ring in the sky.

Of all the fates of men, perhaps the worst is to be hatched a hero. But the second worst, surely, is to be hatched a hero's brother.

APPENDIX

The Shorelandish Calendar

The following is the calendar observed in the River Kingdoms of Palur and Nakhtos; there are minor variations in Aelvia, Rindos, and Agnai. But all calendars are based on the Ring cycle of almost exactly 20.1 days.

The odd .1 day (2 Shorelandish hours) is allowed to accumulate, and then adjusted by an intercalary day every ten Rings. Thus in a 'year' of 20 Rings, the Tenth and the Twentieth Ring each have 21 days instead of the normal 20. The extra day comes at the end of the 'month', and is called Second Ganthis. It is regarded as exceedingly unlucky, especially the Second Ganthis of Twentieth Ring, which is also New Year's Eve. It was during that night that Daelir and Kernin flew over Rathvia without landing (see Chapter 18). Shorelanders do not celebrate New Year's Eve, but the following night of New Year's Day.

The Days of the Ring Month

The Ring is normally at full brightness from about Day 2 (Gorlun's) through Day 10 (Ringripe), half-bright-waxing on Day 1 (New Ring), and half-bright-waning on Day 11 (Last Ring). No-Ring lasts from Day 12 through Day 20 (Ganthis). But there is some variation at the two ends of the 'month' because of the extra .1 day and the intercalation.

Gorlun's Day (etc.) is the day *preceding* Gorlun's night (etc.).

In the following table, where a day has a popular name as well as a patron god, the popular name is printed above the day-number. Day 10, Ringripe, is sacred to both Hinos and Nami, Sun and Earth.

New Ring				Mid Ring					Ring-ripe
1	2	3	4	5	6	7	8	9	10
Suori					Nami	Olari			Hinos
									Nami

Last
Ring

11	12	13	14	15	16	17	18	19	20
Sinis				Prah	Sinolis				Ganthis

(21)
Ganthis